"On your knees, the man shoute

He reached for the back of her neck.

Without otherwise moving, Brigid lashed her right hand up, caught the man by the thumb and secured a *kote gaeshi* wristlock. Twisting sharply, she took a swift step back and kicked the man behind his left knee. He dropped her guns to the floor.

His leg buckled and he went down awkwardly, catching himself by his right hand. Gritting her teeth, Brigid locked the man's wrist under her left arm and heaved up on it, hoping to dislocate it at the shoulder. He cried out in pain.

Captain Saragayn lifted his right hand, the fingers sparkling with jeweled rings. "Our guest does not understand either our language or our etiquette."

In Magindano, Brigid said, "I understand the one and have no tolerance for the other."

Other titles in this series:

James Axler
Outlanders®

WARLORD
OF THE PIT

A GOLD EAGLE BOOK FROM
WORLDWIDE®

TORONTO • NEW YORK • LONDON
AMSTERDAM • PARIS • SYDNEY • HAMBURG
STOCKHOLM • ATHENS • TOKYO • MILAN
MADRID • WARSAW • BUDAPEST • AUCKLAND

Recycling programs
for this product may
not exist in your area.

First edition November 2009

ISBN-13: 978-0-373-63864-2

WARLORD OF THE PIT

Copyright © 2009 by Worldwide Library.

Special thanks to Mark Ellis for his contribution to the Outlanders
concept, developed for Gold Eagle.

I saw a star fall from heaven unto the earth: and to him was given the key of the bottomless pit. And he opened the bottomless pit; and there arose a smoke out of the pit, as the smoke of a great furnace; and the sun and the air were darkened by reason of the smoke of the pit.

—*Revelation* 9:1–2

The Road to Outlands—
From Secret Government Files to the Future

Almost two hundred years after the global holocaust, Kane, a former Magistrate of Cobaltville, often thought the world had been lucky to survive at all after a nuclear device detonated in the Russian embassy in Washington, D.C. The aftermath— forever known as skydark—reshaped continents and turned civilization into ashes.

Nearly depopulated, America became the Deathlands— poisoned by radiation, home to chaos and mutated life forms. Feudal rule reappeared in the form of baronies, while remote outposts clung to a brutish existence.

What eventually helped shape this wasteland were the redoubts, the secret preholocaust military installations with stores of weapons, and the home of gateways, the locational matter-transfer facilities. Some of the redoubts hid clues that had once fed wild theories of government cover-ups and alien visitations.

Rearmed from redoubt stockpiles, the barons consolidated their power and reclaimed technology for the villes. Their power, supported by some invisible authority, extended beyond their fortified walls to what was now called the Outlands. It was here that the rootstock of humanity survived, living with hellzones and chemical storms, hounded by Magistrates.

In the villes, rigid laws were enforced—to atone for the sins of the past and prepare the way for a better future. That was the barons' public credo and their right-to-rule.

Kane, along with friend and fellow Magistrate Grant, had upheld that claim until a fateful Outlands expedition. A displaced piece of technology…a question to a keeper of the archives…a vague clue about alien masters—and their world shifted radically. Suddenly, Brigid Baptiste, the archivist, faced summary execution, and Grant a quick termination. For

Kane there was forgiveness if he pledged his unquestioning allegiance to Baron Cobalt and his unknown masters and abandoned his friends.

But that allegiance would make him support a mysterious and alien power and deny loyalty and friends. Then what else was there?

Kane had been brought up solely to serve the ville. Brigid's only link with her family was her mother's red-gold hair, green eyes and supple form. Grant's clues to his lineage were his ebony skin and powerful physique. But Domi, she of the white hair, was an Outlander pressed into sexual servitude in Cobaltville. She at least knew her roots and was a reminder to the exiles that the outcasts belonged in the human family.

Parents, friends, community—the very rootedness of humanity was denied. With no continuity, there was no forward momentum to the future. And that was the crux—when Kane began to wonder if there *was* a future.

For Kane, it wouldn't do. So the only way was out—way, way out.

After their escape, they found shelter at the forgotten Cerberus redoubt headed by Lakesh, a scientist, Cobaltville's head archivist, and secret opponent of the barons.

With their past turned into a lie, their future threatened, only one thing was left to give meaning to the outcasts. The hunger for freedom, the will to resist the hostile influences. And perhaps, by opposing, end them.

Prologue

As the naked girl waded out of the water like a pearly-skinned Aphrodite, water cascaded from her limbs, the bright sunlight sparkling in the droplets.

For a disoriented instant, Brewster Philboyd felt suspended in the kind of delectable daydream an over-hormoned teenage boy would concoct—standing on a beach as a beautiful nude girl waded through the shallows toward him.

As the girl stepped gracefully through the breakers toward Philboyd, she pushed a diving mask up onto her forehead. She wore a delicate silver chain around her neck, and a tiny jeweled pendant in the shape of a *jagat*, the Hindu symbol of love, nestled between her small, taut breasts. Other than the nine-inch knife scabbarded to the calf of her right leg, Domi wore only the pendant.

As she walked onto the beach, she stared at Philboyd with challenging ruby eyes. "What are you lookin' at?"

Philboyd shook himself and hastily stepped away from the shoreline before the waves soaked his shoes. "Sorry, I was just lost in thought."

Striding past him, Domi stripped off the diving mask

and walked toward her clothes, draped over a large round boulder. "'Long as that's all you get lost in, Brewster."

Philboyd felt his face heat up, but he wasn't sure if it was due to embarrassment or the unremitting California sun, blazing down on the stretch of beach that bordered the barony once called Snakefish.

Gulls wheeled on the thermal currents created by the juncture of the beach and the thundering sea. They soared gracefully through the smoky spume raised by the nearby breakers. There was very little to see except sand, rocks and the long line of combers smashing against seaweed-draped boulders.

The slow tide made gurgling sounds around the base of the rocks. Despite Domi's harsh words, the young albino woman wasn't really hostile, but Philboyd never enjoyed being alone in her company. She had the forthright manner characteristic of other outlanders he had met, but he knew from experience she could be deadly dangerous.

Although she was beautiful despite all the scars marring the pearly perfection of her skin, Domi exuded an aggressive, almost angry energy, so Philboyd pretended not to watch as she got dressed. Her compact body was a smooth symmetrical flow of curving lines with small porcelain breasts rising to sharp points and a hard-muscled stomach. With the droplets of water glittering on her arms and legs, her pale skin looked almost luminous.

As she tugged a black T-shirt over her short-cropped white hair, Domi said in her clipped voice, "Time to get back the ville. Nothin' out there I saw that could cause earth tremors or the sea quakes they told us about."

Philboyd nodded distractedly, glancing out at the whitecaps. "Gedrick claimed most of the tidal disturbances were along this stretch."

Domi pulled on a pair of high-cut khaki shorts. "Didn't see anything. I dived five times."

Born a half-feral child of the Outlands, Domi was blessed with many attributes of those reared in the wilderness, including a natural swimming ability, as well as an exceptional lung capacity.

Reaching into a pocket, Domi withdrew a small rectangle of pressed plastic and metal. Flipping open the cover with a thumb, she punched in a code on the small keypad. "Edwards, you there?"

After a couple of seconds, a deep male voice responded, "Go ahead."

"Me and Brewster are done out here. We're on our way back the ville. We didn't find anything. What about you and Mariah?"

"Negative," Edwards said. "No signs of seismic activity that she could find."

"Gotcha. Stand by."

Folding the cover back over the comm unit, Domi cast a glance over her shoulder at Philboyd. "You ready?"

"As I ever will be," he replied. "I guess it's nice we

got a free California beach vacation out of this, but I don't think Snakefish is in danger of falling into the Pacific anytime soon."

Domi put on a pair of sunglasses and said only, "Me neither."

The lanky astrophysicist fell into step beside her. He stood a little over six feet tall, and in his beige T-shirt and baggy shorts, he appeared to be all protruding elbows, kneecaps and knuckles. Beneath his long-billed cap, his thinning blond hair was swept straight back, which made his high forehead seem very high indeed. He wore a pair of black-rimmed eyeglasses.

Philboyd, like all of the scientists who had arrived in the Cerberus redoubt from the Manitius Moon colony, was a "freezie," postnuke slang for someone who had been placed in cryogenic stasis following the nuclear holocaust two centuries earlier.

Wistfully, he said, "This is the first time I've been to California. It's nothing like the tourist brochures." He paused and added with a wry grin, "Pismo has changed a little since the days of the Surf City."

Domi eyed him quizzically. She padded barefoot across the hot sand. She almost never wore shoes. The soles of her feet bore calluses half an inch thick. "Don't know what you're talkin' about."

Philboyd shrugged. "I don't know, either. I'm just trying to make conversation."

Actually, Philboyd did know, that when the nukes flew and the mushroom clouds scorched their way into the heavens, the San Andreas Fault had given one great final heave and thousands of square miles of California coast dropped into the Pacific. For the past two centuries, the ocean had lapped less than thirty miles from the foothills of the Sierras.

Philboyd knew little about the ville of Snakefish beyond the fact it was the only barony built on the sea and at one time had a small fleet of warships. The walls of the fortress city loomed fifty feet high and at each intersecting corner protruded a Vulcan-Phalanx gun tower. Inside the walls stretched the complex of spired Enclaves. Each of the four towers was joined to the others by pedestrian bridges.

Before the baronial system had fallen, the people who worked for the ville administrators enjoyed lavish apartments, all the bounty of those favored by Baron Snakefish.

Far below the Enclaves spread the streets of the Tartarus Pits. This sector of Snakefish had served as a seething melting pot, where outlanders and slaggers lived. The lanes and footpaths swarmed with cheap labor, and the random movement between the Enclaves and Pits was tightly controlled—only a Pit dweller with a legitimate work order could even approach the cellar of an Enclave tower. The population of the Pits was as strictly and even more ruthlessly controlled than the traffic. The barons had decreed that the villes could support no more than five thousand residents, and the number of Pit dwellers could not exceed one thousand.

Seen from above, the Enclave towers formed a latticework of intersected circles, all connected to the center of the circle, from which rose the Administrative Monolith. The massive round column of white rockcrete jutted three hundred feet into the sky. Light poured out of the slit-shaped windows on each level.

Every level of the tower was designed to fulfill a specific capacity: E Level was a general construction and manufacturing facility, D Level was devoted to the preservation, preparation and distribution of food, and C Level held the Magistrate Division. On B Level was the Historical Archives, a combination of library, museum and computer center. The level was stocked with almost five hundred thousand books, discovered and restored over the past ninety years, not to mention an incredibly varied array of predark artifacts. The top level, or A Level, was reserved for the work of the administrators.

Domi and Philboyd crossed the plank bridge stretching over a canal and walked up the road to the open gates of Snakefish. Although there were no longer guard bunkers outfitted with remote-controlled GEC miniguns, the massive, pyramid-shaped dragon's-teeth obstacles made of reinforced concrete still lined both sides of the road. Five feet high, each one weighed in the vicinity of one thousand pounds and was designed to break the tracks or axles of any assault vehicle trying to gain unauthorized entry.

The two people smelled the interior of the ville long

before they passed through the open gates. Vendors had already opened up food stalls, and the primary items seemed to be dried fish.

Charcoal cookfires made the air smell a bit less fishy, but under the thick scents floated the pungency of poor sanitation and the accumulated stink of hundreds of people. They seemed to be of every shape, size and color, sporting all kinds of garb.

The mixture of building styles was as much of a polyglot as the population. There were old structures dating back to well before skydark, when Snakefish had been an oil refinery, and newer ones that were throwbacks to earlier styles as well as laminated plastic domes and great, squatting stone masses with no discernible architectural design to them at all.

If Domi's and Philboyd's presence caused a stir among the population of Snakefish, they did not detect it. The two people tramped the thronging streets, past shops, past taverns and even open-air dentists' offices without drawing more than a curious glance. Philboyd reflected that by now, word had spread about the arrival of emissaries from Cerberus.

He spied Mariah Falk and Edwards standing near a vendor's tent specializing in small household items. The two people were engaged in earnest conversation with Gedrick, the ville administrator.

Mariah caught sight of him and Domi and gestured toward them. Although Dr. Mariah Falk wasn't particularly beautiful or particularly young, she was attractive.

Her short chestnut-brown hair was threaded with gray at the temples. Deep laugh lines creased the corners of her eyes and curved out from either side of her nose to the corners of her mouth.

A geologist by trade and training, Mariah was another Manitius Moon base émigrée and she was dressed much like him in shorts and a T-shirt. A leather satchel hung from her left shoulder.

Edwards was only a couple of inches taller than Brewster Philboyd but considerably broader of build with overdeveloped triceps, biceps and deltoids. The big shaved-headed man wore a drab-olive T-shirt, green-striped camo pants and high-laced jump boots.

Gedrick was a man of medium height with brown skin. Despite the fact his complexion was completely different from Edwards and his chin framed by a goatee, he exuded a similar attitude of watchfulness.

Gedrick, like Edwards, was a former Magistrate. Although neither man wore a uniform, their right biceps were emblazoned with tattoos that depicted stylized, balanced scales of justice superimposed over nine-spoked wheels. The tattoos symbolized the Magistrate oath to keep the wheels of justice turning in the nine baronies.

Philboyd always felt uneasy in the presence of Magistrates, even those whom he considered friends like Kane and Grant.

Gedrick cast a glance toward the bespectacled astrophysicist and the petite albino woman when they joined their colleagues from Cerberus. For an instant, distaste flickered in Gedrick's eyes when his gaze passed over Domi.

"So you didn't find anything, either?" Gedrick demanded, his voice an aggressive rasp, as if steel wool lined his throat.

Domi shook her head. "Nothing that would give me the idea that this piece of California is unstable. I did some diving out where the tidal disturbances were reported. It seemed ordinary enough."

Mariah Falk declared curtly, "I don't know if that means anything. There are two varieties of tidal stressing that can generate earthquakes—diurnal and biweekly tides. The diurnal correlations would arise from more earthquakes only during the hours when the tidal stress is pushing in an encouraging direction, and biweekly effects are based on quakes when the sinusoidal stressing oscillations are the greatest."

"Be that as it may," Gedrick said, "we've been experiencing ground tremors every other day for the past two weeks. Each time they increase in duration and strength."

"We're aware of that," Edwards said. "But—"

"I know you're aware of it," Gedrick broke in impatiently. "That's why we called upon Cerberus, since you're supposed to have all these fabulous predark specialists on hand. I'm also aware that two other villes have been destroyed by earthquakes in the past four months."

"Mandeville and Palladiumville, yeah," Philboyd

said. "The only common factor is that, like Snakefish, they have become free villes—open to all, run like democracies—with the help of Cerberus advisers."

Gedrick scowled at the taller man resentfully. "Maybe that's the problem. Maybe if we just lock the place down and make it like the old days, our ville will stay standing."

"I don't think you'll have to go those lengths," Mariah said.

"Why not?" Gedrick barked. "We're having the tremors, and you claim there's no reason for them."

Mariah chuckled self-consciously and from her satchel removed several pieces of grit-encrusted rock. "I dug these out of the shoreline, and there's no sign of tectonic fracturing due to shallow oceanic thrust faults. I suppose it's possible that this whole region experiences weak tremors due to the so-called syzygy effect, but after touring the area, I haven't found any evidence of fault lines that could trigger episodic tremor and plate slips. Shallow earthquakes near midocean ridges aren't uncommon in the Pacific, so perhaps you're experiencing residual ripples."

Gedrick's eyebrows knitted at the bridge of his nose. "Two villes being destroyed by earthquakes can't be a coincidence."

Mariah returned the rock samples to the satchel. "I agree, but I don't know what else to tell you."

Domi glanced around, her eyes slitted. "There's not much else we can do here, is there?"

Edwards lifted a broad shoulder in a negligent shrug. "Not really."

Domi stared levelly at Gedrick. "Then, if you'll return our weapons, we'll be on our way."

The brown man gestured toward the Administrative Monolith. "You can pick them up on the way to the mat-trans. Sorry, but the only way we've kept the ville from turning into a bloodbath again is by forbidding all firearms inside the city walls."

"A reasonable policy," Philboyd remarked, affecting not to notice the glare Edwards directed at him.

Gedrick blew out a frustrated sigh. "I may not seem like it, but I do appreciate the help. We never would have gotten the ville back together without Cerberus provid-ing aid. I would have liked to have seen Kane, Grant and Brigid again."

The corner of Philboyd's mouth quirked in a smile. "We're the B Squad. Nowadays, the three heads of Cerberus aren't called in unless something really big happens."

"Like what?" Gedrick asked, tone edged with sarcasm. "When my fucking ville falls down?"

Mariah Falk opened her mouth to answer, then cocked her head toward the rumble of thunder in the distance. Domi tilted her head back, squinting up into the cloudless expanse of blue sky.

"What the hell is that?" Edwards demanded, shield-ing his eyes with a hand and scanning the sky.

Philboyd felt a prickle of dread as he glanced around

the streets. The sound grew louder, as if a great wheeled machine approached. The ground underfoot began to tremble, then it shifted fractionally. Fragments of brick and masonry tumbled from structures. Spiderweb patterns of cracks spread over the surface of the ville walls.

The people in the streets milled about uncertainly. There came the splintering of glass and a chimney toppled over, crashing onto the ground. A portion of a plastic-coated structure came down, and a vendor's tent keeled over. Pieces of the ville walls loosened and rained down, first in flakes then in fist-size chunks. Screaming mothers began shoving their terrified children toward the gate.

A series of consecutive hammering tremors struck the ground from beneath. Rifts split the ground. Rocks and mortar, shaken loose from the walls all around, rained down. Philboyd's legs buckled and he staggered but didn't fall.

Waving his arms, Gedrick bellowed, "Everybody out! Everybody out of the ville! Stay away from the walls!"

Dodging the falling debris, the people stampeded toward the open gate, jostling one another. A small boy stumbled and fell, squalling. Domi scooped him up in her arms and turned toward the Cerberus personnel. "You heard the man! Let's get the hell out of here!" she shouted.

Philboyd started to obey, then froze as the flood tide

of people swirled around him. At the base of a wall a hundred yards away, a moving ripple appeared in the ground, as if a very large animal slid and burrowed just beneath the surface. Little puffs of dust burst up from the cracks in the topsoil.

The furrow inscribed a crescent and halted. Philboyd heard a steady grinding throb. The ground acquired a split and amid a geyserlike spray of dirt, a darkly gleaming metal form heaved up, surrounded by clouds of pulverized grit and sand. A wave of intense heat like that from an opened blast furnace struck his face. His skin felt as if it instantly dried up and shriveled. He recoiled, lifting a hand to shield his eyes. He glimpsed the earth heaving up like a giant wave and rolling toward him in a crushing comber of rock and soil.

A hand closed tightly around his right arm and hauled him backward.

"Move it, asshole!" Edwards snarled into his ear.

A deep fissure opened up in their path and the two men leaped over it. A span of wall toppled down, crushing vendors' stalls. Edwards and Philboyd reeled on their feet, doing their best to maintain their balance on the convulsing earth. A shower of flying gravel pelted them.

Philboyd and Edwards dashed through the gate as the ville walls crumbled, folding inward, block after block, crash after crash. Panting, eyes stinging from dust, they ran across the bridge and joined Gedrick, Domi and Mariah on the far side of the canal. Gedrick bled from a raw gash on his left cheek. He did not seem to notice it.

The three people stared at the Administrative Monolith with wide, shocked eyes. As they watched, it swayed from side to side. Pieces of it fell away. Then the entire tower broke apart and collapsed with an ear-splitting roar.

Tons of rock plunged downward, scattering in exploding fragments. A reverberating, extended thunderclap rolled as the tower cascaded down in a contained avalanche. Thick clouds of dust billowed up, roiling and rising, enveloping the interior of the ville like a gigantic ball of filthy cotton.

Then Philboyd coughed and fanned the grit-laden air. "I guess it's time to call in the three heads of Cerberus."

Chapter 1

Malaysia, the island of Pandakar

The sky rolled with thunderclaps and flashed with bolts of lightning.

So this is the way it'll end, Kane thought wearily. With a bang so big you couldn't even hear a whimper.

Lifting his head, he squinted against the glare of a lightning flash. In the white-blue electric blaze, the night shadows crawling over Pandakar's waterfront looked like caricatures of black animals prowling for prey. Although the men creeping through the rain weren't animals, they were most definitely on the prowl for prey. He figured at this point the odds were ten to two.

Wind-driven sheets of rain fell in a torrential downpour. Gusts of wind tore at the distant tree line. Another stroke of lightning split the indigo tapestry of the sky, turning the hulking ships docked at the piers into ghostly apparitions. Their rain-slick hulls glistened as if as they were painted with quicksilver.

Kane crouched beside the gaping rectangular hole

that had been a window and a fair-size portion of stone wall before the warhead of an RPG had blown it inward in a hailstorm of rubble.

The rain suddenly increased in volume and tempo, sluicing down the sloping roof and through a hole in it. Kane wiped at the warm fluid seeping down the left side of his face and glanced ruefully at the diluted blood shining on his fingertips. He hadn't even been aware of the superficial cut, inflicted during the brief but fierce firefight that had raged all along the docks until ten minutes ago.

He wasn't surprised that the mission had gone sour so quickly, but he raged at the concept that his life and Grant's might end in such a stinking place for such a foolish cause.

"Shit," muttered Grant, who knelt on the floor across from him. He glared at the leak in the ceiling, then out through the gaping hole in the wall. "How much longer do you think this storm will last?"

Kane shook his head. "It's monsoon season in this part of the world. It might last all night or it could stop in five minutes."

Knee joints popping, Grant heaved himself to his feet and peered out at the rain-buffeted darkness. He could see little of the Pacific island called Pandakar beyond the immediate waterfront area.

Grant loomed six feet four inches tall in his stocking feet. He wore a Kevlar vest over a black T-shirt, tricolor camo pants and thick-soled jump boots, which added

almost an inch to his impressive height. The spread of
his shoulders on either side of his thickly corded neck
was very broad. Because his body was all knotted sinew
and muscle covered by deep brown flesh, he did not
look his weight of 250 pounds.

His short-cropped hair was touched with gray at the
temples, but it didn't show in the gunfighter's mustache
that swept out fiercely around both sides of his tight-
lipped mouth. Behind his lantern jaw and broken nose
lay a mind of keen intelligence that possessed a number
of technical skills, from field-stripping and reassem-
bling an SAR 80 blindfolded to expertly piloting every
kind of flying craft, from helicopters to the Annunaki-
built transatmospheric vehicles known as Mantas.

A Colt Government Model .45 pistol hung from his
right hip in a paddle holster, and he held a Copperhead
in his right hand. The abbreviated subgun was slightly
less than two feet long, with a 700-round-per-minute
rate of fire, and the extended magazines held thirty-five
4.85 mm steel-jacketed rounds. The grip and trigger
units were placed in front of the breech in the bull pup
design, allowing for one-handed use.

An optical image intensifier scope and a laser autotargeter were mounted atop the frames. Low recoil
allowed the Copperhead to be fired in long, devastat-
ing, full-auto bursts.

"I don't know who is who out there," Grant murmured, "but I don't care to be caught in a cross fire
again."

"Me either," Kane agreed. His blue-gray eyes took in the details of the slithering shadows in the rain while his mind kept the raw worry about Brigid Baptiste from preoccupying him.

Dressed similarly to Grant in a black T-shirt, Kevlar vest and camo pants tucked into high-laced combat boots, Kane was a tall man, lean and rangy. He resembled a wolf in the way he carried most of his muscle mass in his upper body. His thick dark hair, showing just enough chestnut highlights to keep it from being a true black, hung in damp strands. A faint hairline scar stretched like a piece of white thread against the sunbronzed, clean-shaved skin of his left cheek.

A pair of Bren Ten autopistols were snugged in shoulder holsters, and he cradled a Copperhead subgun identical to Grant's. A canvas rucksack at his feet held spare ammunition clips and other equipment.

Reaching up behind his right ear, Kane made an adjustment on the Commtact's volume control. The little comm unit fit tightly against the mastoid bone, attached to implanted steel pintels. The unit slid through the flesh and made contact with tiny input ports. Its sensor circuitry incorporated an analog-to-digital voice encoder subcutaneously embedded in the bone.

Once the device made full cranial contact, the auditory canal picked up the transmissions. The dermal sensors transmitted the electronic signals directly through the skull casing. Even if someone went deaf, a Commtact would still provide a form of hearing, but if the volume was not properly adjusted, the radio signals caused vibrations in the skull bones that resulted in vicious headaches.

Touching a tiny stud, he opened the channel to Brigid, but only a crackling hash of static filled his head. Scowling, he reached inside the rucksack and brought out a compact set of night-vision binoculars. Kane switched on the IR illuminator and squinted through the eyepieces. Viewed through the specially coated lenses, which optimized the low light values, the riverbank seemed to be illuminated by a lambent, ghostly haze. Where only black had been before, his vision was lit by various shifting shades of gray and green.

Craning his neck, Kane looked toward Captain Saragayn's treasure ship, the *Juabal Hadiah*, the Mountain of Wealth. Even at over a mile away, the ship looked monstrous. The vessel was less of a less of a seagoing vehicle than a huge anchored pavilion, sprawling across several acres of harbor water.

The *Juabal Hadiah* rose to exaggerated heights at stern and bow. The stern was built up in several housed decks, one atop the other. The hull crawled with intricate designs carved everywhere above the waterline, from Asian ideograms to representations of fish and dragons. The prow carried a huge figurehead painted, like the balance of the ship, in gaudy hues of red, yellow and gold. The effigy was of a naked red-haired woman, at least fifteen feet long, with an eighty-eight-inch bust.

Cupping his hands around the lenses of the binoculars to shield them from the rain, Kane tried to find movement on the decks. He saw nothing, whether due to the distance or the rain, he wasn't sure. However, he could make out the huge flag emblazoned with the image of a blazing skull superimposed over a crossed sword and a rifle.

"Pirates," he muttered.

"What?" Grant asked, raising his voice a trifle to be heard over the drumming of the rain.

"Pirates of the goddamn South China Sea," Kane said loudly. "Who would have figured?"

A gust of wind blew streamers of water into his face. Swallowing a curse, Kane rose and went to stand beside the big man.

"*We* should've figured," Grant commented sourly. "Who better?"

Kane assumed the query was rhetorical and so didn't respond. In the world he and Grant shared, the impossible happened often enough to seem commonplace. They had encountered pirates before, like those who prowled the waters off the Western Isles and controlled the island of Autarkic. That term was a catchall to describe a region in the Pacific Ocean of old and new landmasses.

Back during the nuclear holocaust, bombs known as earthshakers had been triggered, seeded months before by submarines along the fault and fracture lines of the Pacific Ocean. ICBM missiles had pounded the

Cascades and the region from western Canada down to California. The concentrated destructive force had ripped that part of the Earth to pieces.

The tectonic shifts and undersea quakes triggered by the atomic megacull raised new volcanic islands. Because the soil was scraped up from the seabed, most the islands became fertile very quickly, except for those in the Blight Belt—islands that were still dangerously irradiated. Pandakar wasn't one of those.

Arriving on a small island in the Straits of Malacca in Malaysia and finding Pandakar to be a stronghold of twenty-third-century pirates was one thing, but landing barely two hours before a bloody insurrection staged by a rival faction was something neither Grant nor Kane could have anticipated. They had been running and hiding along the sprawling waterfront for the past thirty minutes.

Pandakar's population was a surprisingly mixed lot of Malays, Dyaks, Filipinos and quite a few Chinese. Unsurprisingly, the little island stunk of dead fish, mud and the eternal heat of the tropics. Mud-filled holes pitted the narrow streets. Still, Brigid, Kane and Grant had been entranced by the people of all colors with monkeys and parrots for sale. There were vendors of magical charms for the healing of wounds and curing of scurvy. There were sellers of maps who offered charts of submerged predark cities and their treasures.

But at night, the waterfront looked quite different, particularly during a rainstorm, than it had during the daytime. When the Cerberus warriors arrived on Pandakar, they had only caught a glimpse of its stilt-legged huts, plank walkways and piers crammed with sampans and brightly painted outrigger fishing boats. In the rainy darkness, the flickering glow of yellow lanterns cast an unearthly aurora over its byways.

A flash of lightning showed only the faint outlines of two figures creeping between a pair of thick wooden pilings draped with fishnets. With the long streamers of rain falling onto them, they resembled life-size manne-quins attached to puppet strings.

"Looking for us?" Kane whispered.

"I don't think it matters much," Grant replied lowly. "Both sides will probably shoot us on sight."

Kane sighed heavily. "Why does this shit always happen when we're making diplomatic overtures?"

Grant uttered a derisive snort. "You're asking me?"

Diplomacy, turning potential enemies into allies against the spreading reign of the Overlords, had become the paramount tactic of Cerberus over the past two years. Lessons in how to deal with foreign cultures and religions took the place of weapons instruction and other training.

Over the past several years, Brigid Baptiste and former Cobaltville Magistrates Grant and Kane had tramped through jungles, ruined cities, over mountains, across deserts and they found strange cultures every-where, often bizarre re-creations of societies that had vanished long before the nukecaust.

Another crash of thunder exploded overhead, blasting a shock wave ahead of it, concussing with great force against the roof of the structure. A split roof timber shifted with a creak, and wood splinters mixed with dirty water pattered down.

Grant eyed it apprehensively. "We're going to have to get out of here pretty soon, no matter what."

A staccato drumroll wove its way around and through the roar of the storm. Kane and Grant knew the noise wasn't thunder. They ducked, falling almost prone on either side of the cavity in the wall, and peered into the night.

Illuminated by a lightning stroke arcing overhead, they saw a man lying on the ground near one of the pilings, rain slamming into him. Dark liquid ribbons inched away from his body.

A figure slid away from the shadows, and a stab of orange flame spit from between a stack of wooden crates. Shot after shot cracked in the darkness as the subgun sprayed the gloom with bullets. The muzzle flashes strobed.

A crooked spear of lightning spread a curtain of blue-white radiance across the sky. The figures moved swiftly, bent over in crouches. Kane's eyes flitted back and forth, trying to fix the men's position in his mind. Then Grant sucked in his breath and whispered, "They're behind us."

Kane wheeled, unholstering a pistol and leveling it at the doorway in the rear of the hut. The plank door hung askew on crooked hinges. Grant threw himself against the wall, putting his Copperhead against his right shoulder. In almost the same shaved fraction of a second, the door crashed open and three men staggered into the hut.

Chapter 2

They were small, fierce Malaysians, all of them adorned in little more than rags. They carried a variety of pistols and carbines. The tallest man, who stood five foot eight, stared at Grant and Kane in astonishment.

A purple silk scarf enwrapped the Malaysian's forehead, and gold earrings glittered in the lobes of both ears. His face and hands were covered by a network of old scar tracings. A scraggly mustache twisted down around the sides of his mouth, which was open in surprise.

For a long moment no one moved or spoke. Then the man in the purple scarf demanded in passably good English, "Where the fuck did you two come from?"

"Montana," Kane replied, striving to sound nonchalant. "What about you?"

The man ignored Kane's question. "You're not part of Captain Saragayn's crew. I know all of them."

"Are you one of his crew?" Grant asked.

The man's face convulsed with anger. "You don't know who I am?"

"Should we?" Kane inquired.

The man tapped his chest with a thumb. "I'm Mersano." The little Malaysian said the name as if it would explain everything.

Kane pointed to himself and Grant. "I'm Kane. This is Grant. We're trying to find a friend of ours. We got separated when the fighting broke out."

Mersano's eyebrows rose. "A friend? A woman?"

Before Kane could reply, a grenade exploded with a muffled crump, blowing a blast of muck and rock fragments in through the hole in the wall. A brief burst of gunfire followed the detonation, and a bullet chipped stone out of the wall beside Grant's right shoulder. Everyone dropped flat to the floor as three more rounds struck the wall and keened away.

"Their grenade fell short but they'll try again," Mersano said angrily.

"Who will?" Grant demanded. "What the hell is going on here?"

Mersano gestured toward the gap in the front of the building. "Captain Saragayn's crew is trying to kill me and my men."

"Why?" Kane asked.

"Because me and some others tried to boot him out of office," Mersano answered, raising his head and gazing at the darkness beyond the hole. "I think you two ought to throw in with us."

"Good call," Kane commented dryly, turning and aiming his pistol through the gap. He squeezed off a single shot, the Bren Ten slamming like a door.

Immediately a volley of bullets stormed in, ricocheting and chipping out fragments of stone. Kane counted at least four separate muzzle-flashes.

"They've got us pinned down," Grant said. "They'll chuck in more grens once they can get closer."

Mersano chuckled, a harsh, bitter sound. He heaved himself to one knee. "Then it's best not to linger."

Kane cast him a questioning glance. "Do you know of a way out of here?"

Mersano thumbed back the hammer of the big Casull revolver he carried and spoke to his two men in a dialect that neither Grant nor Kane understood. His men nodded in understanding and readied their carbines. Thunder rolled and lightning flared.

"What's the escape route?" Grant asked impatiently.

Mersano sprang to his feet. "Through the hole."

He leaped through the cavity, landing in the mud outside. He crouched, eyes and gun barrel questing for targets. No one shot at him. Over his shoulder, he said quietly, "The captain's men are circling around behind us. No one is paying much attention to the front."

"Define 'much attention,'" Kane demanded.

Mersano's men jumped through the hole in the wall, joining their chief outside. Kane and Grant exchanged glances of weary resignation and then followed the men. They swept the perimeter with watchful gazes. The rain slackened as the heart of the storm moved farther inland.

Their eyes grew accustomed to the darkness, and

Mersano gestured for everyone to follow him. "Move! *Bergerak!* Move!"

As the group of men sprinted across an open expanse of ground, a barrage of gunfire blazed from the interior of the hut. Voices rose in cries of outrage. Geysers of mud spewed up around them as bullets plowed into the ground.

Kane half turned to return the fire. Then he glimpsed a small projectile lancing overhead, seemingly propelled by a ribbon of spark-shot smoke. It arrowed through the gap in the wall of the hut. The interior instantly lit up with an orange nova of flame, surrounded by a dark mushroom of muck. The explosion slammed against his eardrums. The roof lifted up and one wall collapsed outward.

Kane returned his focus to running through the rain over uncertain ground.

"Don't shoot! It's me!" Mersano shouted.

The group ran into a narrow alley formed by several stacks of shipping crates. A tall figure in a hooded rain cape cradling a short-barreled, big-bored LAW rocket launcher stepped out of the shadows to meet them.

"Clarise!" Mersano shouted, showing his discolored teeth in a grin. "I was getting worried about you."

"I was delayed," said a soft female voice touched by a French accent. "A thousand pardons."

Clarise pulled back the hood, revealing a face of surprisingly exotic beauty. She was a tall woman with skin the color of ivory, deep blue eyes and an athletic body with full, proud breasts and strong hips. Her long blond hair glittered with a patina of raindrops.

Clarise cast her suspicious gaze toward Kane and Grant. They met it with neutral expressions. "I don't believe we've met," she said.

Mersano nodded toward the two men. "Grant and Kane. From Montana."

Clarise's eyebrows rose. "Ah. The Americans from Cerberus who've been trying to unite Roamer, robber, Farer and freebooter against a common foe."

"Yeah, that sounds like us," Grant said blandly. "How did you know that?"

"I have my sources," Clarise replied. "How's that job working out for you?"

"Not so bad in some places, terrible in others," Kane answered. "Like Pandakar, for example."

Clarise laughed, but it sounded forced. "If you'd only delayed your arrival by a day or two, your reception would have been quite different. As it is, your timing for a diplomatic effort could not have been worse if you had planned it that way."

Grant scowled. "Yeah, we figured that out after it was too late."

Kane gestured in the direction of the huge treasure ship. "One of our party is aboard the *Juabal Hadiah*."

The humor in Clarise's eyes faded. "Yes, I know. A woman named Baptiste."

Suspicion raised Kane's nape hairs and his hand

tightened around the grip of his pistol. "How do you know her name?"

"I was introduced to her," Clarise said curtly. "Until a couple of hours ago, I was Captain Saragayn's executive officer…and his wife."

"His wife?" Grant echoed incredulously.

"One of five," Clarise explained smoothly. "I would not be the slightest bit surprised to learn the captain has intentions of trying your friend Baptiste out for the sixth."

Kane's shoulders stiffened. "What the hell do you mean?"

"Perhaps we should get out of the rain," Mersano suggested. "This is only good weather for sitting ducks."

He laughed shortly at his own joke although no else did.

"Follow me." Clarise led the men farther down the passageway between the wooden crates. It was extremely dark in the narrow aisle, almost pitch-black.

Far too late, Kane sensed the rush of bodies. He tried to acquire a target for his Bren Ten, but a hard foot whipped out of the gloom and slammed into the pit of his stomach, just above his groin. The air exploded from his lungs, and he folded in the direction of the sickening pain. He staggered, trying to force himself erect, only to feel his shoulders gripped by hands that should have belonged to a great ape.

Kane shook himself violently to break free of the

agonizing grasp. In the murk, he heard Grant's voice blurt a curse, then Clarise shouting in French. A series of smacking, thudding impacts filled the damp, the sound of savage struggle at close quarters.

A man cried out in pain and a white shaft of gunfire blazed in the darkness. A body fell heavily almost at Kane's feet. His assailant shifted his grip from his upper arms to a bear hug, catching him up in a crushing embrace, pinning his arms against his sides. He thought he heard a rib break, but then realized it was the sound of a bladed weapon chopping into a wooden crate.

Sagging forward, Kane shifted his center of gravity into a dead, unresisting mass. His attacker loosened his grip ever so slightly, trying to pull him upright. Planting his feet firmly on the ground, Kane kicked himself backward, smashing the rear of his skull into the nose and mouth of the man standing behind him. He stumbled backward and crashed into a crate. Kane broke free and turned, gasping for air. He glimpsed a shadowy shape rushing toward him, arms outspread, and he squeezed off two shots. He heard a ghastly gurgle and a heavy body toppled nearly at his feet.

Kane leaned against a crate, breathing hard, heart trip-hammering. He heard Grant's voice, "Kane! Where the hell are you?"

He coughed and replied, "Here. Where the hell are you?"

"Getting the hell out of here. Follow my voice."

Kane did so, tripping over two bodies before he

found his companions clustered at the far end of the aisle formed by the shipping crates. They emerged at the edge of the jungle. The green wall of foliage looked thick enough to be nearly impenetrable, but Clarise found a small path. Everyone fell into step behind her, walking single file. Kane's mind toyed with images of poisonous snakes coiled to strike, of scorpions clinging to low-hanging branches and worse forms of wildlife. He knew from prior experience that all jungles held nasty surprises.

Clarise led the way with quick confidence despite the dark. The wind died down to no more than an intermittent breeze. The rain ebbed to a drizzle, then only a spritzing. Lightning still arced across the sky, but the heart of the storm was a couple of miles away. Humidity rose, and streamers of mist curled up from the ground. The world was a primeval, menacing green with night-blooming epiphytes and flowering creepers stretching down from the branches overhead.

They roused a family of langurs, monkeys with white eye rings. There was a brief, outraged chittering as they jumped in great arcs between the trees. No one spoke as they marched. There was the constant pelt and drip of water from the canopy of leaves above them. Kane kept checking his bare arms for the giant gray leeches that dropped from the branches and attached themselves to the flesh.

In the darkness, the danger of straying off the path, and becoming lost was a greater hazard than leeches.

Even in daylight, enveloped within the suffocating heat and humidity and thick foliage it would have been difficult to find the trail.

Then the overgrowth opened up in a small clearing. In the center rose a mat hut built on rickety, leaning stilts. The tips of the thatched roof dripped incessantly with rainwater.

The people quickly climbed up a bamboo ladder into the interior of the hut. The reed walls exuded a cloying, pungent aroma, and the floor was damp. Neither Kane nor Grant relaxed, keeping their weapons close to hand. Mersano produced a candle from a small box and lit the wick with a wooden match.

In the flickering, yellow illumination, everyone stared at the outlanders with a mixture of bemusement and distrust, but no one spoke. Irritably, Kane asked, "Is anybody going to tell us what's going on here?"

Clarise's shoulders lifted in a shrug beneath her rain cape. "Pandakar is a pirate stronghold and has been for the last one hundred years. It's a family business."

"Not surprising," Grant said. "Piracy flourished in this part of the world up until the late twentieth century."

"The extent of it is becoming a little too broad," Kane stated. "Trade lanes and shipping routes are closing down. According to our intel, Captain Saragayn's fleet looted 300 ships last year."

"More like 310," Clarise replied. "He tried to expand onto land, setting up an empire along the China coast.

He seized territory and villages, but the armies of several warlords united and drove him out."

"Saragayn suffered major losses," Mersano interposed smoothly. "He's weak in terms of manpower and matériel. We thought this would be the optimum time to overthrow him."

"Apparently you miscalculated," Kane pointed out dryly.

"Not as much as you might think," Clarise countered. "We drew most of his forces away from his treasure ship. We've got our own people on the inside."

"Like you?" Grant inquired. He looked toward Mersano. "And you're one of his rivals?"

An enigmatic smile touched his lips. "You might say that. I'm his son, back from exile. Most of the captain's inner circle is made up of his bastard spawn who have their own designs on the old man's fortune."

Kane gusted out a sigh. "This is starting to sound complicated."

Clarise chuckled. "We *did* say it was a family business."

"I have my own small fleet," Mersano continued proudly. "My theater of operations is the Sulu Sea. Occasionally we raid along the south China coast, but I prefer the merchant junks. I also run military supplies—guns, food and medicine—to some of the warlords setting up in shop in Indochina. I have my own connections, so I don't need Saragayn."

"Then why are you staging this attack?" Grant challenged.

"Saragayn is considered a devil incarnate, even here where life is not held even to the value of a cigar," Clarise said grimly.

"My father is still ambitious," Mersano went on, "but his ambitions exist now for their own sake. Wealth is only a means to an end with him. He'll never be satisfied. And now he's negotiating with outsiders who've promised him support if he stages a new assault on China."

"These outsiders you mentioned…do they happen to travel under the name of the Millennial Consortium?" Kane intoned quietly.

Clarise's eyes narrowed, her full lips creasing in a frown. "They do. Is it because of them you are here? To prevent that alliance?"

Kane dug into a pants pocket and produced a small button made of base metal. He flipped it toward Clarise, who snatched it out of the air. Holding it close to the flame of the candle, she examined the image inscribed upon it: the stylized representation of a standing, featureless man holding a cornucopia—a horn of plenty—in his left hand and a sword in his right, both crossed over his chest.

"Have you seen anyone wearing that button?" Kane asked.

Clarise nodded. Tossing aside her rain cloak, she turned out the lapel of her shirt and displayed an identical disk. "This should give you an idea of how deep the infiltration has become. Even Saragayn's top officers are required to wear those buttons."

"Who is the consortium emissary?" Grant asked.

"He goes by the name of Mr. Book. Obviously an alias."

"Obviously," Grant agreed. "Is he here now?"

The woman shook her head. "I don't know. Perhaps he got wind of the insurrection and fled, with the idea of returning and cutting a deal with the winner."

Kane smiled without humor. "Yeah, that's the consortium's strategy, all right."

"I placed my men all along the waterfront," Mersano said. "Even aboard the *Juabal Hadiah*. Scores of them are masquerading as laborers, fishermen, deckhands. We thought when the time came, we would strike all at once and seize power quickly."

"We were betrayed," Clarise said softly, bleakly.

"That's all very interesting," Grant stated, "but at this point all we care about is recovering our friend and getting out of here."

"Captain Saragayn won't let Baptiste go now," Clarise replied.

Kane's jaw muscles tightened into knots. "Why not?"

"For one thing," Mersano said, "he might suspect she had something to do with the insurrection."

"Or," Grant interjected, "if she was spotted by the consortium agent and recognized, she could have been ratted out."

"Or," Clarise said, "there could be a simpler explanation—Saragayn wants her for himself. But whatever the reason, if you want Baptiste back, your only option is to ally yourselves with us. I'm sure you've heard the old bromide about the enemy of my enemy is my friend."

"Yeah, we have." Kane blew out a disgusted breath. "Too many damn times."

Chapter 3

After the first warhead exploded, Brigid Baptiste plunged into the crowded emporium of vice, figuring Captain Saragayn wouldn't think to look for her among the prostitutes, gambling tables and cockfighting arenas.

Brigid found it difficult to believe that the huge palace of lust and greed was confined within the hulls of a ship. As far as she had been able to learn, the *Juabal Hadiah* pandered to all tastes, however mundane or perverted. Gambling, drugs, women or even children, she reflected grimly.

Brigid crossed a casino swiftly, trying not to appear intent on leaving. The various gambling stations were decorated with colorful bunting and a band played a variety of musical instruments, blaring forth with a cacophony at a volume she found painful.

From the ceiling hung mirror balls that reflected distorted bird's-eye views of the blackjack, roulette, pai-kow and fan-tan tables. The beeps, burps and bells of slot machines added to the clangor.

Barely audible over the noise rose the murmur of a

dozen languages, as varied as the clothing styles worn by the men and women clientele—white jackets, saris, Malay sarongs and *bajus*.

Brigid felt distinctly underdressed in her black whipcord pants with the cuffs tucked into thick-soled combat boots. She wore a gray T-shirt that accentuated her full-breasted, willowy figure. Her bare arms rippled with hard, toned muscle.

A tall woman with a fair complexion, Brigid's high forehead gave the impression of a probing intellect, whereas her full underlip hinted at an appreciation of the sensual. A mane of red-gold hair fell down her back in a long sunset-colored braid to the base of her spine. Her emerald eyes were narrowed behind the rectangular lenses of her wire-rimmed spectacles as she pushed through the crowd.

Brigid ignored a drink offered to her by a surprisingly buxom Asian woman in a topless outfit and circled a baccarat table. She didn't think she was pursued by Saragayn's security staff. She assumed—she hoped—they had other matters to occupy them. She just kept moving through the low-ceilinged gambling hall.

Her distinctly un-Asian features and coloring did not draw the attention of the patrons. Most of them were too engrossed in their own activities at the roulette wheel and blackjack tables to give her more than cursory glances. Still, she kept the TP-9 autopistol pressed against her right thigh as she walked.

Cages filled with colorfully plumed tropical birds

hung on the walls and they screeched in agitation. They sensed the violence outside on the decks of the huge ship.

The smell of roasting meat drew her toward a small kitchen. Small, sweating men stripped to the waist labored over smoking grills. Cigarettes dangled from their lower lips, and the stench of marijuana mixed in with the odor of flame-seared fat.

Brigid swiftly moved through the kitchenette, barely avoiding being spattered by sizzling grease. She went through the door on the far side and found herself in a cool, dimly lit corridor. Soft red carpeting muffled her steps, and she paused to catch her breath.

Wincing, she flexed the fingers of her right hand, noting that they all moved despite the pain. She had punched Mr. Book in the face, but her knuckles seemed intact. She hoped the same thing could not be said for his jaw.

Reaching up behind her ear, Brigid activated the Commtact and opened the channel to Kane and Grant. She heard only the hiss and pop of static, and she guessed her partners were forced to retreat out of the reception range of the little comm unit. She tamped down the rise of fear, finding it hard to assemble her thoughts.

Kane had told her more than once there was a time to fight and a time to run for cover. She still didn't know what had happened to Kane and Grant, since the situation developed with startling rapidity, but she had taken advantage of it nevertheless.

Upon arriving in Pandakar early in the afternoon, she, Grant and Kane had spent only a short time learning the lay of the land before entering the island's only settlement. Definitely taller than most of the people in the noisy, narrow, crowded streets, the Cerberus warriors let themselves be carried along by the press of bodies, the conical straw hats and the shuffling of feet. The people who looked at them directly did so with blank eyes. A hot wind blew between the wooden houses with their thatched roofs and long eaves that looked like the prows of canoes.

Overlooking the harbor was a vast tumble of reed huts and shanties built on docks. A maze of waterways crowded with canoes and sampans confused the eye but not the nose—the smell of fish overhung it like a cloud.

When Brigid asked locals about Captain Saragayn, the ordinarily friendly faces of the villagers became tight and hostile. Still, they were directed to the waterfront and a private pier leading to the immense treasure ship named the *Juabal Hadiah*.

At first sight, the vessel was impressive. Colored lights flared from the rigging of the huge craft, which was twice as broad in the beam and double the length of any ship docked at harborside. The ship had very high poops and overhanging stems, looking somewhat top-heavy because of the exceptionally tall pole masts and huge sails with batten lines running entirely across the fore- and afterdecks.

The sun cast streaks of copper and gold over the

hulls of the motorized sampans, launches and water taxis clustering around the four boarding ramps that extended down from the ship's port side.

The two Indonesian guards at the security kiosk were suspicious but not overly hostile. They wore grayish-green coveralls with the sleeves hacked off. Web belts cinched their waists and from them hung holstered revolvers.

When Brigid stated their business, speaking the Magindano dialect perfectly, one of the guards grinned at her and then waved meaningfully toward the *Juabal Hadiah* and the carved figurehead of the well-developed, redheaded woman.

"Ordinarily Captain Saragayn wouldn't see any stranger on such short notice," the man said, "but he'd have us lashed if we didn't let you through."

Brigid maintained a stony expression, even when the guard's eyes flicked from her bosom to the gigantic one of the figurehead. The other man took a small trans-comm unit from a pocket and spoke into it softly for a few seconds. Then he folded it up and said roughly to Brigid, "The captain will see you."

Kane and Grant were directed to wait. Since they weren't disarmed, they didn't lodge serious objections, despite hearing the rumble of thunder that heralded a tropical storm front. Both men had learned long ago that when on the home turf of a potential ally, the easiest way to turn him or her into an adversary was to resist local protocol.

One guard escorted Brigid down the long private pier toward the treasure ship looming above them. Exterior galleries ran along each of the decks, with peaked eaves and elaborately carved roof-trees. When they reached a ramp, the guard gestured for Brigid to precede him. Quickly, she climbed it and when she reached the top, she found her way blocked by a door made of bamboo struts.

She noted that the bars were actually steel rods painted to look like bamboo. A young Malaysian woman in a formfitting sheath dress of cobalt blue stared at her expressionlessly. One long bare leg showed through the slit in the skirt. Beyond the door, Brigid saw a wide corridor lit by ceiling bulbs of pale yellow.

A trans-comm unit in the girl's hand buzzed. She quickly lifted it to her ear, spoke one word that Brigid didn't catch and stepped back. Brigid didn't see her touch anything, but the steel-barred door slid aside on a noiseless track.

She stepped over the track and saw a very tall man, dark-skinned and wearing a silk scarf of bright yellow around his head standing in the alcove. The man did not speak, but the black eyes he turned toward Brigid betrayed a contempt of death—either his own or hers. He stepped toward her, moving with a controlled tension as he strained against an invisible leash around his neck.

He held out a very broad hand, and wordlessly Brigid placed her TP-9 autopistol and Copperhead subgun into it. With a jerk of his head, the man escorted her down the corridor. They walked about a dozen yards when they passed a tall blond woman hurrying past. Brigid received only a brief impression of urgency and blue eyes before the man led her into a poorly lit chamber. Her gaze was instantly drawn to the throne-like chair placed atop a dais. Two oval plaques rose from the back, both of them inscribed with Chinese ideograms.

The air smelled of sandalwood incense, and little wind chimes tinkled at the far edge of audibility. Brigid felt a sense of being in a dream or a fairy tale. The man seated in the throne looked as if he had designed his clothes by copying the illustrations found in a children's book about ancient caliphates.

His gold-embroidered tunic was made of shimmering black satin, and a crest of peach-colored feathers sprayed from the jeweled forepart of his bright red turban. She half expected to see pointy-toed slippers on his feet, but he wore sandals, exposing toenails painted a bright red. Brigid guessed he was Captain Saragayn.

Everything looked exaggerated about the man—the sharp, curved nose, thin slit of a mouth, black almond-shaped eyes and his smooth, amber-hued skin gave him the appearance of a raptorial bird. His face was clean-shaved except for a long, thin mustache. An electric aura seemed to charge the air around the throne.

"On your knees!" the tall man barked in Magindano.

Brigid affected not to have understood.

"On your knees, outlander bitch!" the man shouted. He reached for the back of her neck.

Without otherwise moving, Brigid's right hand lashed up, caught the man by the thumb and secured a wrist lock. Twisting sharply, she took a swift step back and kicked the man behind his left knee. He dropped her guns to the floor.

His leg buckled and he went down awkwardly, catching himself by his right hand. Gritting her teeth, Brigid locked the man's wrist under her left arm and heaved up on it, hoping to dislocate it at the shoulder. He cried out in pain.

Captain Saragayn lifted his right hand, the fingers sparkling with jeweled rings. "Our guest apparently does not understand either our language or our etiquette."

In Magindano, Brigid said, "I understand the one and have no tolerance for the other."

Saragayn smiled blandly. "You can let Daramurti up now, I think. Forgive his overzealous attitude. He feels he has more to prove to me now than ever before."

Saragayn spoke in cultured English, a very affected form as if he had learned the language from watching old vids of upper-crust Bostonians.

Brigid obligingly released the man's arm and stepped back. Grimacing, Daramurti pushed himself to his knees and then to his feet. He worked his shoulder up and down and took a menacing step toward Brigid.

Saragayn spoke a single sharp word and the man

picked up Brigid's fallen weapons and took them to him, then retreated to the doorway. Captain Saragayn briefly inspected the guns but said nothing. Watching him, Brigid knew she should have felt fear, or at the very least, apprehension, but instead she felt the tingling warmth of excitement as the prospect of danger spread through her.

For a very long time, she was ashamed of that anticipation, blaming her association with Kane and Grant for contaminating her. Now she had accepted the realization that their own desire for thrill-seeking hadn't infected her, but only forced her to accept an aspect of her personality she had always been aware of but refused to consciously acknowledge.

In the years long past during her life as a baronial archivist, Brigid Baptiste had prided herself on her intellect and logical turn of mind. She was a scholar first and foremost. Back then, the very suggestion she would have been engaged in such work would have made her laugh. Now she was a veteran warrior, and at some point during her time with Cerberus she realized the moments of danger no longer terrified her but brought a sharper sense of being alive.

Her life in Cobaltville's Historical Division had not been fulfilling, but merely a puppet show she had performed so the string pullers wouldn't become displeased and direct their grim attention toward her. Of course, eventually they had. Over the past few years, she had left her tracks in the most distant and alien of climes and breasted very deep, very dangerous waters.

The man on the throne showed the edges of his teeth in a vulpine grin. "I am Captain Saragayn, if you haven't guessed."

"I had. I am—"

"Brigid Baptiste," the man broke in. "A chief field operative for the group known as Cerberus, based in Montana, in the former United States of America."

Brigid smiled with a confidence she did not feel. "Very good. How did you know that?"

"Would you care to guess again?"

Brigid presented the image of pondering the question before replying calmly, "The emissary of the Millennial Consortium either described me or showed you a picture."

Saragayn clapped his hands together in delight. "Excellent. Mr. Book said you were very smart…and very dangerous." A frown suddenly replaced the smile on his lips. "I've already witnessed the dangerous part."

"What else did Mr. Book tell you?"

Captain Saragayn shrugged. "Many things. Mostly about the bit of bad blood between your two houses. Very interesting."

"No doubt," Brigid responded flatly. "Was Mr. Book alone?"

"Yes," a male's voice said from behind her. "Due to a personnel shortage, thanks in large part to Cerberus."

Brigid turned quickly, just as a slender man stepped

around the guard in the doorway and entered the throne room. He wore a one-piece zippered coverall of a neutral dun color. A small button glinted dully on the collar of his garment, and she didn't need to see the image inscribed on it to know she faced an agent of the Millennial Consortium.

"My name is Mr. Book," the man stated coldly. "It's about time we met."

Chapter 4

Brigid's first impulse was to shoot back with a witticism or an insult. But when she looked into Book's eyes, she saw the glint of cruelty in their pale depths, glimmering like the fires of a furnace that had only been banked, not extinguished.

Although of medium height, Book was so excessively lean he appeared taller. His hair was cropped so short it resembled a gray skullcap of bristles. His rawboned, leathery face was deeply seamed, as if it had been cooked by the sun and leached by acid rain until only bone, muscle and sinew were left.

His posture and attitude reminded her of Magistrates she had encountered, and she realized that Book was quite possibly a former Mag, one who had been recruited by the Millennial Consortium. Her mouth went dry as she experienced a rare moment of fear. She opted to remain silent.

Book regarded her broodily. "Brigid Baptiste. And where you are, so are Kane and Grant. The question is why."

Brigid frowned. "What do you mean?"

"You people from Cerberus are enigmas, Baptiste. Oh, I know your names and your histories—renegades from Cobaltville, baron blasters and all that overblown bullshit told about you in the Outlands."

Brigid forced a taunting smile to her face, but she didn't reply. Over the past five-plus years, the Cerberus warriors had scored many victories, defeated many enemies and solved mysteries of the past that molded the present and affected the future. More importantly, they began to rekindle of the spark of hope within the breasts of the disenfranchised fighting to survive in the Outlands.

Victory, if not within their grasp, at least had no longer seemed an unattainable dream. But with the transformation of the barons into the Overlords, all of them wondered if the war was now over—or if it had ever actually been waged at all. Brigid privately feared that everything she and her friends had experienced and endured so far had only been minor skirmishes, a mere prologue to the true conflict, the Armageddon yet to come.

Seeing the smile, Book challenged, "I amuse you?"

"To a point. If our reps are overblown bullshit, why has the consortium black-tagged our files?"

Saragayn stirred in his chair. "What means this 'black-tagged'?"

Staring levelly at Book, Brigid declared, "It means that my friends and I from Cerberus are high-priority targets for the millennialists. There is a big bonus paid to any of their agents who manage to kill us."

Saragayn angled at eyebrow at Book. "Is this so?"

The man nodded and then glared at Brigid. "Why are you here in Pandakar?"

Brigid smiled defiantly. "Take a guess, Mr. Book."

"The cheap heroics of you Cerberus people nauseate me," Book said harshly. "But let's be frank with each other. The consortium's enterprises in America are imperiled by the continual interference of Cerberus. You've destroyed our satraps, killed our personnel and disrupted our operations. You've forced us to move farther and farther from the American shores, yet you keep coming after us. Why?"

Brigid cast a glance at Saragayn. "That's an example of the bad blood you mentioned."

Saragayn nodded. "I gathered as much. I'm interested in your perspective."

Brigid made a dismissive gesture. "Is there any point in that? You've already made up your mind."

Saragayn chuckled. "You severely over- or underestimate me. I am responsible for nearly a thousand people, most of them related to me. Pandakar is surrounded by tides of change, and I do not want my island to be swept away. Therefore, I don't make decisions rashly or choose sides until I've gauged every advantage and disadvantage."

Brigid nodded as if she agreed, although she surreptitiously looked around for another way out of the room. Daramurti still blocked the doorway. "Do you know what the Millennial Consortium really is, Captain?"

"I only know what Mr. Book told me—a union of organized salvagers and traders." Saragayn cocked his head at her in an exaggerated pose of puzzlement. "Is that not the truth?"

"To a point," Brigid admitted, pinching the air between the thumb and forefinger of her right hand. "A very small and very blunt point."

The Millennial Consortium was, on the surface, a group of very well-organized traders who dedicated their lives to recovering predark artifacts from the ruins of cities. In the Outlands, such scavenging was actually the oldest profession.

After the world burned in atomic flame, enough debris settled into the lower atmosphere and very nearly created another ice age. The remnants of humankind had waited in underground shelters until the Earth became a little warmer before they ventured forth again. Most of them became scavengers mainly because they had no choice.

Looting the abandoned ruins of predark cities was less a vocation than it was an Outland tradition. Entire generations of families had made careers of ferreting out and plundering the secret stockpiles the predark government had hidden in anticipation of a nation-wide catastrophe. The locations of those hidden, man-made caverns scattered across the country, filled with hardware, fuel and weapons, had become legend to the descendants of the nukecaust survivors.

Most of the redoubts had been found and raided decades ago, but occasionally a hitherto untouched one would be located. As the stockpiles became fewer, so did the independent salvaging and trading organizations. Various trader groups had combined resources for the past several years, forming consortiums and absorbing the independent operators.

The consortiums employed and fed people in the Outlands, giving them a sense of security that had once been the sole province of the barons. There were some critics who compared the trader consortiums to the barons and talked of them with just as much ill will.

Since first hearing of the Millennial Consortium a few years before, the Cerberus warriors had learned firsthand that the organization was deeply involved in activities other than seeking out stockpiles, salvaging and trading. The group's ultimate goal was to rebuild America as a technocracy, with a board of scientists and scholars governing the country and parceling out the resources where they saw the greatest need. They had taken over the smaller trading groups, absorbing their resources and personnel.

Although the consortium's goals seemed utopian, the organization's overall policy was pragmatic beyond the limit of cold-bloodedness. Their influence was widespread, well managed, and they were completely ruthless when it came to the furtherance of their agenda, which when distilled down to its basic components, was nothing more than the totalitarianism of a techno-tyranny. The final objective sought by the Millennial Consortium was to impose a supranation over the world. The Cerberus warriors had faced millennialists in far-flung parts of the planet.

"Do you know what technocracy is?" Brigid asked.

Captain Saragayn nodded. "Again, only what Mr. Book told me—it is a form of government rooted in science, not politics or religion. It was first developed in the early twentieth century by scientists, engineers and other specialists."

"Yes," Brigid drawled sardonically. "The conclusion reached by these specialists was that an industrialized society governed by a council of scientists and technologists would be far more productive, less prone toward crime and deviation from the standard and certainly not inclined to bomb itself out of existence."

"That's not the case?"

Book started to speak, but Saragayn held up a silencing hand. "I want to hear what she has to say."

Confidently, Brigid declared, "Technocracy is a serviceable set of ideals, I suppose. But it can only function by imposing a dictatorship. That is what lies at the heart of technocracy. The ruling elite are selected through a bureaucratic process on the basis of specialized knowledge rather than through anything remotely similar to the democratic process."

"The Millennial Consortium curtails human freedom, then." Saragayn did not ask a question; he made a statement.

"Basically, yes. Technocracy as envisioned by the Millennial Consortium cannot coexist with freedom."

"You think that is important?" Saragayn asked. "Freedom?"

Brigid cast him a questioning glance. "You don't?"

"I confess I don't quite understand it."

Mr. Book snorted. "It's a strictly emotional concept, illusory. Freedom is also a very great danger because human beings are ignorant by nature and are dominated by the wild side of their consciousness."

"Freedom," Captain Saragayn echoed thoughtfully. "I have heard a few chants of that here, from some of the discontented islanders. Freedom to do what? Freedom from who?"

"From the leash of serfdom," Brigid retorted. "Held by men like you." She inclined her head toward Book. "And you."

"The people of Pandakar are simple, primitive souls," the captain said. "They need a father to look after them and apply discipline. If they did not have that, then the entire system established by my family a hundred years ago falls apart. For example—"

Saragayn paused and his eyes fixed on Daramurti. "My nephew here has served as my bodyguard for over three years. He has been loyal, true and faithful for three years. Then he fell victim to one who did not share those virtues—my wife Clarise. She seduced you, didn't she Daramurti?"

Daramurti's shoulders stiffened, then sagged. He swallowed hard and cast his eyes toward the floor.

"I can't really blame him," Saragayn continued

smoothly. "Clarise is beautiful—and French. That is a heady combination for a young and oversexed man. I am sure he resisted her wiles for as long as he could. But then one day not too long ago, he fell into her bed and after a day and night of vigorous fucking, Daramurti swore to be loyal to her. To that end, he allowed seditionists controlled by my wastrel son, Mersano, to infiltrate Pandakar."

Captain Saragayn sighed, shifted his throne and idly examined Brigid's TP-9, turning it back and forth in his right hand. "Mersano and Clarise's force plan to stage an attack tonight as soon as the storm hits. That should be within the next couple of minutes, I think."

Book's eyebrows rose, his forehead acquiring new creases. "Then why are we standing here, Captain?"

"Ah, calm yourself, sir," Saragayn replied softly. "I intend to trap my enemies, and the best way to do that is to let them think their plot against me is succeeding."

Brigid glanced over at Daramurti. "So you told him of the plan?"

The man did not make eye contact and Saragayn laughed. "Well, of course he did. All of Pandakar is filled with my informants, and the *Juabal Hadiah*—" he used the barrel of the pistol to indicate the ship "—is wired with spy eyes…particularly the bedrooms of my wives. Nothing goes on here without my knowledge. I may pay no attention to it, but I *do* know about it."

"Be that as it may, what precautions have you taken?" Mr. Book asked uneasily.

"It should suffice that I have taken them." Saragayn stared steadily at Daramurti. "With his help."

"*His* help?" Book echoed.

"Although my nephew had sworn loyalty to me, and then to my wife Clarise, ultimately he learned that his primary loyalty lay to himself. He was only too eager to tell me everything I wished to know to protect first his young, impudent cock and then his life."

Saragayn chuckled, a sound like the warning buzz of a rattlesnake. "Isn't that right, nephew?"

Daramurti finally lifted his head. Tears glimmered in his eyes. He looked as fearsome as a small boy caught with a forbidden piece of candy. His mouth opened and closed like a fish stranded on dry land. "I live only to serve you, glorious Uncle. Ever and always."

"Yes," Saragayn whispered. "How well I know that."

The autopistol in his hand blasted out a wave of sound, like a thunderclap. Daramurti's head jerked violently back on his neck. A piece of scalp exploded from the rear of his skull, riding a slurry of blood that splattered the wall of the corridor. He staggered backward and fell heavily.

While the gunshot echoed in the throne room, another explosion shook the bulkhead. Brigid recognized it as the detonation of an RPG. Book stumbled, his eyes widening. "What the hell—?"

Without a word, Brigid wheeled on him, her right fist whipping up fast, connecting with the underside of Book's jaw. The uppercut snapped the man's head back.

Arms windmilling, he toppled off his feet, slamming against Captain Saragayn.

Surging forward, Brigid snagged the barrel of her autopistol and gave it a vicious corkscrew twist, tearing it out of Saragayn's hand and then slashing down with the butt against the crown of his head. Although cushioned by the turban, the blow still landed solidly enough to drive consciousness out of the man's eyes with the suddenness of a candle being extinguished.

Then Brigid turned and ran out into the corridor, leaping nimbly over the corpse of Daramurti.

Chapter 5

Oil lamps glowing from behind panes of yellow glass illuminated the corridor. Brigid considered breaking the glass and dousing the flames because she suspected Captain Saragayn watched her through a closed-circuit spy eye. She doubted he would stay unconscious for long—if he did nothing else for his host, Book would see to his revival.

From outside she heard more explosions, but now they sounded more like thunderclaps. Woven faintly through the racket, she heard the staccato rattle of automatic gunfire. Behind her came the murmur of male voices and thump of running feet. Brigid plunged through the first open door she saw.

She stood in a dim chamber, somewhat Asian in decor but with an Arabian Nights kind of furnishing. There were heaps of big satin and tasseled pillows, tapestries hung from the ceiling and several women of all sizes, shapes and colors stared at her. The only thing they shared in common was nudity. They stared at her silently, their overly made-up faces as immobile as masks.

Brigid put a finger to her lips as she moved deeper into the room, toward an archway at the rear of the cabin. The women stared at her soberly. Astringent smoke curled from a brass brazier set before a multi-armed, many-breasted statue. She stifled a cough as she sidled past. Then the solemn, shivery boom of a gong pressed against her eardrums.

Casting a startled glance behind her, she saw a naked black woman, her flesh glistening with oil, standing before a huge disk of bronze, a mallet in her hands. She struck it again and the heavy note reverberated throughout the chamber. Then three Malaysian men rushed through the door. They wore yellow head scarves like Daramurti and they swung the barrels of their pistols in short arcs. Judging by their bare-toothed grimaces and wild eyes, Brigid figured they were on the verge of panic.

The beaded curtain clattered as Brigid bounded through the arch. The door on the other side swung open easily and she quickly closed it behind her, noting sourly it had no lock. She found herself in a very narrow passageway lit by overhead neon tubes. A small closet opened off to the left, holding cleaning and janitorial supplies.

Grabbing a push broom and a heavy, long-handled mop, Brigid placed the wide head of the broom beneath the doorknob and jammed the blunt end of the handle against the wall, inside the angle where it joined with the floor.

The mop was more difficult to affix, but she managed to brace it just above the knob. Fists and feet began hammering against the door. It shook under the repeated impacts, but the improvised barricades held. She heard a man cursing in Magindano, then the door spit dust and wood splinters as a triburst erupted.

Brigid broke into a sprint down the passageway, navigating through a labyrinth of rusting pipes and wheel valves crisscrossing in all directions. She maneuvered around fuse boxes and cooling systems, all the machinery that kept the giant treasure ship alive. The bulkheads, coated with grease and layers of grime, told her she was very close to the engine room.

When the passage terminated at a closed door, Brigid cursed under her breath, but she knew she could no longer afford to be cautious. Lifting the handle, she took a deep breath, threw the door open wide and plunged into a solid wall of wind- and rain-swept fury.

Staggering on the wet deck, Brigid slammed the door behind her and leaned against it. Rain crashed down in a solid torrent from the dark sky. The downpour pounded her in sheets, virtually blinding her and making it difficult to breathe without inhaling water. In an instant, she was soaked to the skin. She cupped a hand over her nose and mouth so she could breathe without difficulty.

Pressing herself against the superstructure, she found a little shelter beneath the overhang of the deck above. She squinted away from the great crooked fingers of lightning scorching their way across the sky and grimaced at the deafening claps of thunder. Brigid had been in wild weather before, but she had never encountered a monsoon. She wondered if the storm's violence was common in this part of the world or due to the aftereffects of skydark.

After a few minutes, the wind died down to no more than intermittent gusts. The rain slacked off to a steady drizzle. Lightning still arced across the sky, but the heart of the storm had moved away. The humidity rising in its wake was oppressive.

Staring through the shifting sheets of water, she gazed toward the harbor front. She saw bursts of flame and tiny lights strobing in the shadows. Dimly she heard the crump of grenades and the chatter of subguns. A battle raged up and along the quayside. The insurrection was in full swing, proceeding despite the weather.

A twisting thread of red fire streaked up from the darkness, rising into the sky in a wide arc, then lancing down toward the upper decks of the ship. Brigid crouched. Because of a thunderclap, she barely heard the rocket's detonation, but the blaze of the explosion painted the shadows a flickering orange for a couple of seconds. The vessel shuddered. Men and women began screaming. She assumed the first rocket had either fallen short or struck an underpopulated section of the *Juabal Hadiah.*

Brigid pushed herself away from the bulkhead and sprinted along the deck, looking over the railing at the murky water glimmering at least fifty feet below. A man yelled behind her, and she heard the sharp report of a pistol. A bullet thumped the air less than an inch from the right side of her head.

Swiveling at the waist, Brigid squeezed off two rounds. She didn't aim—the shots were fired strictly for effect. She saw no one, but she heard more men shouting in frantic Magindano.

She sprinted along the slippery deck and reached a square hatch and a ladder stretching downward. A closed door was opposite it. She opened the door, set it to swinging on its hinges, then half climbed, half slid down the ladder, listening to the thump of running feet overhead.

On the deck below Brigid scanned the vicinity for either a hiding place or adequate cover from bullets. She rounded a corner and saw a stack of crates. Without hesitation she threw herself behind them and crouched motionless, trying not to breathe too loudly. No one came by so she guessed she had divided her pursuers. She heard more scattered shots, but this time from the direction of the waterfront. A rocket exploded, filling the area with an eye-hurting brilliance. There were more stuttering shots, a series of screams and shouts. The ripping sounds of multiple subguns firing on full-auto came from somewhere nearby aboard the ship.

A small sampan floating less than fifty yards away spit a tongue of flame. She caught a glimpse of a quick, fiery streak, and the ship shuddered under a blow that shook the deck violently. The harbor erupted astern, water rising in a column.

Realizing that the rocket had most likely punched a deep hole in the *Juabal Hadiah*'s hull below the waterline, Brigid rose from her hiding place, made sure the zone was clear, then ran out along the deck again. She ran down a short flight of steps and ducked through a low archway onto a gallery overlooking the stern of the ship. The giant flag of Saragayn, bearing the image of a blazing skull superimposed over a crossed sword and a rifle, hung from a sturdy mast overhead.

A pistol cracked and the sharp reports of an autorifle tore through the fabric of the air, but the shots were not aimed at her.

Returning through the archway, she saw a dozen armed men ranged around the railings of the gallery. They exchanged a flurry of gunfire at point-blank range. Two of them clutched at themselves and folded over. The racket of the gunfire and the whine of ricochets stunned Brigid's senses.

Men rolled on the deck—keening, strangling with their hands, clubbing with empty revolvers, struggling hand-to-hand with knives. She could not differentiate between Captain Saragayn's men and the insurrectionists, and she didn't try.

Taking a breath, she focused her attention on an area of the gallery free of combatants and lunged for it, running flat-out. A man in a coverall suddenly loomed out of the darkness and straight-armed her. His slamming

palm caught her in the upper chest, driving almost all
the wind from her lungs and sending her sprawling.

Brigid slid across the deck on her shoulders and
back. As she did, she squeezed off two quick shots
between her outspread legs. The man's shirt sprouted a
pair of holes and he went over backward. Dragging air
back into her lungs, she climbed to her feet and sprinted
for the railing again.

Before she covered much of the distance, two men
raced to intercept her. Brigid saw them coming, but she
kept going, knowing a retreat back to the archway
would only give them clear shots at her back.

She altered direction, racing toward them, firing with
the TP-9 at the end of an outstretched arm. They
returned fire with handguns and she felt a bullet pluck
at her hair, ripping out a few strands by the roots.

Wincing, she kept her finger pressed down on the
trigger, directing precision bursts. A man's face broke
apart in flying arcs of blood. Then the slide of the TP-9
blew back into the locked-and-open position. Since
stopping or slowing meant an instantaneous death, she
increased her speed, the length of her stride, legs
pumping fast and furiously.

She flung her weapon in front of her. The metal
frame of the TP-9 smashed into the face of Saragayn's
soldier barely half a second before her knee slammed
into his solar plexus. Carried by the momentum of her
rush, she bowled into him and both of them went down.
A shot from the man's pistol went up into the sky.

Going into a shoulder roll, Brigid cartwheeled up and over the man, using his chest as a springboard. She landed on her feet in a deep squat, and then sprang up and onto the Pandakaran. His face was spattered with blood from a laceration on his forehead. Her right foot, with all her weight behind it, drove into his neck. She pivoted sharply and smartly on her heel, crushing his larynx, grinding her foot into his windpipe.

Clutching at his throat, a flood of scarlet spilling from his open mouth, the man went into convulsions, clawing at the deck with his free hand, legs kicking spasmodically.

Brigid raced for the edge of the deck, leaped atop the railing and then jumped feetfirst into the black water far below. As she fell, she inhaled a deep lungful of oxygen and held it. She slammed through the oily surface of the harbor cleanly. The water felt tepid, almost as warm as the air. Water gushed up her nose and filled her sinus passages, trickling into her throat.

She let herself plunge downward, pulled by the weight of her boots and clothes. Brigid tamped down the panic surging within her. Over five years before she had nearly drowned in the Irish Sea, and since that day, she had developed a morbid fear, almost a phobia, of dying by water.

Slitting her eyes open, the brine stinging them, she stared at the roiling surface above her. She glimpsed only intermittent flashes of light. Her ears registered the muffled, multiple thumps of bullets striking the water.

She saw the bubble-laced streaks of the slugs punching into the sea around her.

When her boot soles sank into the soft ooze of the bottom mud, she carefully pushed off at angle, stroking in the general direction of the waterfront. Only when her lungs began to ache intolerably did Brigid decide to surface. She came up slowly near an area of the pier crowded with sampans. She fought the impulse to cough and gasp.

Raking strands of hair away from her eyes, spitting out water, she tried raising Kane and Grant via the Commtact. She received no response and wondered briefly if immersion in seawater had caused the comm unit to malfunction.

Brigid swam underneath the pier. Close overhead was a tangle of timber braces and struts. Long growths of moss dangled from them, like the beards of old wise men she had seen in pictures.

A dull pounding shook the air for a couple of seconds. Looking toward the *Juabal Hadiah,* she saw a plume of white steam billowing out of a hole in her port-side hull. She assumed various combustibles had exploded within the ship. Treading water, she looked for a way to climb out of the harbor without being seen. Voices shouted back and forth, and slowly they diminished in volume.

Brigid swam quietly toward the shoreline, still keeping just beneath the pier, the barnacle-encrusted pilings scraping her arms. She pulled herself along by the cross struts until her feet touched the bottom and she was able to wade. She reached a wooden ladder made of crudely hammered-together slats, and after resting a minute to regain her breath, she climbed it as quickly as she could. The weight of her sodden clothes and boots dragged at her as she pulled herself up, hand over hand.

When Brigid reached the top, she raised her head by degrees so she could see over the edge of the pier. The first thing she saw was the bore of a gun, staring directly into her face like a hollow, cyclopean eye.

Chapter 6

"Taking laps?" Kane asked mildly, lowering his pistol.

Brigid could see him only as a blurred figure, but she knew Kane would cover his relief with an insouciant smile. With her hair a tangled mass plastered to her face and her clothes clinging to her body like a second skin, Brigid felt at a distinct social disadvantage.

Ignoring his outstretched hand, Brigid heaved herself onto the pier. She swept her gaze over Kane, Grant and the four figures clustered in a semicircle near the security checkpoint. "No," she retorted. "What the hell happened to you?"

"When the fighting broke out," Grant answered, "it wasn't healthy to hang around here. The storm didn't help."

Kane gestured to the people standing behind them. "We met up with this group. They suggested we team up with them if we wanted to rescue you."

"As you can see," Brigid said stiffly, "it wasn't necessary."

"This time," Kane put in.

A tall figure stepped forward, pushing a feature-concealing hood away from her face. "So you managed to escape. I thought Saragayn might have installed you in his harem by now."

"I didn't give him the chance." Brigid detected a French accent in the blond woman's voice. "You must be Clarise."

The woman's face registered surprise. "I wasn't sure if you remembered seeing me aboard the ship."

"I never forget a face," Brigid retorted.

"Or much of anything else," Grant rumbled.

Although Brigid Baptiste had spent over half of her thirty years of life as an archivist in the Cobaltville Historical Division, there was more to her storehouse of knowledge than simple training.

Almost everyone who worked in the ville divisions kept secrets, whether they were infractions of the law, unrealized ambitions or deviant sexual predilections. Brigid Baptiste's secret was more arcane than the commission of petty crimes or manipulating the baronial system of government for personal aggrandizement.

Her secret was the ability to produce eidetic images. Centuries ago, it had been called a photographic memory. She could, after viewing an object or scanning a document, retain exceptionally vivid and detailed visual memories. When she was growing up, she feared she was a psi-mutie, but she later learned that the ability was relatively common among children, and usually disappeared by adolescence. It was supposedly very rare among adults, but Brigid was one of the exceptions.

Since her forced exile, she had taken full advantage of the Cerberus redoubt's vast database, and as an intellectual omnivore she grazed in all fields. Coupled with her eidetic memory, her profound knowledge of an extensive and eclectic range of topics made her something of an ambulatory encyclopedia. This trait often irritated Kane and Grant, but just as often it had tipped the scales between life and death, so they couldn't in good conscience become too annoyed with her.

"I'm not surprised you two managed to hook up with the disloyal opposition," Brigid said. She turned her gaze on a slender man with a purple head scarf. "I'll bet you're Mersano."

The man nodded. "That's me."

"Captain Saragayn knows all about your plan."

"Yes, we know," Clarise said with a surprising degree of equanimity. "I am sure Daramurti betrayed me."

"That's exactly what happened," Brigid stated.

"I should have known better than to trust that child."

"That child is dead," Brigid replied matter-of-factly. "The captain blew his brains out."

Clarise's expression did not change. "I assumed as much."

"Any sign of the Millennial Consortium?" Kane asked.

Brigid massaged the knuckles of her right hand. "Yes. I left a sign of Cerberus on his jaw. He claimed his name was Book but he smelled of ex-Mag."

Kane and Grant exchanged a swift, surprised glance.

"You know him?" Brigid asked.

"Of him," Grant answered. "He used to be the division administrator of Mandeville. A real hard-ass."

Brigid snorted. "Isn't that how *all* Mags rep out?"

Both Kane and Grant knew her question was a rhetorical one and so didn't bother to respond.

The legions of black-armored Magistrates were formed as a complex police machine. The Magistrate Divisions of the baronies demanded instant obedience to their edicts, to which there was no possible protest. In a little under a century, both the oligarchy of barons and the Mags that served them had taken on a fearful, almost legendary aspect. The unification program established a social order by which generations of Americans were born into serfdom, slavery in everything but name.

All Magistrates followed a patrilineal tradition, assuming the names, duties and positions of their fathers as though the first Magistrate to bear the name were the same man as the last.

As Magistrates, the courses their lives followed had been plotted before their births. They were destined to live, fight and die, usually violently, as they fulfilled their oaths to impose order upon chaos.

"Book is working for the consortium now," Brigid continued. "And he doesn't like Cerberus one little bit."

A series of gunshots floated from the direction of the *Juabal Hadiah*.

"Can you clue us in as to what's happening aboard my father's ship?" Mersano asked.

"A lot of fighting," Brigid said. "But not as much as you'd think for an insurrection."

Curtly, she related everything she had seen and experienced aboard the treasure ship. "In retrospect, the fighting seemed rather pro forma. The most damage was inflicted by a rocket fired from a boat in the harbor."

Mersano squinted in the direction of the *Juabal Hadiah,* eyeing the steam rising from the hole in the cavity. "She's taking on water."

"But not sinking," Grant commented.

"The harbor is very shallow," Clarise explained. "The ship is built on a foundation of an old stone quay. She might founder a bit, but she won't go capsize or go under."

Brigid frowned. "You'd think the people in the casinos and brothels would have noticed something amiss by now."

Clarise laughed contemptuously. "You aren't familiar with addictive personalities, are you?"

"What's that got to do with anything?" Brigid demanded, peeved.

The ship's whistle suddenly blasted out a deafening hoot. Everyone on the pier jumped in sudden surprise. Another eardrum-compressing wail followed the first.

"That's the abandon-ship signal," Mersano announced excitedly.

Clarise smiled slyly. "It signals more than that, *mon cher.*"

Mersano fixed a questioning stare on her face. "What do you mean?"

Before the woman answered, a muffled explosion came from inside the *Juabal Hadiah*. A corner of an upper deck vanished in a roiling ball of billowing orange-yellow flame and an eardrum-knocking concussion. A flurry of splintered timbers flew skyward. A chemical reek cut into their nostrils.

"That's a bomb!" Mersano blurted.

"One of three," Clarise said calmly. "Linear shaped charges planted in noncritical areas of the ship."

Two more explosions lit up the decks of the ship. A sail billowed like a balloon and then dissolved in flaming shreds. A column of fire punched upward, toppling a mast into the harbor with a tremendous splash. Smoke gouted from portholes amidships.

"Who planted those explosives?" Mersano demanded.

"I did," Clarise answered. "Three hours ago."

"You don't seem too worried about civilian casualties," Brigid observed coldly.

"Like I said…you don't know much about addictive personalities." Clarise's lips drew away from her teeth in a vulpine grin. "There are always more."

A babble of frightened voices wafted to them, quickly resolving into terrified shrieks and screams. A knot of people appeared at the top of the ramp. They fought their way down, several of them tripping and tumbling all the way to the bottom.

"We should probably stand aside," Clarise said smoothly. "Unless we want to be trampled by the stampede."

As the people moved to the far edge of the pier, near the security kiosk, Kane glanced at Clarise. "I don't understand this. If you had set the explosives, why didn't you just light them up instead of staging an armed assault?"

Before the woman answered, the pier became a confusion of shouting, milling and panic-stricken people. Some fell and were trampled, while others were jostled off the sides and into the black waters of the harbor.

When the last of the crowd pelted past, Mersano hefted his big Casull revolver and said, "Let's end this."

Clarise eyed Kane speculatively. "Would you care to accompany us?"

Kane blinked in surprise. "Why should we?"

"Mr. Book," Brigid said softly.

Kane gusted out a weary sigh. "In that case let us indeed end this."

The Cerberus warriors followed the four people. Mersano led the way, down the pier and up the ramp. At the top, one of Saragayn's thugs appeared and flailed out with a rifle butt. Grant grabbed the stock of the rifle and yanked hard. The man lost his balance and pitched headlong over the side with a long scream. He fell into the water between the ship and pier.

As soon as they boarded the *Juabal Hadiah,* a quartet of Saragayn's men fired in their direction from the end of a smoke-clouded corridor. The handgun volley was poorly aimed.

A single shot from Mersano's revolver drilled a hole

through the jaw of a man, punching him backward with such force his head struck the floor first. A scarlet geyser erupted from his mouth and a severed carotid artery.

Kane framed the pirate next to him in the sights of the Copperhead and fired a two-second burst that opened up his chest, propelling him backward in a crimson mist. The other two men retreated.

Clarise took the lead, coughing because of the smoke. She stepped over the dead men without glancing down at their faces. Creaks and groans echoed loudly throughout the interior of the ship, and they felt the deck shift underfoot. Kane began to sweat, worrying about the ship filling with so much water it would slide sideway off the quay.

Entering the throne room, Brigid saw Daramurti's body lying in the same position, a pool of blood spread out around his head. The gun barrels in the hands of Mersano's men darted back and forth like the heads of agitated cobras.

"The *mal vicieux* is not here," Clarise said flatly.

Kane cast Brigid a questioning glance and she translated quietly, "The evil pervert."

They returned to the corridor. A distant murmur of anxious voices reached them. Mersano stiffened. "Hear that?"

A pistol cracked, one shot only. Mersano kicked himself into a sprint, Clarise following closely at his heels. He ran through an open door into what seemed like, at first glance, an art gallery. Jade sculptures, silken wall paintings, elaborate furniture and porcelains filled the room.

Captain Saragayn sat before the dun-clad figure of Mr. Book on a stool carved in the shape of an elephant. The man's upper body leaned forward, and wet crimson spread over the turban in a widening stain.

Book lifted both hands, a small pistol held in his right. He opened his fingers and the gun dropped with a thud to the floor. Quietly he said, "It's done. All taken care of. Everybody just relax."

Mersano eyed Saragayn closely. "You killed my father?"

Book smiled. "I did you a favor, kid. Spared you from committing fratricide. Now we can discuss business like business people instead of egomaniacs."

Mersano glared at Book and stepped closer. "Why should I talk to a treacherous bastard like you?"

"I'm wondering the same thing," Brigid said.

Book's eyes flicked to Brigid, and he nodded in the direction of Clarise. "Why don't you enlighten everyone?"

Mersano swung startled eyes toward the blond woman, who met his gaze with a laugh. She prodded at Saragayn's body with a foot. His body sagged and then fell limply to the floor.

"Don't be so naive, *mon cheri*," she said, reaching out to playfully tousle Mersano's hair. "Your father was very clever, very suspicious. I had to feed him distractions. You were the perfect focus of his attention."

"You had already cut a deal with Millennial Consortium, Clarise?" Kane demanded.

"She did." Book smiled with smug satisfaction. Slowly he lowered his hands. "She brought the consortium here, in fact."

Kane gritted his teeth. "That's a goddamn stupid thing to have done, Clarise."

The woman shot him an angry stare. "Cerberus doesn't have the resources of the consortium—or at least you don't have the kind of resources Pandakar needs. This was a business decision, so don't take it personally."

"It affects us personally," Grant growled, "so we'll by God take it personally."

"You don't know anything about us here," Clarise declared haughtily. "I don't want to make enemies of Cerberus, but Pandakar cannot afford to alienate the consortium, either."

"You can't enter into a partnership with the Millennial Consortium," Brigid declared, "no matter what Book has told you. The millennialists will turn Pandakar into a satrap, a consortium satellite inside of a month. Everybody here will become employees, if not their slaves."

Clarise shrugged. "That's all everybody here on Pandakar was under Saragayn, anyway. Now perhaps the people will have access to medical care and decent food."

"Of course they will," Book said in a silky soft tone. "That's the bargain."

"You don't know what you're giving up," Grant grated.

He turned toward Mersano. "Do you?"

Mersano uttered a bitter laugh and gestured possessively to the items in the cabin. "I grew accustomed to all of this…and then when I was banished, I realized I couldn't do without it. Now I have it back. I'm not going to complain about who gave it back."

Book chuckled. "Then everybody is happy."

Kane's hand clenched hard around his pistol. "You lying piece of—"

Clarise spoke a word and gun barrels snapped up, training on him. She said in a menacing tone, "Do not do anything precipitous, Kane. I have come to like you and would regret giving the order to shoot you down."

Brigid laid a restraining hand on Kane's arm. "We've got to let this one go, Kane. We can't win it."

Book's smiled widened into a thin, mocking grin. "Very wise decision, Baptiste. It doesn't really matter if I'm killed—the contract with the consortium is open. They'd just send another representative to execute it."

Eyes troubled, Clarise said softly to Kane, "You and your friends should leave now."

The grin vanished from Book's face. "That's not a good idea." His voice sounded as cold as a polar night. "The consortium has outstanding warrants on anybody from Cerberus, particularly these three."

Without looking at Book, Clarise snapped, "The contract hasn't been fully executed Monsieur Book. I can still cancel it."

Book did not reply, but the muscles at the hinges of his jaws swelled and knotted.

"Go. I guarantee you safe passage," Clarise said to Kane. "No one will molest you."

Kane glared at Book, who affected not to notice. Then he wheeled and stalked out of the cabin, not looking to see if Brigid Baptiste and Grant followed him. He knew they did—they certainly had no reason to linger.

Once they reached the hatch, the three people stood at the top of the ramp, gazing out at Pandakar. It was still raining, and a haze obscured the harbor front. A stroke of distant lightning split the vault of the night sky.

Grant blew out a disgusted sigh. "This was a big thanks-for-nothing mission."

"We have to make the best of it," Brigid said.

Kane eyed her enigmatically. "We do?"

Then he stepped out into the rain, grateful for its cooling touch.

Chapter 7

Mohandas Lakesh Singh tried hard not to look as if he was worried, but he knew he failed at it miserably.

He stared up at the huge Mercator map spanning the far wall of the Cerberus command center and forced his light brown face to maintain a perfectly neutral expression. Pinpoints of light shone steadily in almost every country, connected by a thin glowing pattern of lines.

They represented the Cerberus network, the locations of all functioning gateway units across the planet. No matter how long Lakesh stared at the indicator light of the Snakefish unit, its glow did not waver or blink. It registered no activity when it most definitely should have.

A headache throbbed behind his eyes as he reluctantly turned away from the map and gazed at the long room with its high, vaulted ceiling and double aisles of computer stations. Most of the time, Lakesh felt like the command center was his personal kingdom or playroom, but on other days it affected him like a medieval torture chamber.

This was one of those days.

He glanced toward the wall shielding the mainframe computer and its priceless database. The operations complex had five dedicated and eight shared subprocessors, all linked to the mainframe. Two centuries before, it had been one of the most advanced models ever built, carrying experimental, error-correcting microchips of such a tiny size that they even reacted to quantum fluctuations. Biochip technology had been employed when it was built, protein molecules sandwiched between microscopic glass-and-metal circuits.

The computer served as the bridge between the worlds of predark and postdark. Lakesh took no pride in the fact of having straddled both of those worlds. A well-built man of medium height, with thick, glossy, black hair, a dark olive complexion and a long, aquiline nose, he looked older than his early fifties, despite strands of gray streaking his temples. In reality, he had observed his 255th birthday only a short time before.

As a youthful genius from Kashmir, Lakesh had been drafted into the web of conspiracy the overseers of the Totality Concept had spun during the last two decades of the twentieth century. A multidegreed physicist and cyberneticist, he served as the administrator for Project Cerberus, and that position had earned him survival during the global megacull of January 2001.

The Totality Concept was the umbrella designation for American military supersecret researches into many different arcane and eldritch sciences, from hyperdimensional matter transfer to temporal phasing to a new form of genetics. Most of the spin-off, yet related projects had their own hidden installations, like Over-project Excalibur, which was based in a subterranean complex in New Mexico.

Lakesh strode up the long aisle between the computer stations. The overhead lights in high-ceilinged room automatically dimmed at sunset and came back on to full brightness at dawn. They were bright now, causing Lakesh to squint at the consoles that ran the length of the walls. Indicator lights flickered red, green and amber, circuits hummed, needles twitched and monitor screens displayed changing columns of numbers.

Only half a dozen people were in the command center, and they resolutely didn't look at him as he passed. He didn't know whether he felt grateful for their studied indifference or annoyed by its transparency. The personnel sitting at the stations were all former Manitius Moonbase scientists.

In the three-plus years since their arrival in Cerberus, the Moon colonists had proved their trustworthiness and ingenuity on many occasions. Most of the people who lived in the Cerberus redoubt acted in the capacity of support personnel, regardless of their specialized individual skills or training. They worked rotating shifts, eight hours a day, seven days a week.

Primarily their work involved the routine maintenance and monitoring of the installation's environmental systems, the satellite data feed and the security network. However, everyone was given at least a superficial understanding of all the redoubt's systems so all Cerberus personnel could pinch-hit in times of emergency.

Grant and Kane were exempt from this cross training, inasmuch as they served as the exploratory and enforcement arm of Cerberus and undertook far and away the lion's share of the risks. On their downtime between missions they made sure all the ordnance in the armory was in good condition and occasionally tuned up the vehicles in the depot.

Brigid Baptiste, due to her eidetic memory, was the most exemplary member of the redoubt's permanent staff, since she could step into any vacancy. However, her gifts were a two-edged sword, inasmuch as those same skills made her an indispensable addition to away missions.

Lakesh entered the antechamber at the far end of the command center. The room held the eight-foot-tall mat-trans chamber, rising from an elevated platform. Vertical slabs of brown-tinted armaglass enclosed the six-sided chamber. All of the official Cerberus gateway units in the mat-trans network were color-coded so authorized jumpers could tell at a glance into which redoubt they had materialized.

Despite the fact that it seemed an inefficient method of differentiating one installation from another, only personnel holding color-coded security clearances were allowed to make use of the system. Inasmuch as their use was restricted to a select few units, it was fairly easy for them to memorize which color designated what redoubt.

Armaglass was manufactured in the last decades of the twentieth century from a special compound that plasticized the properties of steel and glass. It was used as walls in the jump chambers to confine quantum-energy overspills.

Lakesh took a great deal of pride in the Cerberus unit because it was the first fully debugged matter-transfer inducer built after the prototypes. It served as the basic template for all the others that followed.

A metal plate on the elevated platform hung open, exposing a confusing mass of microprocessor boards. Donald Bry lay on his stomach, peering into the aperture, the beam of light from the headlamp casting a halo on the circuitry of the internal emitter array. The elastic strap confined his tangle of coppery curls. A collection of small precision tools were scattered around him.

Bry didn't look up at the sound of Lakesh's approach. Instead he said loudly, "No, Lakesh. Like I told you an hour ago and an hour before that, there's nothing wrong on this end."

In his cultured voice, touched with a lilting East Indian accent, Lakesh retorted, "And like *I* told you an hour ago, I don't expect you to find anything wrong—only to find a way to circumvent the problem. Come up with a work-around."

Bry served as Lakesh's lieutenant in all matters technical, and occasionally he accused his mentor of forcing him to act as either scapegoat or miracle worker. With a sigh, the slightly built man elbowed himself onto his back.

Bry stared up at Lakesh, and the light from the headlamp cut into the scientist's eyes. He flinched, uttering a wordless sound of annoyance. In a tone of aggrieved patience, Bry said, "We've got a transit line signal from this unit to the one in Snakefish, but we can't establish a matter-stream lock. For some reason, that unit is way out of phase with the network. I don't know how I can possibly work around that."

Planting his hands on his hips, Lakesh paced the jump chamber, glaring balefully past its open door to the interior. The polished metal floor consisted of a pattern of interlocking hexagons. Although the gateway represented Lakesh's lifework, he often wished it were otherwise.

A device that could transmit matter—particularly soldiers and weapons—was a more important offensive weapon than America's entire nuclear stockpile. However, matter transmission had been found to be absolutely impossible to achieve by the employment of Einsteinian physics. Only quantum physics, coupled with quantum mechanics, had made it work beyond a couple of prototypes that transported steel balls only a few feet across a room.

But even those crude early models could not have

functioned at all without the basic components that pre-existed the Totality Concept.

As the project's overseer, Lakesh experienced the epiphany and made that breakthrough. Armed with this knowledge, under Lakesh's guidance the quantum interphase mat-transinducers opened a rift in the hyperdimensional quantum stream, between a relativistic here and there. The Cerberus technology did more than beam matter from one spot in linear space to another. It reduced organic and inorganic material to digital information and transmitted it along hyperdimensional pathways on a carrier wave.

In 1989, Lakesh himself had been the first successful long-distance matter transfer of a human subject, traveling a hundred yards from a prototype gateway chamber to a receiving booth. That initial success was replicated many times, and with the replication came the modifications and improvements of the quantum interphase mat-trans inducers, reaching the point where they were manufactured in modular form.

Even then, the mystery of the origin of the technology that made the entire system viable haunted Lakesh. It would be many years before he came across the shocking fact that although the integral components were of terrestrial origin, they were constructed under the auspices of a nonhuman intelligence—or at least, nonhuman as defined by late-twentieth-century standards. Nearly two centuries would pass before Lakesh learned the entire story, or a version of it. Within a year, the proper terminology for the process was replaced in favor of the Cerberus network, or the Cerberus gateways.

To streamline the mass production of the quantum interphase mat-trans inducers, the project was moved from the Dulce, New Mexico, installation and head-quartered in a redoubt on an exceptionally remote mountain plateau in Montana's Bitterroot Range. Only a single road stretched up from the foothills to the plateau, bordered by sheer cliffs that had been carved when acres of mountainside collapsed during the nuke-triggered earthquakes of nearly two centuries ago.

The trilevel, thirty-acre facility built into the side of a mountain peak was constructed primarily of vanadium alloy and boasted design and construction specifications that were aimed at making the complex a secret community of at least a hundred people. The redoubt housed two dozen self-contained apartments, a cafeteria, a decontamination center, a medical dispensary, a swimming pool and holding cells on the bottom level. Redoubt Cerberus was an organized masterpiece of impenetrability.

The plateau holding the redoubt and the road leading up to it were surrounded by an elaborate system of heat-sensing warning devices, night-vision video cameras and motion-trigger alarms. In the unlikely instance of an organized assault against the installation, an electric force field energized with particles of antimatter could be activated at the touch of a button. A telemetric communications array was situated at the top of the peak.

Although official designations of all Totality Concept–related redoubts were based on the phonetic alphabet, almost no one stationed in the facility referred to it as Bravo. The mixture of civilian scientists and military personnel simply called it Cerberus.

Bry's voice brought Lakesh back to the matter at hand. "Anyway, there's no need to stress out. The biolink transponders show the away team is in good health. You need to stop worrying before you give yourself a coronary."

"I've been telling Lakesh the same thing for years," a deep female voice said from the doorway. "He never pays any attention until he collapses."

Chapter 8

Recognizing the voice immediately, Lakesh turned to face Reba DeFore. "I'm not worried as much as I am single-minded, Doctor."

Buxom and stocky, DeFore wore the one-piece white coverall common throughout the redoubt as a duty uniform. She was brown-eyed, and her dark bronze flesh tones contrasted sharply with her ash-blond hair, worn loosely about her shoulders for once instead of being caught back in a severe French braid.

"You become single-minded to the point of obsession when Domi goes out on a mission," DeFore replied. As the chief medic of the Cerberus redoubt, she always spoke her mind. "With Brigid, Kane and Grant on their own mission, she's the most qualified."

"I'm quite aware of that," Lakesh said stiffly. "But she and her team are overdue by nearly five hours. Since the mat-trans unit in Snakefish is apparently malfunctioning, my worries are quite genuine."

"You haven't figured out the cause yet?"

"No," Bry spoke, his tone waspish. "But it's not for lack of Lakesh pushing me."

DeFore frowned at Lakesh. "I thought you knew more about the gateway system than anybody alive."

"Obviously," Lakesh retorted dryly. "But that doesn't mean an unprecedented malfunction could occur, something I or anyone else who worked on the network had never encountered before."

"Dr. Singh," Evanovich called from the control center. "We've finally got some images on the sat uplink."

Lakesh hurried past DeFore. Bry made a move to rise, but Lakesh snapped over his shoulder, "Keep working."

Lakesh walked to the main control console. Evanovich, a blond Moonbase émigré in his forties, obligingly gave up his chair. Lakesh sat before the big VGA monitor screen, and his hands played over the keyboard as though he were a concert pianist.

Across the right side of the screen scrolled a constant stream of figures, symbols and numbers. Near the bottom left corner was a curving sweep of blue-green, mottled with wisps of white.

"There's the Pacific coast," he murmured. "So far so good."

"Wait," Evanovich said.

The view on the screen tightened, penetrating the haze, and more details began to show. Forests appeared as ripples of green texture. At the touch of another key, the country leaped upward. A tapestry of dark, oasis-spotted sand swelled on the screen.

The perspective on the screen changed, rushing downward, through a sky flecked with scraps of white clouds. The plummet halted over a place that was flat and bare, but held structures in the center of it.

The image was slightly out of focus, but Lakesh saw a series of small, outlying constructions arranged in a circle around the bulk of a larger building. Rearing out of the sands was the suggestion of a wall.

Lakesh stared unblinkingly and then swallowed hard. *"Ishvara,"* he murmured hoarsely in Hindi.

Coming to stand behind him, DeFore asked, "What is it?"

Lakesh nodded toward the image on the screen. "This explains why we can't establish a lock on the Snakefish gateway."

Leaning forward, DeFore squinted. "I don't see anything but old ruins."

"Exactly," Lakesh said quietly. "Those ruins are what is left of Snakefish."

"What?" DeFore moved closer. "That can't be."

The view was one of solemn desolation. Dust hung in the afternoon light. Everything looked as if a giant hand had reached down from above and crushed everything into the ground.

Musingly, Lakesh said, "It appears as if most of the ville has collapsed in on itself, fallen into a giant cenote."

"What the hell is that?' the medic demanded peevishly.

"Colloquially known as a sinkhole...a depression in the surface topography that occurs when the bedrock is removed."

"I don't see any sign of the Admin Monolith," DeFore said.

Lakesh touched several sections of the screen with a forefinger. "There and there—and there. The entire building collapsed, carrying the mat-trans unit with it. No doubt it is buried under tons of rubble. The power source is still functioning, still feeding us a live signal, but there is no way the gateway can be activated now, even if it were dug out."

After a thoughtful moment, DeFore said, "At least our team managed to make it out." She nodded toward the medical monitor station. Lakesh followed her gaze.

On the screen he saw an aerial topographical map of what used to be the state of California. Superimposed over it flashed four icons. The telemetry transmitted from Domi's, Edwards's, Falk's and Philboyd's subdermal biolink transponders scrolled in a drop-down window across the top of the screen.

Everyone in the installation had been injected with the transponders, which transmitted heart rate, respiration, blood count and brain-wave patterns. Based on organic nanotechnology, the transponder was a nonharmful radioactive chemical that bound itself to an individual's glucose and the middle layers of the epidermis. The computer systems recorded every byte of data sent to the Comsat and directed it down to the redoubt's hidden antenna array. Sophisticated scanning filters combed through the telemetric signals using special human biological encoding.

All of the icons, including Domi's, glowed a steady green, much to Lakesh's relief.

"Without access to the satellite uplink in the Admin Monolith," Lakesh said musingly, "they're incommunicado."

Swiveling in his chair, he addressed a trim black man seated at a console and wearing a headset. "Friend Banks?"

"Yes, sir?"

"No signal from our away team in Malaysia?"

"Not yet."

"Keep trying to raise them over the Manta's satcomm channels. As soon as you get a response, patch me in."

"You got it."

DeFore laid a comforting hand on Lakesh's shoulder. "Everything is under control. You can relax."

He forced a laugh and patted her hand. "I don't know if I would agree with that assessment, Doctor. It is certainly no coincidence that the ville of Snakefish falls down when our people are there investigating why other villes had fallen down."

DeFore arched an eyebrow. "Are you suggesting that the earthquakes were intentional? Artificially induced?"

He nodded. "I am."

"Is that possible?"

"Very much so. Earthquakes are caused by the sudden release of energy within a limited region of the rock strata due to tectonic stress. When stresses in rock masses have accumulated to a point where they exceed the strength of the rocks, it leads to rapid fracture. The fractures usually tend to travel in the same direction and may extend over many miles along a certain fault zone.

"An artificial means of inducing earthquakes was experimented with many times, from the excavation of bedrock to the detonation of underground nuclear devices."

"That doesn't seem very efficient," DeFore commented.

Lakesh shrugged. "Anything that changes the local fault field and can produce a fracture or a slippage can trigger an earthquake. Another method was the electromagnetic excitation of quartz mineral deposits through use of microwaves. The extent of the damage we see in California seems due to a deep-focus slippage."

"What's that?"

"It's a pattern to describe quake zones that dip into the Earth at a forty-five-degree angle."

Skeptically, DeFore asked, "How could something like that be artificially induced?"

"I have my theories." His tone held a dark undercurrent of foreboding.

DeFore caught her breath, hesitating before asking. "You don't suspect that one of the overlords is behind this, do you?"

Lakesh shook his head. "Not at the moment. But we can't rule them out, either."

DeFore compressed her lips, knowing he spoke the truth. Years ago, Lakesh had created an underground resistance movement of superior human beings to oppose the hybrid barons and their hidden masters, the Archon Directorate.

The barons and the Cerberus exiles alike had believed the barons were under the sway of the Archons, a mysterious race who had influenced human affairs for thousands of years. Allegedly, the sinister thread linking all of humankind's darkest hours led back to a non-human presence, which conspired to control humanity through political chaos, staged wars, famines, plagues and natural disasters.

The nuclear apocalypse of 2001 was all part of the Archon Directorate's strategy. With the destruction of social structures and severe depopulation, the Archons established the nine barons and distributed predark technology among them to consolidate their power over Earth and its disenfranchised, spiritually beaten human inhabitants.

But eventually the Cerberus exiles had learned that the elaborate backstory was all a ruse, bits of truth mixed in with outrageous fiction. The Archon Directorate did not exist, except as a vast cover story, created in the twentieth century and embellished with each succeeding generation. The only so-called Archon on Earth was an entity named Balam, the last of an extinct race who had once shared the planet with humankind. All of the barons believed that they acted as the plenipotentiaries of the Archons.

For several years, Kane, Brigid and Grant had struggled to dismantle the machine of baronial tyranny in America. They had devoted themselves to the work of Cerberus, and victory over the nine barons, if not precisely within their grasp, did not seem a completely unreachable goal—and then unexpectedly, over two years before, the entire dynamic of the struggle against the nine barons changed.

The Cerberus warriors learned that the fragile hybrid barons, despite being close to a century old, were only in a larval or chrysalis stage of their development. Overnight, the barons changed. When that happened, the war against the baronies themselves ended, but a new one, far greater in scope, began.

The baronies had not fallen in the conventional sense through attrition, war or coup. No organized revolts had been staged to usurp the hybrid lords from their seats of power; no insurrectionists had met in cellars to conspire against them.

The barons had simply walked away from their villes, their territories and their subjects. When they reached the final stage in their development, they saw no need for the trappings of semidivinity, nor were they content to rule such minor kingdoms. When they evolved into their true forms, incarnations of the ancient Annunaki overlords, their avaricious scope expanded to encompass the entire world and every thinking creature on it.

The overlords were engaged in reclaiming their ancient ancestral kingdoms in Mesopotamia. They had yet to cast their covetous gaze back to the North American continent, but it was only a matter of time.

Before that occurred, Cerberus was determined to build some sort of unified resistance against them, but the undertaking proved far more difficult and frustrating than even the cynical Kane or the impatient Grant had imagined. Two years after the disappearance of the barons, the villes were still in states of anarchy, of utter chaos with various factions warring for control on a daily basis.

A number of former Magistrates, weary of playing the roles of ronin, masterless samurai or fighting for one transitory ruling faction or another that tried to fill the power vacuum in the villes, responded to the outreach efforts of Cerberus.

A few of the former Mags joined Cerberus and made up the core of the CATs—the Cerberus Away Teams. A few others remained in the former baronies and attempted to rebuild them, establishing a new model of a democratic system.

"Although I can speculate as to the causes of the earthquakes," Lakesh declared, "the primary pattern is the three destroyed villes had managed to pull themselves out of the abyss of anarchy."

He paused and took a long breath, releasing it in a

sigh. "Some force opposes a new society that isn't based on the old god-king system as practiced by the barons."

A line of consternation appeared on DeFore's forehead. "But since the barons are gone—"

"Lakesh," Banks called from the comm station. "I've got the transmission from our team in Malaysia. Brigid is waiting to talk to you."

Chapter 9

The navigational computers directed the Manta ships on a trajectory across the Pacific toward the coastline of California.

The blazing glory of dawn flamed in the sky as the Manta automatically dropped its airspeed to five hundred miles per hour.

The change in speed roused Kane from a fitful slumber and he came to full alertness. Swiftly, he oriented himself, reaching for the handgrip control. Kane studied the turbulence data fed to him by the LARC—the low altitude ride control—subsystem. The numbers scrolled across the inner curve of his helmet's visor, and he reduced the Manta's airspeed.

Kane wore a bronze-colored helmet with a full-face visor. The helmet itself was attached to the headrest of the pilot's chair. A pair of tubes stretched from the rear to an oxygen tank at the back of the seat. The helmet and chair were a one-piece, self-contained unit. A dozing Brigid sat strapped into a small jump seat in the rear of the cockpit.

Turning his head to the left, he saw Grant's Manta

flying less than ten yards from the tip of his wing.
"Grant," he said. "You awake?"

"Are you?" Grant's surly query echoed within the
walls of his helmet.

"I'm not sure yet."

He studied the Manta, noting that if he didn't know
otherwise, he would have no idea who was piloting the
craft. The pair of Transatmospheric Vehicles held the
general shape and configuration of manta rays, and as
such they resembled little more than flattened wedges
with wings. Sheathed in bronze-hued metal, intricate
geometric designs covered almost the entire exterior
surface.

Deeply inscribed into the hulls were interlocking
swirling glyphs, cup-and-spiral symbols and even elaborate cuneiform markings. The hulls, although they
appeared to be composed of a burnished bronze alloy,
were of a material far tougher and more resilient.

The craft had no external apparatus at all, no
ailerons, no fins and no airfoils. The cockpits were
almost invisible, little more than elongated symmetrical oval humps in the exact center of the sleek topside
fuselages. The Manta's wingspans measured twenty
yards from tip to tip, and the fuselage was around fifteen
feet long.

Of Annunaki manufacture, the Mantas were in
pristine condition, despite their great age. Powered by
two different kinds of engines, a ramjet and solid fuel
pulse detonation air spikes, the Transatmospheric

Vehicles could fly in both a vacuum and in an atmosphere. The Mantas were not experimental craft, but an example of a technology that was mastered by an ancient race when humanity still cowered in trees from saber-toothed tigers. Metallurgical analysis had suggested that the ships were a minimum of ten thousand years old.

"This is a hell of a detour," Grant said, the ship-to-ship comm system accurately conveying his frustration. "I'd made plans to visit Shizuka when we got back today."

"CAT Alpha is stranded," Kane said. "We can't leave them to find their way home on their own."

"I don't know why not," Grant replied. "It's only about a thousand miles from Snakefish to Cerberus. A hike like that would toughen 'em up…give 'em character."

Brigid stirred in the jump seat. "If Domi gets any more character, she won't be fit for any human company whatsoever."

"When did you wake up?" Kane asked.

"About a minute ago." She yawned and said, "Besides, if Snakefish was destroyed by an earthquake, the investigation is now in our laps."

"Yeah," Grant rumbled. "I was afraid it would be something like that."

"That's usually the case," Kane said. "We're the ones who have reps to live up to, remember."

"Speak for yourselves," Brigid replied sourly. "Being a living legend isn't at all like it should be."

"No argument there," Grant declared. "But we are who we are. And we've earned our reps."

Even Brigid couldn't deny that. They were the infamous Cerberus warriors, the baron blasters, and their reputations were fearsome. Anyone who lived near any of baronies had heard tales of Kane, Grant and Brigid Baptiste, the rogue Magistrates and archivist who had continually escaped and outwitted all the traps laid for them by various barons of different villes.

For their part, Kane and Grant found that blurring the line of demarcation between legend and fact had proved very useful on occasion.

They were credited with killing Baron Ragnar in his own bed, and although no one knew how they managed it, they were also held responsible for the fall of the villes and disappearance of the barons.

"Closing on the coordinates of Snakefish," Kane reported.

He and Grant again notched back the Mantas' airspeed. As they did so, dawn became a sunny morning. The snowcapped peaks of the Sierra Nevadas thrust up from the horizon. Along a hundred miles of the coast they saw nothing resembling a shoreline, only a sharp range of cliffs as if an unimaginably huge knife blade had slashed through the state.

Once the Cascades came into view, Grant and Kane dropped altitude to a thousand feet and cruised above a panorama of rolling terrain. Lifting his gaze, Kane looked out over the blunt prow of the Manta at the rugged foothills spreading out beyond the tableland.

The instrument panel of the Manta was almost comical in its simplicity. The controls consisted primarily of a handgrip, altimeter and fuel gauges. All the labeling was in English, squares of paper taped to the appropriate controls. But the interior curve of the helmet's visor swarmed with CGI icons of sensor scopes, range finders and various indicators.

Both Kane and Grant had easily learned to pilot the Mantas in the atmosphere, since they had handled crafts superficially like them, the Deathbird gunships the two men had flown when they were Cobaltville Magistrates. But when they flew the first of the four TAVs down from the Manitius Moon colony where they had been found, they came to the unsettling realization that the ships could not be piloted like winged aircraft while in space.

A pilot could select velocity, angle, altitude and other complex factors dictated by standard avionics, but space flight relied on a completely different set of principles. It called for the maximum manipulation of gravity, trajectory, relative velocities and plain old luck. Despite all of the computer-calculated course programming, both men learned quickly that successfully piloting the TAV through space was more by God than by grace. But so far, the Mantas had proved to be trustworthy in all maneuvers and atmospheres.

"Here we are," Grant announced.

Kane looked down and experienced a queasy sense of disbelief. He husked out, "My God."

They soared over a small mountain of rubble, the slopes littered with crushed stone and splintered wood. The steel girders and walls were tumbled and twisted in utter ruin. Rocks strewed the area. They saw a number of dull-eyed people huddled around small fires. They glanced up with vague interest as the Manta ships flew over and then circled. Even at such a height, Brigid could see faces filled only with listless despair.

Grant and Kane engaged the vectored-thrust ramjets of the Mantas and dropped the TAVs straight down, bringing them gracefully to rest facing the gate. Fine clouds of dust puffed up all around.

The two men switched off the engines, and they cycled down with piercing whines. Opening the seals of their helmets, Grant and Kane unlatched the opaque cockpit canopies and slid them back. Everyone disembarked, sliding down the wings to the ground.

Silently they surveyed the destruction with astonished eyes. Evidently the tremors had struck with a particular ferocity at the Admin Monolith, reducing the proud tower to little more than a heap of debris. People crept through the rubble and a few curious faces turned toward them. Hanging over the twisted wreckage that had once been Snakefish was an oppressive pall that seemed hostile.

"Hey!" At the sound of the sharp female voice the Cerberus warriors whirled, hands reflexively going for gun butts.

They relaxed a trifle when they saw Domi trotting toward them from the direction of the beach. Brewster Philboyd, Mariah Falk and Edwards followed at her heels.

When she reached the Cerberus warriors, Domi's eyes flashed like polished rubies. "About time—where you been?"

"Nice to see you, too," Kane countered, not bothering to blunt the edge of sarcasm in his tone. "I hope we didn't inconvenience you too much."

Breathing hard, Philboyd jogged up. "Don't listen to her. I for one am overjoyed to see you guys. The past twenty-four hours have been pretty nerve-racking."

Brigid glanced at the rubble. "I don't doubt it."

The right side of Philboyd's face looked red, as if he had been exposed to the sun for too long.

Domi sighed and dry-scrubbed her white hair in frustration. "Sorry. Got worried. Bein' stuck here in an indefensible zone. Got no weapons but my knife and what we improvised."

Grant narrowed his eyes. "What happened to your guns?"

"Ask him." Edwards pointed toward a brown-skinned man who sauntered toward them with a make-shift spear in one hand. A fresh gash showed on his left cheek.

"Hello, Gedrick," Kane called. "Are you all right?"

He nodded. "About as well as could be expected."

"Why'd you disarm our people?" Grant demanded.

"I confiscated their guns," Gedrick answered. "As per the ville ordinance."

"Ordinance?" Grant echoed incredulously.

Gedrick nodded. "With fewer guns in the hands of hotheads, it cuts down on the daily bloodbaths we used to have here. It worked, too."

Kane bit back the observation that the ordinance also cut down on the ville's ability to defend itself. He knew Gedrick could cope with reasonable confidence against ordinary dangers, but acts of nature that destroyed his ville and wantonly killed innocent people were things no one could anticipate.

"How many casualties?" he asked.

Gedrick shrugged. "No way to tell for sure, but I'd judge that ninety percent of us managed to get out before the walls and the monolith came tumbling down."

Kane glanced toward Mariah. "Are you all right, Dr. Falk?"

The woman rubbed a shoulder, but she grinned in response, laugh lines deepening at the corners of her eyes. "Who wouldn't be after spending the night on a California beach? All we needed was marshmallows and surf music to really set the mood."

Ignoring the remark, Grant said, "You're the geologist. Did this seem like a normal earthquake to you?"

The woman's grin turned into a frown. "There really isn't such a thing. But no, in my estimation this quake wasn't the result of natural causes."

"Explain," Brigid said.

Mariah opened her mouth to respond and then cut her gaze over toward Philboyd. "Time to report what you saw."

Philboyd nodded. "Right before we evacuated the ville, I saw—just for a second—some kind of machine rising up out the ground. It had burrowed beneath the walls."

Brigid raised an eyebrow. "Burrowed?"

"Yeah. It also generated an incredible amount of heat. Even though I was standing quite a distance from it, I still got this." Gingerly, he touched the reddened flesh on the right side of his face.

Brigid stepped closer, eyeing the tiny blisters rising from the skin. "Looks like a radiation burn."

"Yeah, that's what I thought, too."

"I didn't see any machine. Never heard of a mechanical mole," Gedrick said grimly.

"Like I told you before—we have," Domi said waspishly. She gestured to herself, Brigid, Grant and Kane. "Tell 'im."

Brigid and Gedrick locked gazes. Matter-of-factly, she stated, "We've seen such machines."

"We even blew one up," Kane interjected.

Gedrick gusted out a weary sigh. "I was afraid of that."

"Why?" Grant asked.

Gedrick gestured toward the far side of the debris field. "Because that means what I thought was an earth slippage is actually a track."

Chapter 10

Gedrick led the Cerberus personnel around the perimeter of rubble, skirting tumbled masses of stone and concrete, picking his way over the litter. They walked across an open field that tilted sharply upward to a rock wall where fruit trees lifted their limbs to the sky. There were very few trees—the area surrounding the ville walls were usually kept cleared of vegetation as a precaution against a surprise attack.

One of the official reasons for fortifying the villes was a century-old fear of a foreign invasion from other nuke-scarred nations. It had never happened, mainly because no country's army was large enough or well-equipped enough to establish anything other than a remote beachhead.

Then there had been the threat of mutant clans, unifying and sweeping across the country. Legend spoke of a charismatic mutie leader who had once united the clans against humanity, but the war hadn't quite come off. However, the memory of the threat was burned deep into the collective minds of the baronial hierarchies. It had burned so brightly that a major aspect of the early Program of Unification had been a campaign of genocide against mutie settlements in ville territories.

Gedrick stopped at the crumbling edge of a ditch, a little less than four feet wide. The soil within it alternated from powdery grit to fist-size clods. Gedrick pointed toward the ville, silently indicating how the furrow snaked in under the debris of a wall, and then he swung his arm in the opposite direction. The ditch stretched across the field, disappearing into the base of a bluff.

"I thought this was one of the ville's drainage ditches," Gedrick said. "But it's not."

Beneath a shading hand, Kane gazed at the dark line curving over the surface of the ground, running in a southerly direction. "Looks to me like something was digging its little heart out."

"That doesn't mean it was a mechanical mole," Edwards muttered disdainfully.

"I saw what I saw," Philboyd retorted doggedly.

"A few years back, after we blew up the Archuleta Mesa installation, we came across a digging machine," Domi stated.

"Came across?" Gedrick repeated doubtfully.

"It came across *us*," Brigid said wryly. "It burst up out of the ground right in front of us."

"How big was it?" Gedrick asked.

"Not all that huge," Grant answered. "About the size of a Sandcat."

"Speaking of which," Gedrick declared, turning and gesturing toward a distant copse of aspen trees, "I've got one stashed there."

"Got one what?" Domi demanded.

"A Sandcat. Thought maybe we use it to backtrack this trail, assuming it was made by a tunneling machine."

Kane squinted toward the cluster of trees. He barely made out a blocky shape parked beneath the broad boughs. "Why is it out there?"

Gedrick's lips twitched in either a feeble smile or a moue of distaste. "It's for my personal use."

Grant eyed him speculatively. "Were you planning a road trip?"

Gedrick shook his head. "You know how it is, Grant. You always should have an escape route in case your presence is no longer desired."

"Due to an uprising, you mean?" Brigid inquired.

"Exactly. The citizens here seem to be happy with the way things are…as long as they get the food and comforts they want. But if one day the amount of food is rationed and the comforts aren't quite as comfortable…"

Gedrick trailed off, shrugged and added, "They could turn not just unhappy but downright homicidal."

"Hence the exit strategy," Kane concluded. "I thought you were an elected official."

"More or less," Gedrick replied diffidently.

Domi uttered a scoffing laugh. "That means you didn't have a candidate running against you, right?"

"Hey, nobody else wanted the job," Gedrick said defensively. "Besides, nobody else was qualified."

"Well," Philboyd said, "the citizens sure as hell are going to run out of food soon…and their comforts aren't so comfortable. Are you going to exit, stage right?"

Gedrick glowered at him. "I haven't decided yet. But I'm keeping that option open."

Kane felt a sudden surge of anger. The Cerberus personnel had been briefed only sketchily by Lakesh about the political setup of Snakefish, and he realized that he had barely half listened to it as it was.

As a Magistrate, he had been trained to consider and question all possibilities and exigencies about a mission. He knew that to be careless in the details was to jeopardize the odds of survival. Kane and Grant had learned never to open a door without considering an enemy waiting behind it. They never walked into a room without expecting a possibly lethal surprise.

In the five-plus years since joining Cerberus, the two men accepted the grim reality of a quick and unanticipated death in the lost corners of the world. They had survived for so long against great odds by knowing everything that could be known about a given situation and a potential adversary.

Kane took his risks with the objectivity of a professional gambler, playing the odds and the percentages. He, Brigid and Grant had been in tight situations many times before and in more than a few of them he hadn't expected to survive. But he and his friends always did, even if they lost some blood, flesh and peace of mind in the process.

Lakesh had once suggested that the trinity they formed when they worked in tandem seemed to exert an almost supernatural influence on the scales of chance, usually tipping them in their favor. The notion had both amused and intrigued Kane. He was too pragmatic to truly believe in such an esoteric concept, but he couldn't deny that he and his two partners seemed to lead exceptionally charmed lives.

"Gedrick, if you cut and run from your people now, there won't be any coming back," Domi warned.

"I didn't think there would be," the man retorted.

"Do you have a destination in mind?" Brigid asked.

He smiled at her. "I was thinking about Cerberus."

"Not a fucking chance," Domi snapped. "You run from here, you just keep running."

While the people talked, Mariah Falk bent over and picked up a handful of soil from the edge of the ditch. She rubbed it between both palms, producing a gritty, crunching sound. Then she cried out. "What the hell—?"

She shook the dirt out of her hands, then examined her right palm. A splotch of fresh blood glistened there. "Glass!" she exclaimed. "Glass cut me."

Eyes narrowed in concentration, Brigid glanced at Mariah's hand, saw the cut was superficial and then knelt at the burrow, carefully probing with her fingers. "Soil with a high silca content is turned to glass by extreme heat," she said. "Vitrification."

"I am aware of that," Mariah said stiffly, kneeling beside her. "Lightning strikes turn sand into fulgurites."

"How hot are we talking?" Grant asked.

Brigid lifted a small wedge-shaped object, holding it between thumb and forefinger. She blew off a surface coating of grit to reveal a chunk of dark glass. "Between 800 and 1500 degrees Fahrenheit. Remember Washington Hole? That's all heat-fused, vitrified glass."

Kane and Grant exchanged sour glances. They weren't likely to forget Washington Hole, the so-called hell zone of hell zones. These were places where the geological or meteorological effects of the nukecaust prevented a full recovery. The passage of time could not completely cleanse the zones of its hideous, invisible plagues.

"So whatever made this tunnel," Brigid continued, "generated extreme heat energy…most probably in the form of microwave pulses."

Philboyd gingerly fingered his face. "That would explain how I got burned."

Brigid rose, dusting off her hands. She surveyed the area and said, "If this tunnel was dug by a machine, it came and went in the same direction. It just reversed course and followed the same path it had dug to get here. That would make leaving a little easier than arriving."

Grant knuckled his chin thoughtfully. "Access and egress along the same getaway line. Makes sense."

Kane turned to Gedrick. "I want to take a look at your exit strategy."

The man frowned in confusion for a couple of seconds, then chuckled. "Let's go."

He led the Cerberus personnel across the open field. They passed through an area where the injured of the ville were laid out on blankets and pallets. About twenty people were huddled there, some cradling broken arms, others with crude splints tied around their fractured legs. A woman holding an unconscious little girl with most of her head swathed in bloody bandages reached out for Gedrick's hand as he walked by.

He hesitated, an expression of pity creasing his face, but he continued walking across the field.

"There aren't too many serious injuries," Gedrick said quietly. "But what we do have are more than we can cope with. All the medical facilities were in the Admin Monolith."

Kane grunted noncommittally. "You better set up a burial detail before you leave, then."

Gedrick shot him a sharp glance but didn't reply. He walked through the closely growing trees and into a small clearing where the Sandcat was parked. The vehicle was known by assorted names: fast attack vehicle, armored personnel carrier or simply a wag, but was most often referred to as a Sandcat.

Built to serve as an FAV rather than a means of long-distance ground transportation, the Sandcat featured a pair of flat, retractable tracks that supported the low-slung, blunt-lined chassis. The armored topside gun turret held a pair of USMG-73 heavy machine guns.

The Cat's armor was composed of a ceramic-armaglass bond, protection against both intense and ambient radiation. The gun appeared to be a transparent half dome, but at the touch of a button microcircuitry would engage, feeding an electric impulse to the chemically treated armaglass bubble. It would instantly become opaque when exposed to energy-based weapons, such as particle-beam emitters—not that there was much chance of encountering such weapons. Like most everything else used by the Magistrate Divisions, the Sandcat was based on an existing predark framework, built to participate in a ground war that was never fought.

Kane and Grant walked around it, inspecting the tracks and the dull gray chassis. They opened the rear hatch and inspected the equipment, finding boxes of bottled water and self-heat MREs, as well as a medical kit. Grant tapped the lid and angled questioning eyebrows at Gedrick.

"There are not enough painkillers, antibiotics or bandages to help more than one or two people," Gedrick said. "Who do I choose to treat and who do I choose to let suffer?"

"You could have at least parceled out the food and water!" Domi said angrily, her ruby eyes glittering.

"It's still not enough for even half rations for a quarter of them," Gedrick shot back. "But go ahead, take it all."

Domi reached for it, but Kane laid a restraining hand on her arm. "Hold on that."

The little albino glared at him in angry astonishment. "What? Why?"

"We're going to need the provisions in here."

"Who's 'we'?" Gedrick demanded suspiciously.

Kane pointed to himself, then to Brigid and Grant. "We is. We're going to take the Sandcat and backtrail whatever dug the tunnel. The Mantas have supplies in the cargo hold, about as much food, water and medicine as you've got stashed here."

"Even so," Edwards said, "that's still not a lot to go around."

Kane nodded. "That's why Brewster here will take one of the Mantas and fly back to Cerberus and fetch more."

Domi opened her mouth to object, but Grant said, "Brewster is the only one besides us who is fully rated as a Manta pilot. He can take you back to the redoubt."

"No," she said defiantly. "I should go with you."

"That's not how we divided the duties of the away teams," Brigid reminded her. "Besides, Lakesh is very worried about you."

Domi made a negligent gesture. "I'll talk to him on the Manta's sat comm, tell him I'm all right."

"You still need to return to Cerberus," Grant told her. "You're the next one in the chain of field command if something happens to us. We shouldn't all be out on away missions at the same time."

Domi regarded him gravely but said nothing.

"If I leave in the next hour, I can be back with food, water and medicine by nightfall," Philboyd said.

"You might want to bring DeFore with you, too," Kane said.

"Who's DeFore?" Gedrick asked.

"Reba DeFore," Grant answered. "The closest thing to a certified medical doctor inside of a couple of thousand miles. She'll set up a field hospital."

Kane gazed levelly at Gedrick. "We're commandeering your exit strategy, Gedrick. If you want, we'll take you along…at least for a ways."

Pursing his lips, Gedrick presented the image of pondering Kane's offer, and then he shook his head. "This responsibility thing gets under your skin, I guess. I can't leave my people now. I don't know whether we're going to rebuild or move on, but I'll stick with them."

He smiled thinly, his eyes shifting from Kane to Grant to Brigid. "But you knew that already, didn't you?"

Kane nodded. "We did."

"Like you said," Grant intoned, "this responsibility thing gets under your skin."

Chapter 11

Kane gazed through the ob port at the rolling hills and the plunging canyons. The first light of dawn just touched the edges of the eastern sky, turning the indigo into a tapestry of pale orange.

Despite the fact that the furrow was fairly easy to see, the trail led over ridges, down into shallow coulees and through tangled underbrush. Brigid sat in the copilot's seat and tried to read a map by the light provided from the instrument panel. Squinting through the rectangular lenses of her wire-framed eyeglasses, she kept checking their route against the compass.

"We're heading due south," she announced loudly to be heard over the engine roar. "I think we're on our way to Mexico."

"Why do you say that?" Grant asked from a rear passenger seat.

She pointed to the map and then to the compass. "Snakefish is roughly located in the same area as old San Diego. That places us only a few miles from the Mexican border."

Kane tightened his hands on the steering wheel. "Think we'll see Welcome To Mexico signs?"

"I seriously doubt it," Brigid answered. "There's no need for borders now."

The Cerberus warriors had left Snakefish three hours earlier with only thin soup and cups of coffee for an unsatisfactory breakfast. The predawn air, so close to the ocean, was cold, wet and penetrating. It made Kane's old injuries ache.

The goodbyes with the other Cerberus personnel were brief. Brewster Philboyd planned to fly one of the Mantas back to the redoubt in Montana at first light. Once there, he would exchange Domi for Reba DeFore and medical supplies, as well as other provisions.

By the time the morning sunlight bathed the distant hills in hues of orange and russet, Kane's aches and pains were even more pronounced. He was forced to take the Sandcat on wide detours, around ravines and riverbeds. The FAV jounced and bounced as he piloted up and down gullies and over shallow river crossings. The vehicle sang a perpetual groaning protest in every joint, seam and rivet. The racket made by the metal tracks return rollers was an incessant clatter, as was the roar from the diesel engine.

Grant complained about the pummeling, but nothing could be done. He sat in the rear storage compartment, which was large enough to accommodate six extra troops on two sets of fold-down jump seats that could also be used as beds.

As the sun rose higher in the sky, the Sandcat rolled through scattered pockets of ruins—houses leaning in on themselves, roofs cocked sideways, the burned-out shells of old service stations and fast-food restaurants rising from the arid landscape like headstones.

When the Sandcat punched through a tangled snarl of mesquite, they emerged onto a two-lane blacktop road. The asphalt had a peculiar ripple pattern to it, and weeds sprouted from splits in the surface. Kane, Brigid and Grant had all seen the rippling effect before—it was a characteristic result of earthquakes triggered by nuclear bomb shock waves.

Kane downshifted and braked the Sandcat to a halt. From a clip on his web belt he took a compact set of binoculars. Pushing his sunglasses back, he brought them to his eyes, peering through the ruby-coated lenses. He swept them over the gently rolling, sandy terrain, then stared along the black ribbon of ancient roadway stretching out to the horizon. Along the left side of it he saw the humped furrow creasing the ground. It disappeared into a sprawling jumble of rubble several miles in the distance.

"It looks like our mole is paralleling the road here," he said. "At least for a while. We're getting into desert country."

Grant leaned forward between the two seats and glanced all around at the parched terrain as if expecting to see something other than a dead land stretching away in drifting dunes of ocher and saffron.

"Riding on the road will spare our backsides," he grunted. "We can make better time."

Kane cautiously then released the clutch and the Sandcat lurched forward. He carefully upshifted through the gears and guided the vehicle in a lumbering course down the center of the interstate.

Now that they traveled on a road, even one as rutted and potholed as it was, the ride was much smoother and considerably faster. The big engine throbbed steadily without missing a beat, and the suspension didn't squeak or creak.

They passed around bottles of water as the heat of the day increased. "Baptiste, is there really a machine that can tunnel for this kind of distance?" Kane asked.

Brigid swallowed a mouthful of water before answering. "There used to be. They were called Subterrenes."

Leaning forward so he could hear, Grant inquired skeptically, "Like a submarine, only one that traveled on dry land?"

"Exactly. They were used in the last years of the twentieth century to construct underground military bases as part of the COG program."

Kane nodded. "Figures."

As many as fifty years before the nuclear holocaust, a long-range construction project was undertaken by a program known as Continuity of Government. The program was perceived as the ultimate insurance policy should Armageddon ever arrive. Hundreds of subterranean command posts were built in various regions of the country, quite a number of them inside national parks, hiding in plain sight. The size and complexity ranged from little more than storage units to immense, self-sustaining complexes.

"After we had that encounter with the tunneling machine outside of the Archuleta Mesa," Brigid said, "I looked for more information in the Cerberus database. There were several different types of Subterrenes, but the largest and most efficient operated by melting its way through the rock and soil, actually vitrifying it as it traveled and leaving a neat, solid-glass-lined tunnel behind it."

"How could it generate that intense heat?" Grant asked.

"By a compact nuclear reactor that circulated liquid lithium from the reactor core to the tunnel face, where it melted the rock. In the process of melting the rock the lithium lost some of its heat. It was circulated back along the exterior of the Subterrene to help cool the vitrified rock as the machine forced its way forward."

"That sounds superficially like what Brewster reported," Kane said. "The main question now is who has one and why are they using it to destroy the villes?"

"I guess if we keep following the track," Grant replied, "we're bound to find out."

The Sandcat rolled down the straightaway for only

another mile before Kane was forced to stamp on the brakes. The road was bisected by an earth slip, the cut as clean as a surgical incision. Beyond lay a great plain of parched desert terrain, dotted only with sagebrush, cacti and octotilla shrubs.

Kane hissed out "Shit" between his teeth, then said, "I knew it was too good to last. Everybody hang on to something."

He let up on the brake and the Sandcat eased forward. The front end teetered precariously, tipped and plunged, carving its own path over the rock face. Miniature avalanches cascaded beneath the tracks. Kane wrestled with the wheel, downshifting, upshifting, braking and riding the clutch.

When the vehicle reached the bottom, Kane fixed the position of the ground furrow in his mind and steered toward it. The Sandcat rolled over the dead, sterile soil, throwing up rooster tails of dust.

Grit sifted in through ob ports, and all of them were forced to don goggles to protect their eyes. Brigid wrapped a bandanna around her nose and mouth. They tried closing the windows, but the interior quickly became like that of an oven.

Within half an hour, they came across a tiny village of brown adobe huts. The streets were empty of all life and movement except for wind-driven eddies of dust. Kane stopped the Sandcat so they could stretch their legs and eat.

The Cerberus warriors checked the perimeter and

noted bullet pocks in the walls of the buildings. The houses were empty of just about everything, even furniture.

"I think this place was raided," Grant said reflectively. "By slavers, maybe."

"Maybe," Kane replied. "Or maybe the people here just decided to pull up stakes and move on."

"Couldn't blame them," Brigid said.

The three of them ate from the MRE packs automatically, mechanically. The packages contained all the minerals, vitamins and proteins a human needed to keep healthy, but they all seemed to share one of two flavors—bland or repulsive. No middle ground seemed to exist, and even the most undiscriminating of palates eventually ended up in a form of shock. Taste buds refused to function.

Brigid scanned the area. The terrain sloped to hills that seemed to be covered in brown dirt. Dust devils, tiny whirlwinds, sprang up and vanished.

"Not much of a country," Grant grunted.

"Unless you're into smuggling," Kane said. "Or slave trading."

He looked for a stem of grass to chew but gave up after a few moments. There was nothing within reach but a stunted variety of prickly pear that looked withered from the heat and lack of moisture.

Crumpling up the MRE pack, he eyed the position of the sun in the sky and said, "Let's go. We've got at least six more hours of daylight left."

Grant switched places with Brigid, and the Sandcat continued traveling over the flatlands, crushing thorny shrubs and squat, scrubby trees so short they were more like overgrown bushes. Jagged rocks and boulders pushed up on all sides.

The rad counter on the instrument panel was the only way to tell if they were entering a hell zone, a region where ambient radiation still lingered at lethally high levels. They skirted one such zone and for nearly an hour the needle of the rad counter wavered, edging between orange and red.

The few bits of vegetation they saw were leached of all color, a monochromatic shade of gray. All of the shrubbery crunched to powder under the treads of the Sandcat, vaporizing like sculptures made of ash. The three people didn't relax until the rad counter ticked over into the yellow zone.

Within minutes of leaving the hell zone, Grant suddenly said, "We've got company."

Kane looked through the right window. A half a dozen men on horseback paralleled their course, riding at a swift canter. Even through the clouds of dust, he was able to make out the outlines of broad-brimmed sombreros and the glint of weapons.

Kane slowed, keeping his eyes on them. His right hand went to the butt of his holstered pistol.

"We can outdistance them easy enough," Brigid said with a studied nonchalance. "No need to lure them into a firefight."

Kane cast her a questioning glance, then forced a laugh. "You're right."

He pressed on the accelerator and the Sandcat surged ahead.

The Cerberus warriors had all heard tales of self-styled "toll takers" in the Outlands, coldhearts who staked out and barricaded a section of road and charged exorbitant and sometimes bloody fees to travelers. Most of the toll takers were Roamers, outlaws who paid lip service to overthrowing the cushioned tyranny of the villes to justify their criminal activities.

The Sandcat rolled past the burned-out ruins of a village. The outlying area was nothing but several acres of shattered brick and concrete with rust-scabbed reinforcing bars twisting around the rubble like gnarled, skeletal fingers.

"Something is going on out here," Grant observed sourly. "Looks like those buildings collapsed, just like in Snakefish."

Brigid leaned forward between the seats, her posture tense. "Slow down a little."

Kane did as she said, downshifting. "What?"

She pointed through the forward ob slit. "Look at the track there. What do you see?"

Thumbing dust away from the lenses of his goggles, Kane followed the furrow they had been trailing for hours. A dozen yards ahead, a deep groove in the ground intersected it, then branched out, curving along the face of a low hillock.

Bringing the Sandcat to a halt, Kane stepped out to examine the track, following it to the base of the hill. He lifted the goggles and grimaced. His eyes stung due to the searing light reflecting off the sand. The heat rose in shimmering waves, never relenting. The sun tightened a screw of pain into the back of his head.

He kicked at the edge of the furrow. "Another Subterrene?"

Grant and Brigid joined him. "I don't think so," Brigid said.

Grant gestured. "Yeah, the motion pattern is different. It's not as wide and the ground doesn't look as broken."

Kane opened his mouth to respond—then they heard the screams.

Chapter 12

Lungs laboring, feet slogging in the sandy soil, Kane, Brigid and Grant reached the crest of the hill and stumbled to an unsteady halt. They stared down into a shallow, bowl-shaped depression, their minds not immediately comprehending what their eyes saw.

At first glance, it appeared that four people, all of them with dark skin and hair, struggled to keep a small, shrieking boy from being drawn into a funnel-shaped hole by a length of gray vine. The vine wrapped around the child's right leg was stretched taut. Two adults gripped him by the arms and dug their heels into the ground, but judging by the grooves cut into the soil by their feet, they were slowly dragged forward.

While the Cerberus warriors watched in confusion, another vine whipped out of the hole and fastened itself around the boy's left ankle. He screamed in terror as a thin layer of ground burst upward. Through the shower of grit, Kane received a fragmented impression of a creature humping up through the sand.

Kane snatched his autopistol from his holster and

kicked himself off the crest of the hill. He snapped, "The Ouroboros!"

As they ran down the face of the slope, a creature heaved itself from the hole. It resembled a garden slug, but its leprous gray mass, colored by splotches of tan, was over twelve feet long and nearly half that wide. A blunt, featureless head bobbed on the end of a rubbery neck. Two stalks jutted from the head, and they bore round eyes on tips that swiveled in different directions at the same time. The neck extended at least four feet and was almost as thick as the boy's entire body.

With a moist, sucking sound, a round, pulsing orifice opened on the underside of its head. Coiling and uncoiling tentacles surrounded the rim. The slug emitted a high-pitched hissing sound, like steam escaping from a faulty valve. More tentacles lashed out, whipping and flailing.

The Cerberus warriors, Kane in particular, knew the creature from Outlands folklore, the Ouroboros Obscura, the giant mutant worm of the deserts. Anyone born in postdark America had heard rumors of its existence drifting in from hell zones. Outlanders had sworn to the stories of the predatory beast, mutated and adapted to life underground.

Several years before, in the alkaline deserts of Utah, Kane had very nearly been devoured by an Ouroboros. He knew how dangerous the creature could be, with a resilience that bordered on invulnerability.

He barely noticed the reaction of the people when he,

Brigid and Grant took up positions around the mutant monster. The Ouroboros reacted to their arrival by hissing angrily and rearing up, its circular mouth opening wide to reveal a ring of small inward-pointing teeth like a lamprey's. The orifice glistened wetly. A tentacle shot out, missing Kane's face by a slender margin.

Kane staggered on the uneven ground, brought up his Bren Ten and aligned the unprotected flesh of the creature's head and neck in front of the bore. His finger squeezed the trigger, and the pistol spit thunder and flame.

The bullet sliced through one of the tentacles wrapped around the boy's leg. The giant slug reared back, lifting its blunt head, and with a slithering sound uncoiled the other tentacle from around the boy's ankle. The adults dragged him away as the Ouroboros twisted toward Kane. Opening its round maw wide, it emitted a sound like that of someone spitting. A jet of colorless liquid flashed through the air.

Kane ducked frantically, but a jet of fluid splashed his cheek, and droplets splattered the lenses of his goggles. His skin instantly began to burn as if exposed to a hot coal.

Arching its body, the Ouroboros plunged headfirst beneath the sand and in a billowing puff of dust, disappeared.

Brigid came quickly to Kane's side, wiping at the caustic liquid on his face with her bandanna. As she dabbed at the drops on his goggles she asked, "Is it gone?"

He shook his head. "I don't know. The one I dealt with in Utah was pretty goddamn tenacious."

Grant, his Copperhead cradled in his arms, glanced toward the five people. They were all Hispanic and all very frightened. They wore simple clothing of white linen, pants and shirts that looked like a uniform. The left breasts of the shirts bore small insignia patches— a simple symbol of several concentric rings surrounding a black center.

The single female among them looked very gaunt, her black hair a dry, hayrick tangle, her dark skin roughened by the sun. She also looked to be at least five months' pregnant. Light glinted dully from the metal manacle affixed around her right ankle. The other adults wore similar shackles.

"Slaves," Grant grunted.

"Runaway slaves," Brigid corrected.

Slavery had been a common trade in the Outlands, but after the fall of the baronies, the Cerberus personnel had hoped the practice would become less widespread because it was less profitable, with fewer buyers.

Kane opened his mouth to speak to the people when the hiss of shifting sand reached his ears. He whirled, leading with his gun. The Ouroboros burst up from the ground, sand sifting down from its mass of rubbery flesh.

The thickly muscled flat tail of the creature flipped

up and battered deep into Kane's midsection, slamming him off his feet and driving him against Brigid. She staggered to one side, crying out in wordless fear. All the breath left Kane's lungs in an agonized bleat between his teeth.

Kane was only dimly aware of collapsing to the ground in a heap, but he knew the monster's open maw, dripping with acidic saliva, hovered above him. He forced his body into a roll.

Grant fired his Copperhead, the triburst homing in on the mutant's head. The rounds punched holes in its back amid little squirts of dark ichor. Shuddering ripples ran through the slug's gray skin and it burrowed swiftly beneath the sand again, clouds of dust flying up from beneath it.

Kane painfully rose, spitting out grit. "Did you kill the son of a bitch?"

Copperhead at his shoulder, Grant scanned the area, turning in a complete circle. "I don't know. Tagged it solid, though."

Brigid, gripping Kane's second Bren Ten autopistol in a two-handed grip, looked in all directions. "I think it left."

"I wouldn't count on it," Kane bit out. "What the hell kind of thing is it, anyway? A mutated sandworm?"

Brigid shook her head. "The *nereis virens* is known as the sandworm, but they aren't anywhere near as large as the Ouroboros. There *have* been reports of giant caecilians, a species of burrowing amphibian that lives underground. But this creature seems more like a gastropod, most likely the result of genetic engineering."

"It can't be very intelligent, then," Grant stated.

"It's efficient, though," Brigid replied. "The acid it spits is most likely powerful digestive juices that it can expel."

"That's efficient?" Kane inquired dourly. "I'd call it disgusting."

They felt a faint trembling beneath the soles of their boots. The Mexicans felt it, as well, and drew away. An elderly man holding the boy in his arms, shouted, "*¡Cuidado!*"

Kane, Brigid and Grant were thrown from their feet when the Ouroboros suddenly burst up through the soil directly under them.

Kane cartwheeled and landed hard on his back, the wind forcibly leaving his lungs in a grunt. Jarred by the impact, his fingers lost their grip and his Bren Ten skittered away. He glimpsed both Grant and Brigid sprawling and rolling. The Ouroboros lunged at him, its round mouth gaping wide.

Kane threw himself to the right, reaching frantically for his pistol, but a pair of tentacles snapped out and locked around his left leg, instantly constricting in painful grips. They dragged him toward the creature's open mouth. Clawing at the ground, Kane dug in his heels, but he continued to be pulled toward the creature.

"*Señor!*"

Turning his head, Kane saw a young man scooping

up his pistol and tossing it to him underhanded. Kane snatched it out of the air and aimed at the pulsating maw of the Ouroboros. He fired with a steady drum roll, the reports coming so close together they sounded like a series of multiple handclaps overlapping one another.

At the same time, Brigid and Grant opened fire, instinctively shifting position to catch the creature's head in the apex of a triangulated cross fire. The rounds blew away the Ouroboros's eye stalks and ripped deep gouges in its rippling flesh. Black liquid drooled from the creature's mouth. The crushing pressure on Kane's leg subsided as the tentacles released. The body of the Ouroboros thrashed wildly like a worm impaled on a fisherman's hook.

The giant worm writhed backward, working its way tail first into a hole. It squirmed, leaving a trail of ichor. They heard the crunching sound of its escape as it burrowed away. The ground lifted up in a curving ripple. Brigid, Grant and Kane stood, weapons at the ready, waiting for it to return. They breathed hard, dirt and dust adhering to their sweat-slick faces.

They looked at one another, lowered their goggles, then turned toward the Mexicans who huddled together, staring at them with wide, dark eyes. Kane glanced toward the young man who had thrown him his weapon and touched his brow with the barrel in a salute. *"Gracias."*

The youth offered a jittery smile. *"Por nada."*

Lungs still laboring, Brigid said, *"Amigos."* She

pointed to herself, then to Kane and Grant. *"Amigos. Companeros."*

The elderly man placed the boy on the ground and shuffled toward them, walking with a limp. Gray speckled his unkempt black hair. His wrinkle-netted face held no particular expression, having much the same color and texture as the leather sandals on his feet.

"We speak English," he said in a pleasantly accented voice. "Thank you for your help. You saved my grandson, Ramon. Thank you."

"You're welcome," Grant replied. "Do you live in that village over there?" He hooked a thumb over his shoulder in the general direction of the ruins.

The man hesitated before saying, "We did before it was destroyed."

"How was it destroyed?" Brigid asked. "By an earthquake?"

"Yes," the young man said bitterly. "An earthquake. We were returning to it, looking for any of our belongings that might have survived and could be salvaged."

"Returning *to* it?" Kane repeated. "Returning from where?"

The pregnant woman said simply, "Mictlanx."

"Where's that?" he asked. He took a closer look at her and realized that she was probably pretty when she had a chance to be.

The woman's face registered surprise. "It is not a place, *señor*. It is a who. You do not know of Mictlanx?"

Although Kane caught the flicker of recognition in Brigid's eyes, he said, "No, we don't. You may have guessed that we're not from around here."

A short stocky man inquired suspiciously, "You are outlanders?"

"You might say that," Grant said. "Is that a problem?"

"Not at all," the elderly man said. He took a deep breath. "My name is Luis. This is my daughter Carmenita, her son Ramon, my nephew Felip…and my brother, Pepito. We have been traveling for the last five days, barely a day ahead of those who would recapture or kill us."

Grant made quick introductions and then nodded toward the manacles on their ankles. "You're slaves?"

"Yes," Felip growled. "Taken from our home by Mictlanx and his Diableros. Nearly a week ago, thirty-two of us were freed from bondage by the magic of Maruja. We are all that is left."

"Who is Maruja?" Kane asked gruffly. "Or does that happen to be a what this time around?"

Carmenita's lips creased in a faint smile. "No, Señor Kane. Maruja is our liberator. She is a very powerful *brujix*."

Grant frowned. "A what?"

"A witch," Brigid stated. "For lack of a better term."

"I could've guessed," Kane muttered.

"Where is she?" Grant wanted to know.

"She lives in the forest," Felip said. "In the Municipio de Aquismon. She wars on Mictlanx."

"Ah." Kane nodded. "That explains everything."

Luis fixed him with a penetrating stare on his face, as if trying to ascertain if he was joking. "Señor Kane… you have already been so kind to us, but I ask this not for myself but for my daughter and grandson—"

"We have food and water we can share," Brigid said.

Luis's seamed face collapsed in relief. "Oh, *gracias.*"

"We might even have some tools to get those manacles off you," Grant declared.

"But we expect some information in return," Kane interposed.

Eagerly, Felip said, "Anything you want to know! We have been two days without food and a full day with no water."

Grant turned toward the slope. "I'll go bring the Cat around."

Kane checked the position of the sun and said, "I don't think there's much point in going any farther today, Baptiste. We might as well make camp for the night."

"I agree," she said.

In a low voice, Kane said, "I saw how you reacted, Baptiste. Does the name Mictlanx mean something to you?"

Brigid smiled without humor. "Only mythologically. Mictlanx was the god of the Aztec underworld."

Kane gusted out a sigh and knuckled his eyes. "You know, I almost said that."

Chapter 13

Grant drove the Sandcat over the hill and parked it. The Cerberus warriors unpacked their gear while Felip and Ramon found enough dried shrubbery to provide tinder. Brigid built a small fire and balanced a cooking pot over the flames. Tidbits from the MRE packages were mixed with bottled water to make a tasteless but sustaining meal.

No one complained about the quality of the food. Watching the little boy, Ramon, spoon the stew from a mess tin into his mouth with a single-minded intensity, Grant commented, "That child hasn't eaten since his last meal."

By the time the family had eaten their fill, sundown was nearing, purpling the high sky. From the Sandcat's toolbox, Grant found a hacksaw with three extra blades. Felip accepted the task of cutting through the manacles around everyone's ankles. He began with Carmenita, sawing at the shackle's hinge.

Brigid sat across from Luis and asked, "All right, tell us your story. What happened to you?"

Luis sighed, ran his hands through his hair, bowed

his head and then sighed again. The old Hispanic man had the irritating habit of prepping himself before answering any question.

"We lived in the village of Santo Cristobel," he said. "You saw what was left of it. I have lived there most of my life, since I was younger than Ramon here."

Grant arched a skeptical eyebrow. "What could you find to live on out here?"

Pepito chuckled through a mouthful of stew. He swallowed noisily. "There are underground streams that flow into little valleys all over this part of the country. We grew vegetables and caught fish."

"And we traded," Carmenita said, wincing as the motion of Felip's saw blade heated the metal of her manacle. "It wasn't an easy life, but we were free."

Kane reflected that living anywhere in the Outlands was a harsh test of endurance, and even barely surviving sometimes qualified as the miraculous. The last vestiges of skydark still lingered.

From what he understood, the years following the nukecaust had been a period of nature gone amok. The hundreds of very nearly simultaneous atomic explosions had propelled massive quantities of pulverized rubble into the atmosphere, clogging the sky and blanketing all of Earth in a thick cloud of dust, debris, smoke and fallout.

For over two decades it was as if the very elements were trying to purge the Earth of the few survivors of the atomic megacull. The exchange of nuclear missiles did more than slaughter most of Earth's inhabitants—it distorted the ecosystems that were not completely obliterated.

After eight generations, the effects of the skydark were more subtle, an underlying texture to a world struggling to heal itself. But the residue still let itself be known from time to time, in the form of wild weather fronts or chem storms that brought acid-tainted rain. Chem storms were the most common manifestation, with downpours of acids and heavy metals that could strip flesh from bone in less than a minute.

"Then," Luis said grimly, "the Diableros came."

At the mention of the name, Ramon leaned against Carmenita, his face showing fear.

"Who are the Diableros?" Kane asked.

"They are more like whats," Carmenita said, reaching out to stroke Ramon's head.

Kane rolled his eyes. "You need a scorecard to tell the difference between the whos and the whats out there."

"The Diableros are practitioners of *brujeria,*" Pepito said.

Grant scowled. "What?"

Curtly, Brigid said, "*Brujeria* is the Spanish word for witchcraft or sorcery. Both men and women can be witches—*brujos* and *brujas*—respectively, but men who practice black magic, or evil witchcraft, are known as Diableros."

"Oh," Kane said, trying to sound mystified.

"It has been a belief among some of our people that when the Diableros appear in greater number," Luis continued, "it is a portent that Montezuma has been reborn and will once more become a mighty ruler."

"Montezuma?" Grant inquired. "Is this the same guy the revenge is named after?"

Brigid barely repressed a smile. "In a way. Montezuma was the last Aztec emperor, ruling all of Mexico from about 1503 until he was killed by Spanish conquistadores in 1520. He was renowned as a mystic, but in the folklore of the native people of the Southwest he became the embodiment of arcane wisdom and magic."

Luis eyed her with new respect. "You are very learned. Are you a scholar?"

"Something like that," Brigid admitted. "More of a historian. A collector of information."

"Montezuma possessed great supernatural powers," Pepito announced earnestly. "He flew upon the back of a giant eagle to build Tenochtitlan—Mexico City. He was a wise ruler and a greatest of all *brujos*. Stories of his feats spread everywhere."

Brigid cast a glance toward Kane and Grant. "As you can hear for yourself, Montezuma became a great culture hero. There were legends of the eternal sacred fire Montezuma had kindled in an underground tunnel, so the souls trapped in the underworld could warm themselves. If anyone found the sacred fire, he would become immortal with unlimited magical powers."

She paused for a thoughtful second and then added, "That corresponds to the Greek myth of Prometheus."

"Maybe so," Kane said impatiently, "but what did these Diableros look like?"

Luis squeezed his eyes shut. "Terrifying, Señor Kane. They wore black armor and helmets…their eyes were covered with visors the color of blood. When they pointed their hands, thunder spoke and people died. They boasted they did the will of Mictlanx and we must obey, or we would be killed."

He inhaled a deep breath, then slowly exhaled it. "Some of us resisted. Our village was destroyed. We were put in chains and forced to march."

With a semimusical chime, the manacle around Carmenita's ankle sprang open and fell away. Felip cried out in satisfaction. *"¡Excelente!"*

Sighing with relief, Carmenita rubbed the callused band of flesh formed by the shackle. She breathed, "*Gracias.* I've worn this for three months…ever since I spurned Mictlanx."

Grant's forehead acquired creases of consternation. "You were his woman?"

Luis reached out for her. "You do not have to speak of it."

Carmenita squared her shoulders and gazed directly into Grant's face. "I must. Yes, I was his woman. By force. He took me."

She touched her swollen belly. "He fathered the child I now carry. That is one reason why he will send trackers to bring me back. He will kill the rest of my family, but he will spare me…until the child is born. He wants the child to be the heir of Montezuma's sacred flame."

"You're getting a little ahead of yourself," Brigid said. "You don't really believe Mictlanx to be an incarnation of the god the underworld, do you?"

Luis snorted. "Of course not. We are poor, but we are not stupid. We knew the man who went by the name of Mictlanx was a fraud when he first appeared. He seeks only power."

"Yeah," Kane said dryly. "We sort of guessed that."

Everything came down to the price of power, he reflected bleakly. Those who sought it, those who possessed it and those who suffered under it. For the scattered survivors of the nukecaust and their descendants, the price of power was tragically high. Many of them were forced to live beyond any concept of law or morality. Many more willingly chose that path.

Rather than rebuilding a civilization around which a new, wiser human society could rally, it was far easier to lead the lives of scavengers and nomads, digging around in the remnants of the prenuke world. A fortunate few managed to build power bases on what was salvaged. Still, power was measured in human blood— those who shed it and those who were more than willing to spill it.

When the Program of Unification was established, the anarchy and barbarism that had ruled the postnuke America for over a century was curtailed, and power was no longer measured in human blood, but the human spirit, the seat of the soul. The nine barons knew—or they were taught—if the soul could be controlled, then humanity could be bound in heavy harness.

Power existed not to accrue wealth or luxury or long life or happiness, but only to gain more power. Everything else—love, honor, compassion—was irrelevant. Those who controlled its price controlled not just the world, but every human being who lived in it and was born into it. The atomic megacull made the planet the property of someone else, and humans like himself were exiles on the world of their birth.

Grant stood up, brushing off his pants. He walked around the Sandcat, toward the far side of the perimeter. "I'll be back in a minute. Hold on the storytelling until I get back."

Felip handed the hacksaw to Pepito, who began sawing at the shackle on his ankle. "Careful now," Kane cautioned. "We don't have that many spare blades."

Addressing Carmenita, Brigid asked, "If Mictlanx put you back in slavery, why do you think he cares about bringing you or the baby back?"

The woman shrugged. "I do not know. Sometimes he was tender and caring to me. Other times, vicious and cruel."

With a forefinger, Felip inscribed a circle beside his right temple. *"Loco en cabeza."*

"A madman," Luis offered.

A drumming of heavy hoofbeats came through the

ground. Luis jumped to his feet, face contorting in terror. "The trackers! They have found us!"

Carmenita rose, as well, face tightening. "I expected them."

Kane glanced toward the hill and then gestured toward the open rear hatch of the Sandcat. "Everybody get aboard. We'll button you up. Don't make any noise. Don't even breathe loud."

Ramon, Felip, Carmenita, Luis and Pepito clambered quickly inside the vehicle. Kane had just closed and latched the hatch when a small column of mounted men rode over the crest of the hill. They were six men astride big horses, and neither Brigid nor Kane liked their looks. They wore wool serapes, wide-brimmed sombreros and were festooned with weaponry. Bandoliers crisscrossed their chests, with long machetes and big showy handguns at their hips.

"We've seen them before," Brigid said quietly.

Kane nodded. "Yeah…you should have let me lure them into a firefight."

Grant's voice filtered over their Commtacts. "What the hell is going on?"

"Stay put," Kane told him. "Can you see?"

"Yeah. Nasty bunch."

"Stay hidden, but we'll keep our channels open."

The men crowded close to the Sandcat on their horses. All but one of them dismounted. The leader, a big-bellied Mexican wearing a huge sombrero, sat in a black saddle studded with silver conchos. Spurs jingled at the heels of his boots. A necklace of human ears hung from around his neck. The blood on them still looked fairly fresh.

The man stared with frank admiration—first at the Sandcat, then at Brigid. His dark eyes fixed on her and he murmured, "Ah, *chiquita.*"

"Do you mind telling us who you are?" Kane asked.

The man looked Kane up and down, noting his weapon. He smirked. "A gringo pistolero, eh?"

Kane said nothing in response. He recognized the type. It was impossible to predict what the man might attempt. The man ran a thumb over the untrimmed mustache sprouting along the line of his upper lip. "My name is Calavera. Tuco Calavera. Does the name mean anything?"

"Should it?" Brigid asked.

Calavera shrugged. "Possibly if you lived around here. Since my name means nothing, that means you are strangers. Outlanders. And therefore, I have the right to kill you."

Chapter 14

Kane let a lazy smile play over his face and his hand hovered close to his holstered pistol. "Is that a fact?"

Calavera shifted in his saddle with a creak of leather. "It is indeed a fact...but that doesn't mean I will exercise that right. I am here on different business."

"Which is?" Kane asked.

"The apprehension of runaway slaves."

"Slaves from where?" Kane asked.

"It doesn't matter, does it?"

"Who hired you?" Brigid inquired.

Calavera grinned at her with his brown teeth. "You want to meet him, *chiquita?*"

"That depends on who he is."

Tuco Calavera jammed a blunt cigar into the corner of his mouth, leaned down and said, *"¡Fuego!"*

A small Mexican, barely five feet tall, struck a sulfur match against the sole of a boot and applied the flame to the end of the cigar. Kane watched Calavera, but he was also aware of what his men were doing. They circled the Sandcat, tugging at the door handles, peering through the ob ports, kicking at the tracks.

Grant's voice whispered, "They're trying to break into the Cat."

Kane inclined his head to let Grant know he had heard him. Calavera puffed on the cigar for a thoughtful moment, his face screened by wreaths of malodorous blue-gray smoke. Slowly he straightened.

"Have you never heard of Mictlanx?" he asked.

Brigid frowned. "Unusual name. He hired you?"

Calavera smiled. "He did. He is the authority in this region, and I act in his name. When I tell him about you, he'll want to know your name—*both* of your names."

"What if we don't want to give them?" Kane asked.

Calavera glowered at him. "I can *make* you give them, pistolero."

Kane uttered a short, derisive laugh.

"You don't believe me?"

"I believe you can try," Kane replied. "Not quite the same thing as accomplishing it."

Calavera snorted, then puffed a smoke ring toward the sky. "We're not enemies, you and I. We can talk like equals, like men, can't we?"

"Then do it," Kane retorted flatly. "And tell your crew to stop trying to vandalize my vehicle."

Calavera spoke sharply and the men shuffled away from the Sandcat, returning to cluster around their chief. "They are curious, *señor.* Your machine is a fine thing. We saw it earlier today. We followed the trail it made. Funny thing—the trail it made is the same as the runaway slaves we are seeking."

"Do tell," Brigid said with studied indifference.

"There were many more slaves," Calavera stated, patting the necklace of ears, "and we caught up with them all but for five. I'm not too interested in four of them, but the fifth is a woman. She is *enceinte.* Pregnant."

"Haven't seen anybody out here but you," Kane said. Even in his own ears, his words sounded transparently false.

One of the men sidled over to Calavera and whispered to him urgently. The man bent down and listened intently. The man pressed something into Calavera's hand and then stepped away.

Calavera lifted the sawn-through shackle and held it close to his face, turning it this way and that. "This is an interesting thing to find out here, wouldn't you say, pistolero?" he murmured.

Kane whipped his Bren Ten from its holster a shaved fraction of a second after a long-barreled revolver appeared in Tuco Calavera's hand. The fact it was a single-action six-shooter gave him just enough time to leap aside. A tongue of red fire blazed from the bore, and Kane felt the passage of the heavy bullet very close to his right ear.

Almost in the same instant, he squeezed the trigger of his Bren Ten, knowing as he did so that he had snapped off the round a shade too quickly. The bullet creased the right side of Tuco Calavera's face, inscribing a livid burn from chin to temple before punching a neat hole in the brim of his sombrero.

The man howled in furious pain, dropping the manacle to clap a hand over his wound. As he recoiled, he drove his spurs into his horse's flank. Squealing in pain, the animal reared, forelegs lashing out. Hooves slammed into two of Calavera's men, bowling them off their feet. The horse bucked frantically and triggered a panic-stricken chain reaction among the other mounts. They neighed and reared, jostling one another, stamping and snapping.

Brigid drew her own autopistol and whirled toward a Mexican who thumbed back the hammer of his single-action revolver. She squeezed the trigger, putting two bullets into the slave tracker's chest. As he staggered, he fired his pistol and the heavy round ripped through the loose fabric of Brigid's tricolor desert-camouflage pants at the left thigh.

Voicing a roar, Tuco Calavera lost his seat on the saddle, his sombrero flying from his head. He went up, then crashed to the ground. He twisted back and forth, swearing in Spanish, trying to avoid being trampled by the horses.

The slave trackers shouted in confusion, unholstering their big revolvers and unsheathing machetes. With no one to give them orders, they reacted in a disorganized rush, moving on anger and fright.

An older man sidled toward Kane, waving a knife blade to and fro. He slashed at Kane's belly with it.

Kane was barely able to sidestep the attack. The backswing of the knife dragged along the right side of his shirt, parting the khaki as if it were so much tissue paper.

Kane brought down his gun barrel, smashing it into the man's forearm. The blow almost missed, but the impact was sufficient to throw the man off balance for a second. Kane took advantage of that second, driving a hammer blow with his left fist against the back of the Mexican's head.

The blow landed solidly and drove the slave tracker off his feet. He slammed into the ground face-first. The dagger flew from his hand. Kane delivered a vicious kick to the ribs, lifting his opponent off the ground and rolling him over a half dozen times before he came to a faceup stop against the left rear tire of the Sandcat.

Holding her pistol in a two-fisted grip, Brigid aimed at a young man with a drawn machete.

"*¡Capitulación!*" she shouted. "Surrender!"

The Mexican's face contorted in a snarling smile, revealing a mouth of broken, cavity-speckled teeth. "*Puta!*" he spit, and lunged for her, whipping his machete up over his head.

Kane and Brigid heard the stutter of a Copperhead and a triburst of 4.85 mm rounds sliced through the air. A trio of dark dots appeared on the slave tracker's face. Crimson spray erupted from the back of his head and his body slammed to the ground.

Grant sprinted into the combat zone, Copperhead held against his shoulder, a bloodred thread of light stretching from the laser autotargeter. The abbreviated

If offer card is missing write to: Gold Eagle Reader Service • 3010 Walden Ave., P.O. Box 1867, Buffalo NY 14240-1867

BUSINESS REPLY MAIL
FIRST-CLASS MAIL   PERMIT NO. 717   BUFFALO, NY

POSTAGE WILL BE PAID BY ADDRESSEE

GOLD EAGLE READER SERVICE
3010 WALDEN AVE
PO BOX 1867
BUFFALO NY 14240-9952

NO POSTAGE
NECESSARY
IF MAILED
IN THE
UNITED STATES

magazine of the subgun held only fifteen rounds, and in untrained hands could be fired dry in the space of two seconds. Grant, however could squeeze off triorbursts with deadly accuracy.

With a thunderous drumming of hoofbeats all of the horses bolted, stampeding from the gunfire and scream- ing humans. Two of the slave trackers ran after them, shouting in plaintive tones for them to return.

The survivors, facing automatic weapons in the hands of people who knew how to use them with expert lethality, hesitated, then threw down their pistols and blades and raised their hands.

Tuco Calavera slowly rose to his feet, eyes seething with hatred. His face wound did not bleed, but Kane knew the man would bear the mark of his bullet for the rest of his life. Calavera glanced around for his pistol, saw it on the ground half buried beneath hoof-kicked sand, and realized he would never be able to reach it before being shot down.

"Very clever, Señor Pistolero," he said grimly, brushing himself off. "A hidden compatriot. What you gringos call an ace on the line. Very clever."

"Not so much," Kane said. "You were just very stupid."

"Now what?" Calavera demanded. "You will kill me and my men?"

"That's not necessary. Your men can go on their way, try to catch their horses."

Calavera's expression did not change. "And what of me?"

"I think we'll keep you here, at least for a little while."

The man's eyes widened. "Why?"

"That's a good question," Grant said. "Why?"

"Information," Brigid said. "If you work for Mictlanx, you can probably tell us quite a bit about him."

For the first time, Calavera showed fear. "He will kill me and my family."

"Somebody always has to die," Grant rumbled. "Sometimes it's somebody who deserves to, like you. Maybe even your family."

Brigid Baptiste was not surprised by Grant's and Kane's apparent coldheartedness.

It was difficult for Brigid to keep in mind that the two men had spent their entire adult lives as killers—superbly trained and conditioned Magistrates, not only bearing the legal license to deal death, but the spiritual sanction, as well.

Both men had been through the dehumanizing cruelty of Magistrate training, yet had somehow, almost miraculously, managed to retain their humanity. But vestiges of their Mag years still lurked close to the surface, particularly in threatening situations. In those instances, their destructive ruthlessness could be frightening.

Kane gestured with his Bren Ten toward the men standing with their hands up. They shifted their feet uncertainly. *"Vamose,"* he ordered.

The men glanced over at Tuco Calavera and Kane said angrily, "Don't look at him. I hold your misbegotten lives in my hand, not that overstuffed bastard."

When they still didn't move, Brigid rattled off a stream of rapid-fire Spanish. The Mexicans reacted with trepidation, and slowly they stepped back toward the lengthening shadows, keeping their eyes fixed on the Kane and his pistol.

"I translated for you," Brigid said.

Kane smiled ruefully. "Thanks. One day I'll get serious about becoming bilingual."

His smile vanished when he took a step closer to Calavera, eyeing the heavyset man closely. "Get rid of the rest of your weapons."

Calaveras stared at him with wide, innocent eyes. "I swear by the blood of my mother—"

Kane struck him across the face with the barrel of his autopistol. Although he did not put even a fraction of his strength into the blow, Calavera was still rocked back on his heels.

"Do you want me to repeat it?" Kane demanded.

Probing the inside of his cheek with his tongue, Calavera turned his head and spit a little jet of scarlet onto the ground. Then, with an air of aggrieved royalty, the man patted himself down. From hidden pockets and pouches, Tuco Calavera removed a folded straight razor, a single-shot derringer, a knife with a four-inch blade and a set of brass knuckles.

Kane watched him drop the collection at his feet. It required a conscious effort of will on his part to keep from triggering his pistol and planting a bullet in the man's forehead. He might not have been a Magistrate any longer, but his ingrained Mag pride was offended by the slave tracker's arrogance. He felt the old Magistrate sense of righteous superiority rise in him.

Grant smiled at the litter of weaponry around Calavera's feet. "You believe in this 'be prepared' business, don't you?"

Calaveras shrugged. "It is a difficult life out here, *señor.*"

"It's a life of your choosing," Kane declared, his pale eyes gimlet hard.

"I work to maintain order," Calavera replied defensively. "Like the Magistrates in your own country."

"You're nothing like a Magistrate," Grant growled.

"And how would you know, *señor?*" Calavera challenged. "I enforce the laws."

"Maintaining order, enforcing the law…that's a good motivation for people with a just purpose," Brigid said, "but inevitably that purpose attracts beasts like you, who join up because it provides a good cover for your own thirst for power. It gives you a semblance of legitimacy."

Tuco Calavera blinked at her in owlish confusion. "I do the work assigned to me by Mictlanx. He is the authority here," he said plaintively.

"Who gave him that authority?" Kane asked.

Calavera stared at him silently for a few seconds, as if confused by the question. "He assumed the authority. And why not? Who better? He is the greatest of the Magistrates of your land, as are his deputies—the Diableros."

Chapter 15

Grant slipped a pair of nylon cuffs around Calavera's wrists, snugging them so tight that his arms were drawn up against the small of his back.

The sky at sunset looked like a falling curtain of blues and grays, smeared with angry flame-red streaks. The moon's pallid glow turned the wasteland into a panorama of dulled silver.

Grant tested the cuffs asking, "Too tight?"

"*Sí,*" Calavera said flatly.

"Good."

The man's stoic expression did not alter except when Brigid opened the Sandcat's rear hatch, allowing Luis and his family to clamber out. At the sight of them, Calavera knotted his jaw muscles in anger and directed an accusatory glare at Kane. "You lied to me."

"Shame on me," Kane replied blandly.

The glare Carmenita fixed on Calavera was so full of venom and loathing, the Cerberus warriors half expected the man to avert his gaze. Instead, he tried to draw himself up in a parody of injured pride.

"If I had a knife," Carmenita whispered, "I would

carve off two pieces of you for every ear hanging from your disgusting necklace—and make you eat them."

Luis reached out, snatched the necklace of human ears from around Calavera's neck and spit directly into his face. He hurled the trophy far into the gathering gloom.

Pepito looked at the two corpses sprawled on the ground and gestured for Ramon to stay inside the Sandcat. "We heard the fight…these men brought their fates upon themselves," he said with a grim satisfaction.

"They did indeed," Grant agreed. "Keep the kid inside the Cat until we get the bodies out of sight and clean up the zone a bit."

Felip, Luis and Pepito assisted in dragging away the bullet-blasted corpses of the slave trackers. Carmenita kicked dirt and sand over the blood trails. "We should make you do this," she hissed at Calavera. "You led these men to their deaths."

"I take it you and Tuco here are acquainted," Brigid commented.

The woman nodded, eyes still glittering with hatred. "He is a *sicario*…a contract killer."

"Not true," Calavera protested, holding his head at a defiant angle. "I do my duty as an authorized deputy of Mictlanx."

"Sit down," Kane ordered.

Calavera glanced down, and slowly and clumsily eased himself to one knee.

"I said *sit* down." Kane kicked him in the chest,

driving him onto his back with a whoof of forcefully expelled air.

"Kane—" Brigid began warningly.

"I'm not going to hurt him," Kane said between clenched teeth. "Not too seriously, anyway."

Securing a grip on the Mexican's collar, Grant heaved him to a sitting position. The man tried to recover his breath, gasping like a landed fish.

"Now we're going to start talking," Kane stated, looking toward Carmenita and then at Calavera. "And we're going to be direct. Who the hell is Mictlanx?"

"I know him only by that name," Carmenita said. "He speaks Spanish like one of us, but I do not think he is Mexican. Not a full-blood, anyway."

"His Diableros have names," Felip ventured. "As do his familiars."

"Familiars?" Brigid echoed in surprise.

"That is what Maruja called them," Luis said. "But they seemed like scholars to me." He nodded in Brigid's direction. "Much like you."

"They are his advisers," Pepito said. "Counselors. But they are only men, not demons."

Carmenita declared, "All we know is that the Diableros first came to our village nearly six months ago, riding in a vehicle much like that one." She waved toward the Sandcat. "They claimed they acted only in the service of Mictlanx, the warlord of the pit, and they were conscripting us to his service, too."

"*Sí,*" Ramon said dolefully. "The Diableros told us

we could enter the service of Mictlanx willingly or by force, but we *were* in his service no matter what."

Pepito nodded, lips compressed. "We tried to resist. But then came the night of the underground thunder."

Kane, Grant and Brigid all exchanged glances but said nothing.

"Then our village began to fall down," Pepito continued, voice quavering. "We rushed out into the night, terrified, with only the clothes on our backs. Our homes, our stores, even our church collapsed."

"The Diableros were waiting for us," Luis interposed. "With their shackles."

"*He* was there, too," Ramon said, kicking dirt toward Calavera. "They marched us for two days across the wasteland. Those of us who had been injured when our village collapsed were left to die."

"Marched you where?" Brigid asked. "Earlier you said Municipio de Aquismon."

"It is an area of rain forest and jungle," Carmenita said. "A land of witches, a land haunted by the ghosts of the old Aztecs. It is where the entrance to the underworld can be found—Sótano de las Golondrinas."

Brigid's brow furrowed. "That translates as 'basement of the swallows.'"

Luis nodded. "*Sí.* Do you know of it?"

"A little," Brigid replied. "Sótano de las Golondrinas is an enormous pit cave, a cenote or a sinkhole. The entrance measures approximately 160 by 205 feet, from the lowest point of the entrance is a drop to the bottom of 1094 feet. Those measurements make it the largest cave shaft in the world. At the bottom of Sótano de las Golondrinas are numerous openings to a multiplicity of different crevices, passages, crawlways and tunnels that were never mapped or investigated."

"Ah, it is more than that," Luis said, a knowing smile creasing his weathered features. "The Sótano de las Golondrinas was known by the Aztecs as the Xoloclif. Legend says it was formed by the sacred waters of death. They marched to the entrance once in a year to give a princess in sacrifice to the underworld, to become the bride of Mictlanx.

"The last princess to be sacrificed was named Calmalli, but Mictlanx did not accept her sacrifice because he had decided to punish the Aztecs. When the water touched Calmalli's body, the anger of Mictlanx opened a big chasm and formed the deepest hole of the sacred cave. A whirlpool swallowed the sacred water of death and left the caves dry."

Neither Brigid, Grant nor Kane responded, letting the old man tell his tale.

"Bitter days fell upon the Aztecs," Luis went on, "plagues that killed the warrior societies, then conquistadores came with their powerful weapons. Montezuma prayed at the entrance to the Sótano de las Golondrinas and a miracle appeared—thousands of snakes came slithering out of the cave. The biggest and most beautiful snake was Calmalli herself!

"The snakes attacked the Spanish and drove them

back. After the victory, Montezuma gave Calmalli his sacred flame to hide. She and the other snakes transformed into swallows and flew inside the cave. Since then, the cave has been their home."

Luis concluded the tale with an expectant glance from Brigid to Kane to Grant. "That of course is only a legend," he added.

Brigid smiled wanly. "Of course, but I'm sure it has a basis in fact."

Luis's raised shaggy eyebrows. *"¿Que?"*

"Yeah," Grant rumbled sourly. "And when you've got snake-people in the same legend as caves, then that basis has one name."

"The Annunaki," Kane intoned. "Dammit. You don't suspect the overlords have anything to do with this, do you?" he asked.

Brigid shook her head in frustration. "Who knows? On the surface, this doesn't seem big enough for them to get involved with."

"Yeah," Grant drawled sardonically. "On the surface. But that's the operative term, isn't it? Whatever is really going on *is* under the surface. And I have the most unpleasant feeling that's where we'll be going."

Chapter 16

The Sandcat clanked onward, toward gently rolling hills covered by sparse green grass. In the distance rose stands of cedar and pine-oak trees. Beyond stretched the blue-shadowed peaks of the Sierra Madre Oriental.

Sitting in the passenger seat, Brigid looked out at the midmorning sky. "We're well out of the dead zone."

"Finally," Grant grunted, flexing his hands on the steering wheel.

For the past two hours they had crossed seemingly endless miles of desert with only prickly pear, the occasional barrel cactus and spidery ocotillo with its brilliant red streamers to break up the monotony of the flat tableland.

Brigid hitched around to look at Kane, sitting with a trussed-up Tuco Calavera. The heavyset Mexican looked miserable, but Brigid wasn't sure if his discomfiture wasn't simply due to the close proximity of Kane, who stared at him dispassionately, his eyes hidden behind the impenetrable lenses of sunglasses.

"How's our guest?" she asked.

"He's no guest of mine," Kane stated emphatically.

"He barely qualifies as a prisoner. Until he starts giving us useful information, he's ballast. Not even that—he's a parasite."

He fingered his nose. "And a pretty stinking one, too."

The Cerberus warriors had left the little group of escapees at dawn, giving them two days' worth of food and water—enough so they could reach the hidden springs and gardens that Pepito had mentioned. Before they departed, the shackles were removed from their ankles, even though it cost them a hacksaw blade.

They weren't too concerned about Calavera's men returning, since they appropriated the weapons the slave trackers left behind. According to Luis, all of them knew how to use them.

Brigid suggested bringing Calavera along, to act as both a guide and a source of information. So far, the Mexican had supplied little of either, except to indicate a general direction in which to travel.

The ride became rougher when the Sandcat entered the hill country leading up to the mountain range. Grant maintained a steady speed of slightly below thirty miles per hour. He eased off the accelerator only when the FAV chugged its way up an exceptionally steep slope. The engine and transmission whined with the strain.

As the Sandcat topped the brow of the ridge, they saw a vista of solemn desolation spread out below them. Trees lay uprooted, many of them splintered by boulders that had rolled down from the slopes. Great cracks split the ground.

"Earthquakes here, too," Brigid observed. "Perhaps as a result of the Subterrene's testing."

Kane surreptitiously eyed Calavera for a sign of a reaction to the word, but the man's face remained impassive. "Do you know what she's talking about, Tuco?" he asked.

Calavera shook his head. "No."

Grant carefully drove the Sandcat down the bluff and maneuvered it around the litter of broken shale and over a tree trunk. The sun overhead shone down bright and hot, which made the dead men hanging from crosses at the top of a bluff look very unreal. Turning the wheel, Grant steered the Sandcat toward the base of the hill in order to get a better look.

From crudely nailed crossbars at the top of the posts, three men dangled head down, ropes cinched tight around ankles. Squawking birds fluttered around the corpses, pecking and hacking away bits of flesh. They had already been at the bodies for several days, feasting on all the soft organs and tissues. The eye sockets were raw, red cavities.

Kane turned toward Calavera. "Mictlanx's doing?"

The man swallowed hard, his dark complexion turning the hue of old ashes. "No, *señor.* Maruja is responsible for this. The bitch even signed her handiwork."

Squinting, Kane saw the corpse in the center had a hand-lettered sign apparently nailed to his groin. He couldn't quite make out the words, since the medium used was blood, but Brigid intoned, *"Muerte El Diableros."*

"Death to the Diableros," Grant said, releasing the brake.

The Sandcat continued on, detouring around deep rifts in the ground. More trees filled the terrain, green and tall, with cool shadows stretching in between. The vehicle snapped off saplings and tore through underbrush as it entered the tree line.

Grant drove into a clearing and stopped, turning off the engine. "Let's stretch our legs a bit. The engine is getting thirsty, too." He tapped the fuel gauge. The needle wavered only a hairbreadth above the *E.*

The Cerberus warriors disembarked, Kane dragging Calavera out with him. Brigid broke out MREs and bottled water while Grant and Kane removed a jerrican filled with diesel fuel from the rear. The sun was hot, but in the shade the breeze was almost too cool for comfort.

"Are you hungry?" Brigid asked Calavera.

"Sí, I am. But—" He shrugged, to indicate his hands pinioned behind his back. "If you could cut me loose just long enough—"

She smiled coldly. "I've been in this business a long time, Tuco. You can either let me feed you or you can go hungry."

The man's black eyes glittered with momentary resentment, and then he nodded in resignation. "Feed me then, *señora.*"

"It's *señorita*," she retorted, opening the package.

"I thought you were the woman of the man Kane."

Brigid took out a small piece of dried meat, holding it between thumb and forefinger. "No."

"Grant, then?"

"No. Do you want to eat or ask questions?"

"I am just curious. It seems unusual for a woman as beauteous as you to be alone."

"I'm not paired off," she said, a hard edge entering her tone. "That doesn't make me alone. I'm part of a team."

Calavera opened his mouth to respond, and Brigid crammed the piece of meat into it, effectively silencing him. He chewed noisily, glaring at her from beneath grizzled brows. She repressed a smile.

Normally, Brigid shied away from examining the bond she shared with Kane. On the surface, there was no bond, but they seemed linked to each other and had the same destiny. She recalled another name she had for Kane: *anam-chara.* In the ancient Gaelic tongue it meant "soul friend."

From the very first time they met, he was affected by the energy she radiated, a force intangible yet one that triggered a melancholy longing in his soul. That strange, sad longing only deepened after a bout of jump sickness both of them suffered during a mat-trans jump to Russia several years before. The main symptoms of jump sickness were vivid, almost-real hallucinations.

She and Kane had shared the same hallucination, but

both knew on a visceral, primal level it hadn't been gateway-transit-triggered delirium, but a revelation that they were joined by chains of fate, their destinies linked.

She concentrated on feeding Calavera and tried hard not to think about the message conveyed from the future Kane of some thirty years hence, regarding their relationship. She was glad she and Kane never discussed the issue at length. For all his fighting prowess—or maybe because of it, Brigid wasn't sure—Kane thought first with his emotions. That was alien to everything Brigid Baptiste held dear.

Still, there was no denying she, Grant and Kane had come a very long way in distances that could not be measured in mere miles from the day they had escaped from Cobaltville, some five years before. As veterans of the Magistrate Division, both Kane and Grant were accustomed to danger and hardship, but nothing like they and Brigid had exposed themselves to since their exile.

Brigid occasionally wondered how Kane's and Grant's regimented, ville-bred minds had managed to adapt to all the new, and on the face of it, insane situations they had found themselves in over the past five years. But somehow she and his friends had not only adapted, but learned an entirely new set of superior skills.

"Careful, Baptiste," Kane said, walking around the Sandcat. "If he bites you, we don't have a powerful enough antibiotic to save your hand."

Brigid sighed and placed the rim of a water bottle against Calavera's lips. He drank greedily, but after three swallows, Kane reached over and pushed the bottle away.

"Enough," he said. "We're not going to be making pit stops every five minutes. Besides, until we find some potable water, we'll have to ration what we have."

"The Río Pánuco is nearby," Calavera said. "We must cross it to reach our destination. The water is very clean."

"That must be because you've never bathed in it," Kane remarked.

"Can we knock off the asides about his hygiene?" Brigid asked exasperatedly.

Kane ignored her as he recapped the water bottle. "How many people does this Maruja have working for her?" he asked.

The Mexican shook his head. "No one really knows. She could work alone for all we know."

"One woman didn't kill and hang those men up to dry," Brigid said.

Calavera gave her a searching stare. "You do not know Maruja. Pray you never do."

Kane uttered a scornful laugh. "You mean she's worse than the leader of a gang of slave trackers who wears the cutoff ears of his victims as a fashion statement?"

"I know little about her," Calavera said. "I have only seen her a couple of times, and then from a distance."

Grant opened up the driver's door of the Sandcat and announced, "Saddle up. We're burning daylight."

They climbed aboard and continued on, driving deeper into the forest. Branches whipped at the sides of the Sandcat, dragging along the armored hull. The deep growl of the engine replaced the placid silence of the woods with an incessant roar. Birds flapped from their roosts, squawking in outrage.

Looking between the trees, they saw the surface of the Panuco River winking in the late-afternoon sunlight. The rushing water foamed white around boulders, the current running swiftly southward. From bank to bank, the river spanned a hundred feet.

Grant paralleled the river, keeping a line of trees between the Sandcat and the bank. When the bridge appeared at the last moment, he slammed on the brakes. The tracks kicked up showers of dirt and leaves. The rear end slewed a few feet to the right.

The bridge looked to be in no condition to hold the weight of even one of them, much less that of the Sandcat. The main timbers were cracked and splintered, and the planks hung down crookedly, the ends only a few inches above the surface of the river.

Grant hammered on the wheel in angry frustration with his fist. "Now what?"

Calavera shifted in his seat. "There is a ford beyond that bend. If you are careful, you can get this machine across. That is where my men and I came over."

Grant peered forward toward the bend, then sighed.

"All right. We'll give it a try...not like we have much choice."

The Sandcat rolled past the bridge, following the course of the river upstream. After a couple of minutes, Calavera said, "Here, *señor.*"

Grant braked and stared across the river. He saw a small strip of sand that followed the water's edge on their side of the concourse. "I don't know about this," he said uncertainly.

Kane opened the door, saying, "Let me take a look."

He walked carefully to the edge, noting that the river, although not particularly deep, flowed exceptionally fast. As Calavera said, he found the ford—a flat rock ledge projecting into the river, extending from bank to bank. He guessed it was the remnant of an old dam, made of concrete and crushed stone.

As Kane turned to return to the Sandcat, he heard a woman scream.

Chapter 17

Kane edged onto the shelf of the rock, looking up and down the river.

"Hey!" Grant shouted. "What's going on?"

"Hold on a second," Kane called in response. "I heard something."

He waited, head cocked, listening, but he could not locate the source of the scream. Then he saw the woman clinging to a half-submerged tree that had toppled from the far bank. It hung down at a forty-five-degree angle in the roiling white water.

Although she floundered less than two yards from the underwater ledge, she was up to her neck in the quick current. Her features were obscured by the long black hair plastered to her face, but she screamed again, *"¡Ayuda! ¡Por favor! ¡Ayuda!"*

Cupping his hands around his mouth, Kane shouted, "Hang on!"

The woman removed one hand from the tree trunk long enough to rake hair away from her face. She stared at him with big black eyes. Sounding half strangled, she called, *"¡Intentaré hacer todo lo posible!"*

Coming up behind him, Brigid translated, "She said she'll try her best."

Kane unleathered his pistol and handed it to Brigid. "Cover me, Baptiste."

She lifted her eyebrows in surprise. "You think there's something suspicious here?"

"I don't know." Kane gave the opposite bank a swift visual appraisal. He saw nothing unusual in the dark green woods, but that could have been the main reason this spot was chosen for an ambush. "But let's take no chances."

Kane stepped into the river, balancing himself on the stone ridge. The icy water drew a surprised curse from him. Almost immediately his feet, protected as they were by high jump boots, went numb. The current tugged at him, an invisible force working to dislodge his boot soles from the rock. The woman uttered a choked cry as her fingers slipped on the bark on the tree. Her black hair streamed around her shoulders. The face she turned toward him was full of despair.

"Hang on!" he shouted.

"*¡Me temo que si!* I can't!"

He realized that she replied first in Spanish, then in English. He said, "I'm going to reach out to you! Grab my hand."

Reaching a point directly opposite her, Kane planted his feet firmly and leaned forward as far as he dared, stretching out his left arm. The fingertips lacked only a few inches of touching the tree trunk. Spitting out water, the woman removed her right hand from the tree and lunged desperately for his hand. She missed.

The woman lost her grip and screamed only once before the white current swept her away. Kane dived in after her, no longer considering the possibility of a trap. The chill current slammed him downstream in tumbled confusion. Blinking the water from his eyes, he saw the woman's head bobbing in the foam.

Stroking toward her, Kane managed to catch her hand, felt her fingers slip through his and caught at her again, grasping her wrist. This time her arms slid around him tightly, given strength by terror and panic.

Her body pressed against his and they both went under, propelled in a headlong rush downriver. The current carried them around a bend, where the waterway narrowed. He felt their bodies whipped forward, pushed faster and faster. The current bumped and banged them against the irregularities of the bottom, rolling them over and over.

He fought his way to the surface, coughing. Through water-occluded eyes, he glimpsed foam glistening white in the sunlight. He and the woman shot toward a stretch of white-water rapids, the river swirling and pouring around half-submerged boulders.

Holding the woman tightly, Kane twisted his body to one side, kicking and flailing. Sputtering, he tried to check their catapult toward the rocks. The current pushed them against the opposite bank where the shallow water provided him with footholds. Tree limbs, like gnarled fingers, reached down toward the river. He pulled the woman up with him, hauling her bodily toward the tree. Using the branch and roots as hand-holds, they clambered their way up the muddy bank until they reached the top. They both sat down, gasping for breath.

"Are you all right?" he asked, breathing hard.

"*Sí*, I think so." The woman hugged herself, shud-dering violently. "*Gracias*. I did not think there was another person around for many miles."

A cool breeze bit clammily through his wet clothing, and Kane shivered. "What were you doing here?"

"Trying to ford the river." Her teeth chattered. Her English, although heavily accented, was understand-able and melodious to the ear. "Foolish to try it alone, with the current running so fast."

Before he could ask her more, Brigid and Grant yelled at them from upstream.

Kane stood up, shouting, "Over here!"

Grant trotted into view, followed closely by Brigid. She paused and stared, hands on her hips, expression in-scrutable. One of Grant's rare grins showed white teeth beneath his mustache. "What *is* it with you anyway?"

Kane ignored the query, assuming it was an oblique reference to the many times he ended up in the company of comely young women, regardless of the circum-stances and setting. "Bring the Cat."

"Who is she?" Brigid asked.

"I don't know yet," Kane replied. He helped the shivering woman to her feet. "You'll be all right in a minute. Who are you?"

The woman dragged a tangle of wet hair away from her face. "My name is Maruja."

EVEN AS DISHEVELED as she was, Maruja was one of the loveliest women Kane had ever seen. Standing several inches over five feet tall, she had the blue-black hair, matte-tan complexion and deep brown eyes of a pure-blooded Latina. Her brows were thick and naturally arched. Her white blouse hung half off her shoulders, and beneath it a dark green skirt, her body was long limbed, high waisted, full breasted and lithe. Her voice was throaty, her mouth seductive and full lipped. Silver-and-turquoise jewelry glittered at her wrists, fingers and throat.

Her eyes searched Kane's. "Is something wrong?"

"Why?" he asked.

"You seemed to recognize my name."

"No, it's a lovely name," he said inanely.

Maruja smiled at him uncertainly. "I am grateful to you for saving my life. What are you called?"

"Kane."

She nodded toward Grant and Brigid, who were returning to the Sandcat. "And your friends?"

"Grant and Baptiste."

"There are not many *norteamericanos* in this region. I recognize all the others around here."

"How many are there here?"

Maruja veiled her eyes with long, sweeping lashes. "Is that important?"

Kane shrugged. "You never can tell."

"And why are you here?" She took a half step away from him. "Do you intend to join your countrymen?"

"Do you know where I can find them?"

Maruja hesitated before saying, "Perhaps. There are a few in El Rey."

"What were you doing out here by yourself?"

"Collecting herbs—roots and such. I am a healer, a *brujix*. Do you know what that is?"

Before Kane could craft a response, he heard the roar of the Sandcat's engine upstream. "Why don't we go to the ford. We can get dry, and you can have something warm to eat or drink."

The invitation won out over Maruja's apprehension. They walked along the river's edge. She shivered in the breeze and pushed aside a thick strand of black hair blowing across her cheek.

"You'll need to get out of those wet clothes," Kane commented.

She cast him a suspicious glance. "And what will I wear?"

"I think Baptiste has a change of clothes you can borrow. If not, there are blankets."

"I have business to attend to in El Rey. I can't travel through the forest and mountain passes in a blanket."

"You'll have to until your clothes dry, unless you

care to take your chances with pneumonia. If you get sick, we can't take care of you."

Maruja's eyes flashed with anger, but she made no reply. By the time they reached the ford, the breeze had strengthened, cold and raw, biting through Kane's wet clothing so he shivered as much as Maruja.

Crossing her arms over her breasts and vigorously rubbing her arms, Maruja said, "I will take you up on your offer, Señor Kane."

The aristocratic note in her voice made Maruja seem as if she granted him a favor. She lifted her skirt when she stepped over a log. She wore a pair of rope sandals on her feet. Her legs were long and firm. Her right had a slender-bladed dagger about six inches long strapped to the calf.

He repressed a smile. Her attitude somewhat reminded him of the women of Sky Dog's Lakota band who were the Cerberus redoubt's nearest neighbors and most steadfast allies. He found himself liking Maruja already, partly because she seemed part of the same natural world as Sky Dog's tribe.

Reaching the ford, they waited until Grant drove the Sandcat across the river, the prow cleaving a path through the water. He steered the FAV up the bank, the treads finding secure purchase on the rocky ground.

"So," Maruja said. "It is just you and Grant and the woman you call Baptiste who travel inside that beast?"

"Them," Kane answered, "and our guide."

"Guide?"

Offhandedly, Kane replied, "Just somebody we picked up about sixty miles back."

Maruja eyed him skeptically. "There's not much to find sixty miles back—except an abandoned village."

Grant parked the Sandcat and turned off the engine. He and Brigid disembarked. "You both look miserable," Brigid observed as she walked around the vehicle and opened up the rear hatch.

From a metal chest in the cargo compartment, she took a thermal blanket, a khaki shirt and jeans. Maruja peered into the vehicle at the back of Tuco Calavera's head, but if she recognized him, she gave no sign.

Grant and Kane considerately turned their backs and waited while Maruja stripped out of her clothes and draped herself in the blanket. She and Brigid spoke in low tones. While the woman quickly donned the garments Brigid had offered, Grant asked quietly, "Did she give you a name?"

Kane nodded. "She says her name is Maruja."

Grant's eyes narrowed. "The witchy woman Tuco is so afraid of?"

"Same name, maybe not the same witch woman."

Grant snorted. "It can't be a coincidence unless Maruja is a real common name in these parts."

"Should we introduce her to Tuco?"

"I don't see how we have much choice. He's going to get out of the Cat eventually, if nothing else but to take a leak."

At the sound of footfalls, the men turned to see

Maruja approaching them. Although she slowly buttoned up her shirt, she allowed them a glimpse of ample cleavage.

"You are right, Señor Kane," she said, smiling. "I feel much better. You look as if you can use a cup of something hot yourself."

Grant stepped toward the Sandcat, saying, "I'll get you a self-heat package of coffee."

"Where is your guide?" she asked. "I grew up in this area, so I should know everyone who claims they are familiar with the region."

Grant opened the side door and pulled out Tuco Calavera, his hands still bound at the small of his back. As soon as he saw Maruja, his eyes went wild with shock and disbelief.

"Maruja!" he shrilled.

The woman did not alter her expression, but her hand plunged inside her partially unbuttoned shirt and came out gripping the dagger Kane had seen strapped to her leg.

Maruja lunged for Calavera, the knife in her fist pointing at his eyes like an accusatory finger.

Chapter 18

Kane grabbed Maruja by the shoulders, and to his dismay, he could barely restrain her. She struggled violently, her body alive with furious muscle, surprisingly hard and wiry.

A stream of hard-edged Spanish obscenities hissed from between her teeth.

The Mexican snarled in response.

Grant hauled Calavera back a few feet, safely away from the tip of Maruja's glittering knife. Brigid grasped the woman's right wrist, trying to hold it immobile. "Knock it off! We agree Calavera is human excrement, but at the moment, he's valuable to us."

Maruja glared first at Calavera, then at Brigid. "As a guide?"

"Yes," Kane said. "He led us to you, didn't he?"

Twisting her head up and around, Maruja regarded him with an incredulous stare, then she sagged in his grip. She relaxed her fingers around the handle of the knife, permitting Brigid to take it from her.

Kane released the woman, and Maruja rubbed her

shoulder where his fingers had clamped. "Do you know what Calavera really is?"

"A slave tracker," Grant said. "Or so we've been told."

"And you trust him?"

Calavera's lips writhed back over his discolored teeth. "*Puta,* if they trusted me, would my hands be bound?"

In a low, deadly monotone, Maruja said, "Tuco Calavera is a thief, a *bandido,* a child killer, a torturer. He was an outlaw before Mictlanx came along."

"Yeah, we figured as much," Kane said.

"Where did you find this *puerco?*" Maruja demanded.

Curtly, Brigid explained about rescuing the small group of runaway slaves from both the Ouroboros and Calavera's men. Maruja's eyes softened with sadness. "Only Luis and his family escaped?"

"We're afraid so," Grant answered. "But they mentioned your name, told you helped them to escape from Mictlanx."

She nodded. "*Sí,* them and many others. I crept into the base camp of Mictlanx and cut their chains."

Calavera, feeling protected by Grant, spoke in a defiant, accusatory voice, "You murdered many innocent men in the process!"

"Innocent?" Maruja shrilled, stepping toward him but checking herself. "Men?" Throwing back her head, she barked out a scornful laugh. "They were *puercos!*

No—worse than pigs, because pigs cannot help being pigs. But they died squealing like pigs!"

She pointed a beringed forefinger at Calavera. "My only regret is that you were not among them. You are the worst of the lot—a torturer, a rapist!"

Calavera squared his shoulders. With hands bound behind him, it was not easy. "They defied the will of Lord Mictlanx."

Maruja's face twisted into a mask of contempt. "He is no lord—he is a man. His name is Ramirez."

Kane stiffened, the shock of recognition turning the base of his spine cold. "Ramirez?"

"*Sí*. He is one of your country's renegade Magistrates."

"From which ville?" Grant asked.

Maruja lifted a shoulder in a shrug. "Snakefish, I believe. Does it matter?"

"It might," Kane replied, "if it's the same Ramirez I'm thinking of."

"He's dead, isn't he?" Grant asked. "You left him in Redoubt Yankee, right?"

Kane hesitated before answering defensively, "We *all* left him there, remember? We got too distracted by the Operation Chronos tech to worry about whether he was alive or dead."

"There was no sign of him the next time we visited the place," Brigid said.

Grant frowned. "That doesn't mean a whole hell of a lot. After we left, he could have come to and used the mat-trans unit there to jump to another redoubt."

"What are you talking about?" Maruja asked peevishly.

Kane answered, "Mictlanx—Ramirez—might be someone we've come across before. A Magistrate, like you say."

"He also has other Magistrates at his command, not to mention snivelling little cowards who wear rainbows."

Brigid pursed her lips. "By rainbows you mean little rainbow insignias on their chests here?" With a finger, she inscribed a U shape over her heart.

"*Sí,*" Maruja answered confidently. "They wear green uniforms."

"They're archivists," Brigid said. "Historians."

"*Sí,* I have heard Ramirez call them that."

The archivists in the Historical Divisions wore bodysuits with chemically treated rainbow insignias that allowed them to pass through security checkpoints. Despite the common misconception, archivists were not bookish, bespectacled scholars. They were primarily data-entry techs, albeit ones with high security clearances. A vast amount of predark historical information had survived the nukecaust, particularly documents stored in underground vaults. Much more data was digitized, stored on EMP-resistant computer diskettes.

No information was sometimes better than half information, but the archivists could not make that judgment call. Their primary duty was not to record predark history or evaluate the veracity of the data, but to revise, rewrite and often times completely disguise it. The political causes leading to the nukecaust were well-known. They were major parts of the dogma, the doctrine, the articles of faith, and they had to be accurately recorded for posterity.

"You seem familiar with his operation," Grant observed.

"I am indeed, Señor Grant. I was once the woman of Ramirez."

Brigid's eyebrows rose. "Carmenita made the same claim."

"It is a true claim," Maruja said frankly. "Mictlanx— Ramirez—chose her to carry his heir when I proved barren."

Kane repressed a groan. "Don't tell me all this hostility boils to being a woman scorned."

Maruja favored him a slit-eyed stare. "Don't be insulting. I was taken and held by force, like Carmenita. When he had no more use for me, I was released. I went back to my village, determined to keep Ramirez from making this land his personal kingdom."

"Where's your village?" Grant asked.

"Take me there. I will tell you all I know."

"How far is it?" Brigid inquired, glancing into the sky.

"If we leave now, we will arrive before sunset."

Kane studied the woman, looking for signs of dishonesty. "Why hasn't Ramirez taken it over?"

She chuckled throatily. "You'll see why once we're close."

Kane exchanged glances with his two partners. When they nodded, he said, "Deal. But promise me you'll behave yourself around Tuco during the trip."

Maruja smiled sweetly. "Of course. May I have my knife back?"

"I don't think that's a good idea," Grant said uneasily.

"If you wish my people to accept you, to trust you," Maruja said reasonably, "then you will need to prove to them that you are worthy of trust. Rolling into El Rey with me as a disarmed prisoner will only guarantee you their suspicion, if not hostility. You might as well take your chances with Ramirez head-on, relying on Calavera to guide you properly."

"Well, when you put it that way," Grant said gruffly.

Brigid passed the knife hilt first to Maruja. She took it with a gracious smile. "*Gracias.* It is not really a weapon, you know. It is more of a ceremonial instrument. I use it for digging up roots and medicinal herbs."

Calavera threw back his head and brayed out a laugh. *"Estupida puta—"*

Sunlight flashed from the fingers of Maruja's right hand, so swift and brief, it was like a subliminal glimpse of quicksilver. Calavera's laugh turned into an inarticulate gurgle. The knife blade had struck into the Mexican's open mouth and became fixed, the point piercing his brain. The pommel protruded like a grotesque tongue.

Then, as if he had suddenly become very tired, his knees buckled and he collapsed slowly to the ground. He lay there, his feet twitching spasmodically.

Maruja stalked over to his body and wrenched the knife free. Swishing the blade through the air to shake off blood drops, she said casually, "Of course, I also use my knife to dispatch vermin when they get on my nerves."

Bending, she groped over Calavera's shirt pocket and withdrew a black cigar. She planted it in the corner of her mouth and grinned in Kane's direction. "Do you have a light?"

Kane gaped at her, surprised into speechlessness by the swift efficiency of the killing. Then he returned her grin. "I *knew* there was something I liked about you."

Chapter 19

After some discussion, they reached the decision not to bury Tuco Calavera, although Grant and Kane dragged his body into the underbrush. Impassively, Maruja watched them work while puffing on the malodorous cigar. Brigid fanned the air in front of her face but voiced no objection.

They climbed into the Sandcat and rolled through the forest, heading toward the mountain range.

"How is it you are acquainted with Ramirez?" Maruja asked.

Kane, sitting in the front seat, hitched around to face her. "If he is the same man, and I have a feeling he is, then he's a Magistrate who was sent to capture and kill us a few years back."

Maruja blew a stream of smoke out the side window. "I see that he was not successful. Why was he sent to perform such a task?"

"We were classified as criminals in the baronies," Brigid stated. "Worse than criminals actually. Terrorists and baron blasters."

Grant's hands reflexively tightened around the

steering wheel, and his jaw muscles knotted. Like "sec man," the term "baron blasters" was old, deriving from the rebels who had staged a violent resistance against the institution of the unification program a century before. Neither Kane nor Grant enjoyed having the appellation applied to them—their ville upbringing still lurked close to the surface, and they had been taught that the so-called baron blasters were worse than outlaws. They were terrorists incarnate.

Maruja's eyes narrowed. She looked from Brigid to Kane to Grant. "Are you—you are not...Cerberus?"

Brigid nodded. "That's exactly who we are."

Maruja smiled. "Ah." Smoke puffed from her mouth in a little cloud. "Now it makes sense."

"What does?" Kane asked.

"Why you are here. Mictlanx—Ramirez—threatens your own land, does he not?"

"You could say that," Brigid admitted. "That's what we're trying to ascertain."

Maruja tapped a half inch of ash from the end of the cigar. "And what is this Operation Chronos facility you mentioned where you last saw Ramirez?"

"That's a little hard to explain," Kane said.

"Once again," Grant rumbled, "you prove your gift of understatement is unparalleled."

The seat of Operation Chronos, code-named Redoubt Yankee, was built on one of the Santa Barbara Islands, disguised as a satellite campus of the University of California. As one of the finest and most secret research establishments in the world, its engineering and computer centers were second to none. Its accomplishments in the field of physics were never matched, much less exceeded. The personnel of the installation managed to crack the so-called cosmic code.

According to Lakesh, the cosmic code was vernacular for the unified field theory. It referred to the mathematical reconstruction of the first few seconds of the big bang when the universe was a primal monobloc without dimensions of space.

Since discovering Redoubt Yankee, Cerberus had joined forces with people of nearby New Edo to secure it. Twenty expatriates from the Manitius Moonbase were permanently stationed in the installation, working to refurbish the sprawling complex and make it a viable alternative to the Cerberus redoubt in case it ever had to be abandoned.

"Well?" Maruja's impatient interrogative drew Brigid's attention back to the present.

"Well what?"

Maruja gestured with the cigar. "What about Operation Chronos?"

"Like Kane said, it's hard to explain. It's very complicated—very technical."

The Mexican woman's brows knitted at the bridge of her nose. "And too far above a lowly *brujix* to understand, eh?"

"That's not what I meant," Brigid retorted. "Your question can't be easily answered."

"So I should not seek out the answers—or ask the questions?" An angry edge entered Maruja's voice. "Only an educated person like you can understand the answers?"

Rather than be put on the defensive Brigid shot back, "Not necessarily—but it would help to have a basic grounding in hyperdimensional physics. And with all due respect, I don't think you have one."

Maruja glared at her. "I am not stupid, *señorita*."

"I didn't say you were…just that you're not in the position, through no fault of yours, to comprehend what I tell in response to your questions."

Maruja shifted in her seat, rudely turning her back, blowing cigar smoke out of the window. Brigid repressed a smile, but regretted the woman chose to take offense. As an archivist, she had been in a unique position to seek out answers and oftentimes she found the mysteries far more disturbing than any possible solutions.

The Sandcat rolled steadily through areas of pines and cedars and then entered canyons that gashed through the foothills of the Sierra Madre Oriental. Overhead, the crags seemed to scrape the clouds.

Leaning forward, Maruja directed Grant which trail to follow, and they climbed a treeless slope to a hogback ridge. From there they looked northward toward the mountain range extending before them. The highest peaks were snowcapped.

Grant steered along a rocky rampart as the sun began

to sink. The first hints of twilight deepened around the Sandcat, a sea of russet and indigo flowing from the western sky.

"I thought you said we'd reach your village before nightfall," Kane said.

Maruja shrugged. "It is not always easy to be exact." She glanced at Brigid challengingly. "Just like it is not always easy to get answers."

The ridgeline debouched into a rugged path that swerved around rock formations and gullies. Kane swore as the Sandcat yawed and nearly pitched him from his seat. The path swung down into a dry arroyo with a lazy serpentine motion. Pebbles clattered noisily beneath the vehicle's tracks. Grant suddenly slowed the FAV to a crawl, hitting the brakes and downshifting.

A group of six Mexicans blocked the path. They were all uniformly big men, swarthy, and wore leather belts studded with cartridges and pistols. They stared openly and suspiciously at the Sandcat but did not challenge them. Kane looked past them and saw a deadfall of high-stacked boulders on both sides of the arroyo. He guessed that it wouldn't take much to start an avalanche and either bury or disable an interloping vehicle.

Maruja leaned her head out of the side window. She called to them and although their expressions did not change, their postures became more relaxed. They stepped aside and one waved grandly. He said loudly, *"Bien entra."*

After traveling another half a mile they were challenged a second time, this time by a man seated on the back of a mule, with a double-barreled shotgun cradled in his arms. As before, once he saw Maruja, he allowed the Sandcat to pass.

After less than a mile, the arroyo opened into a wide, flat area with cultivated fields. The crops were corn and beans. Beyond the fields lay the village of El Rey.

The village looked surprisingly clean, with its flat-roofed buildings and narrow, crooked lanes. Candles burned in the windows, and on every dwelling dried bundles and mesquite dangled from the roof overhangs. In the center of the plaza stood a whitewashed church with a crudely carved cross on top.

The Sandcat rolled down the main thoroughfare, dust rising in clouds from beneath the clanking tracks. Children shouted as they ran abreast of it. Squawking chickens and squealing pigs scuttled from its path. From open doorways stood black-haired, lustrous-eyed girls and scowling, mustached young men. They openly fingered the handles of machetes sheathed at their hips. They also saw two men sporting shaved heads with mirrored sunglasses masking their eyes. Compact MAC-11 subguns hung from lanyards around their neck.

"Not a very welcoming community," Brigid observed.

"You can hardly blame us," Maruja replied. "Outlanders always mean trouble."

Earlier, Maruja had told them about the many times

over the past century that freebooters, raiders and Roamers had come through El Rey—and left their mark in one fashion or another. They came, they saw, they conquered. Even if the visits were not violent—a rarity—they conquered the women of the village, and for that insult, the men were always wary, always sensitive to a perceived slight.

Following Maruja's instructions, Grant parked the Sandcat in front of a one-story building of adobe with the words *Toro Bravo* painted above the bat-winged doors.

"The Brave Bull cantina?" Kane inquired. "Why here?"

"If you want information about Mictlanx, this will be the place," Maruja replied. "But that information may not be easy come to by. You may have to trade."

Brigid glanced at her distrustfully. "You mean bribe? With money?"

Maruja shrugged. "If you're lucky, that is all they will ask in return."

Chapter 20

They disembarked. For the benefit of watching eyes, Grant made a very exaggerated show of sealing the Sandcat's ob ports and locking the doors. They entered the Toro Bravo cantina, and despite the flickering lamplight, Kane saw the interior was very neat, the bar top, tables and floor exceptionally clean.

The mustached man behind the bar sat on a high stool and absently strummed a guitar. His eyes were half-closed, vacant. Other than the bartender only two men were present. They sat at a corner table, nursing ceramic cups, a glass bottle half-full of clear fluid between them.

Maruja strode deliberately toward them. The man facing the doors glanced up at her approach, his expression registering first dismay, then even a bit of fear. He exclaimed, "Maruja! We haven't seen you in a couple of days."

"I haven't been in El Rey for a couple of days—that's why you haven't seen me, Tarquin."

Tarquin spoke English with no trace of an accent. He was of medium height, with a weather-beaten face and long, dark blond hair gathered in a knot at his nape. His nondescript clothing looked threadbare to the point of falling apart.

The other man hitched around to gaze first at Maruja, then at the Cerberus warriors. Silver threads shot through his shock of hair, and a grizzled leonine mustache framed his mouth in a horseshoe shape. His bleak gray eyes flickered not with fear when he looked at Maruja, but with recognition when his gaze passed over Kane, Grant and Brigid Baptiste.

He wore hand-stitched road leathers, vest and pants. The brown material showed faded stains and scuffs. A stiff glove made of cross-stitched leather encased the man's right hand and wrist. Only two fingers and a thumb protruded from it. He kept his left hand out of sight, beneath the table.

Maruja gestured to the two men. "This is Tarquin and Three-Fingers Lebeaux. They were once part of Mictlanx's operation until he had no more use for them."

Lebeaux snorted and gestured with his deformed hand. "Don't stand on ceremony when you can sit on it."

The Cerberus warriors pulled chairs away from other tables and sat down. Without preamble, Maruja poured liquid from the bottle into a cup, filling it. Taking a slice of lemon from a tin saucer, she took a spoonful of salt from a little dish and shook it into the juncture between her left thumb and index finger.

Picking up the glass, she stared directly into Kane's eyes and intoned, *"Salud."*

She tossed the liquor back in one swallow, then touched her tongue to the salt and sucked at the lemon. Her expression did not change. She pushed the bottle toward Kane. "Your turn."

"No, thank you," he said mildly. His eyes flicked from Lebeaux to Tarquin. "A little information first."

Lebeaux smiled lazily. "Why should we tell you shit about shit, Kane?"

Kane was not surprised Lebeaux recognized him. Pix of him, Grant and Brigid had been circulated to every Magistrate Division. All of the nine villes in the continent-spanning network had engaged in a cooperative search for the three of them. As the years went on, tales of their exploits gave rise not only to rebellious thoughts, but also to acts of resistance.

Kane shrugged. "If you already know who I am, I suppose I should find out who you are."

The bearded man sneered. "Maruja told you my name."

"Your name means nothing," Grant rumbled. "We know an ex-Mag when we see one."

"Lebeaux is a cockroach," Maruja snapped. "But he has proved useful to me on occasion. He can do so again."

"Not very respectful," Lebeaux said, looking at the woman with feigned reproach.

"That's because there's not much about you to

respect." Maruja inclined her head toward his right hand. "Didn't Mictlanx cut off two of your fingers?"

"His name is Ramirez," Lebeaux replied. "Mictlanx, my ass. What do you want to know about him?"

Tarquin shifted in his chair, casting Lebeaux a warning glance. "There's a matter of payment first."

"Mictlanx turned out both of you?" Brigid inquired. "If so, you don't owe him anything."

"Mebbe so," Lebeaux retorted. "But we owe you three renegades even less."

Grant grunted. "Do you even know what a renegade is?"

Before Lebeaux could answer, he said flatly, "A renegade is someone who betrays a cause or a faith or a group of people who trusted him. That's not any of us."

Lebeaux's eyes narrowed. "The three of you betrayed unity didn't you?"

"There never was unity," Brigid stated matter-of-factly. "It was a lie, another control mechanism."

Nearly a century before, Unity Through Action was the rallying cry of the early Program of Unification. It awakened the long-forgotten trust in a central government by offering a solution to the constant state of hardship and fear—join the unification program and never know want or fear again. Of course, any concept of liberty had to be forgotten in the exchange.

Lebeaux's lips twisted in a smirk. "Like I'd believe anything you'd say."

He turned toward Tarquin. "Am I right?"

Tarquin nodded. "So right."

Quietly, Kane said, "You're both a couple of turds. If I was a cat, I'd cover you up with dirt. You should've been flushed away when the baronies fell."

As Kane hoped, Three-Fingers Lebeaux's face twisted with fury. Snarling wordlessly, he sprang out of his chair, thrusting for Kane's throat with the knife in his left hand. Kane leaned away from the blade and stood up. Grant pushed his chair back, but Kane said casually, "Don't bother."

Lebeaux swung the knife at Kane's midsection with a side-arm slashing motion. Kane stepped aside and the man made a half cut, half thrust at his groin, seeking to sever the femoral artery. Kane chopped the edge of his right hand down on the man's wrist. Lebeaux cried out as the knife clattered to the floor.

Eyes glittering with rage, Three-Fingers Lebeaux assumed a martial-arts combat stance, one that was exceptionally familiar to Kane. Magistrate martial-arts training borrowed shamelessly from every source— from tae kwon do to savate to kung fu. The style focused primarily on offense rather than defense.

"Come on," Lebeaux said tauntingly. "Let's see if you can fight as good as you talk shit."

Kane smiled gently. "Say when."

As he half expected, Lebeaux launched a roundhouse kick at Kane's head in a lightning-swift crescent. Kane moved into the arc, backfisting the man's leg to the left, causing him to stagger while he tried to maintain his balance on one foot.

Lebeaux managed to keep his feet and he swung his deformed right hand, the clawlike fingers seeking his eyes. Kane ducked and came up inside, catching Three-Fingers' arm and trying to pull off the glove of hard leather. It was laced tightly around the wrist with rawhide.

Lebeaux wrenched his body free and hammered at Kane's head with his left hand. Kane staggered, the blow much more powerful than he expected.

Lebeaux snorted out a contemptuous laugh. "There's some unity through action for you, you bastard!"

He slugged Kane in the jaw a second time, the punch jarring him. With a surge of shame, Kane realized that even half-drunk and at a disadvantage due to a crippled hand, Lebeaux was a trained Magistrate and therefore was a formidable opponent.

Lashing out with his right hand, Kane secured a grip on Three-Fingers' nose. He twisted hard. Blood spurted from both nostrils like opened faucets, and the man howled in agony. When Three-Fingers clapped both hands to his face, Kane kicked him in the crotch and he sank to his knees, clutching at his groin.

"Here's a little more unity for you," Kane rasped, then drove a left boot against the side of the Lebeaux's jaw. The man fell over, unconscious.

Kane picked up Lebeaux's knife from the floor and returned to the table, picked up the bottle and upended it into his mouth. The tequila burned its way down his throat like a flow of liquid fire.

Maruja gazed at Kane in frank admiration. *"Magnifico."*

"Yeah," he said wryly. "Wasn't it just."

"Took you longer than I figured," Grant observed dourly. "You're getting soft."

"He was a lot more determined than I thought he'd be."

Brigid, eyeing the sprawled form of Three-Fingers Lebeaux, murmured, "Indoctrination is hard to break, no matter how often it's proved to be a lie."

Neither of her friends disagreed. For most of their lives, Kane, Grant and Brigid Baptiste had subscribed to the same unity-through-action doctrines. In the case of Kane and Grant, they had dedicated their lives to serving them. As Magistrates, the two men enforced the laws of the villes, enjoying their reputations of being both ruthless and incorruptible.

Then the three of them stumbled over a few troubling questions, and when they attempted to find the answers, all they discovered were far more troubling questions. In the process of looking for answers, they became exiles on the planet of their birth.

Kane stared at Tarquin. "Do you need the same kind of persuasion as your boss?"

"Three-Fingers ain't my boss," Tarquin shot back, as if the notion scandalized him. "He's barely my partner."

Grant leaned back in his chair and folded his arms over his chest. "Good to know. You're not an ex-Mag?"

The man shook his head in furious negation. "Fuck no!"

"Can you take us to Mictlanx?" Brigid asked.

Tarquin's expression instantly became evasive. "I could, but why should I?"

"For the sake of El Rey—and your own," Maruja said grimly.

Three-Fingers Lebeaux groaned and slowly pushed himself up from the floor. He worked his jaw back and forth and squinted toward Kane. "You fight dirty."

Kane shrugged. "So do you. We're both ex-Mags, right?"

Lebeaux slowly and stiffly rose to his feet. He said, "The main drawback with my current handicap is I can't give you the finger. And since I can't, I might as well tell you what you want to know."

Chapter 21

Three-Fingers Lebeaux sat down and reached for the tequila bottle. Kane laid the man's knife on the table in front of him, but Lebeaux made no move to pick it up. He wasn't concerned if he did or not—he knew that under the table, Brigid's hand held her pistol, the barrel pointed at Lebeaux's groin.

"What do you want to know?"

"Does Ramirez have a digging machine?" Grant inquired. "A tunneler that causes earthquakes?"

Lebeaux didn't answer immediately, but Tarquin's eyes widened. Taking a swig of the liquor, Lebeaux winced and said, "He has. Ramirez calls it a Subterrene."

"Where did he find it?" Brigid asked.

"Right here," he drawled. "In Sótano de las Golondrinas."

"How did he find it?" Brigid pressed.

"He looked for it, what else?"

Brigid's lips compressed in irritation. "How did he know that the Subterrene was in Mexico?"

Tarquin snickered as if the question were ridiculous. "How do you figure he did, Baptiste? The archives."

Brigid's green eyes turned jade hard, emerald cold. "You're an archivist, too, aren't you? From what Historical Division?"

Lebeaux hawked up from deep in his throat and spit on the floor.

"Hey!" the outraged bartender shouted.

"Sorry, Pedro," Lebeaux called.

"My name is Miguelito," the man snapped angrily.

Lebeaux pointed to himself and to Tarquin with a gnarled thumb. "We're both from Snakefish."

"That is not news," Maruja said disdainfully. "All of you Diableros come from there."

"Not all of us," Lebeaux replied. "Just the inner circle."

Gazing levelly at Brigid, Grant and Kane, the man said, "A couple of years back, after the baron disappeared from the ville, Ramirez and the rest of us Mags did our able best to hold the place together. But everything got all fucked up—factions fighting one another, revolts, counterrevolts. It just wasn't working. So Ramirez told us there was a better way. He wanted to start over in a new place, but he needed an edge."

"And he came to the Historical Division to find one," Tarquin said smugly. "He went through the archives, looking for any predark tech that he could get his hands on. He seemed to know there were places, testing facilities, where it was stored."

Tarquin paused, sighed and added, "Don't know how he learned about it, but he was right."

Grant, Kane and Brigid suppressed the urge to look at one another. They guessed that once Ramirez revived in the Operation Chronos installation, he familiarized himself with the technology still in operation there and accepted the concept of a much larger and more complicated world than he had envisioned. It was also a world that offered far more opportunities than he assumed existed, due to his limited upbringing in Snakefish.

"So he found out about the Subterrene?" Brigid asked.

Lebeaux nodded. "That ain't all. Ramirez found out about something called the Archon Directorate, too. Said the Archons were behind the nukecaust and everything else."

"*Sí,* I have heard Ramirez talk of the Archons, too," Maruja said quietly. She glanced toward Kane. "Have you heard of them?"

"You might say that," he replied. "The Archons and the Archon Directorate aren't what you think they are."

"Oh no?" Tarquin challenged. "I saw some of the files myself. Do they exist or don't they?"

Grant shifted in his chair uncomfortably. "That's a yes and a no," he said evasively.

When no one elaborated, Lebeaux continued, "Anyway, Ramirez's idea seemed like the best one at the time."

Maruja's eyes glittered with contempt. "To seek out and find a place where the people couldn't fight back, take over and enslave them?"

"That's the way of it, *hermana*," Lebeaux said dismissively. "There are only two kinds of people life in the in the world—slaves and slave owners."

Kane tamped down the anger that rose within him. "There's a third kind," he said flatly. "You might've heard of them. They're called Cerberus."

He slid his pistol from its holster and laid it on the table beside Lebeaux's knife. "That kind is really, *really* hard on the slave owners."

Lebeaux snorted, reaching for the bottle. "I don't take threats kindly."

"Good thing, because I never make them with any kindness. I'm offering you a choice—help us to find Ramirez."

"Or die?" Tarquin asked faintly.

Grant nodded. "Oh, yeah. There *is* that."

Brigid brought out her own pistol, but rather than placing it on the table, she aimed it directly at Lebeaux's head. She intoned, "There *is* that, indeed."

MIGUELITO AGREED to rent rooms to the outlanders, although Grant preferred to sleep in the Sandcat to prevent theft. Lebeaux and Tarquin both had permanent quarters above the cantina. The ex-Magistrate promised to meet them there the next day at dawn.

Maruja accompanied the Cerberus warriors out of the Toro Bravo, walking with them to the parked Sandcat to collect their belongings and so she could reclaim her own clothes.

As Kane opened up the rear hatch, Maruja said softly, "We are being watched."

Grant glanced toward a pair of shaved-headed men standing in the shadows of an overhang. "I noticed them when we arrived. Who are they?"

"Spies. Agents of Mictlanx. They will question Three-Fingers Lebeaux and Tarquin and then leave before us."

"To set up an ambush?" Brigid inquired.

"Possibly."

Kane handed Maruja her blouse and skirt. "They're just allowed to come and go as they please?"

She shrugged. "They buy supplies, so as long as their money is good—"

Grant snorted. "Damn mercenary setup."

Maruja pierced him with a challenging glare. "You have to know Mexico before you can judge it. Revolutions come and go here, often with the seasons. El Jefe, the chief today, might be hanging from a cottonwood tree tomorrow and somebody like Three-Fingers, with a little ambition, might be in charge the day after. So everybody plays both sides of the street, as you anglos say. We look the other way when Mictlanx's spies come to town because tomorrow they may be running the place."

"That's all well and good," Kane said. "But we can't let them take back word of our arrival or get ahead of us so they can spring a trap."

"If you kill them," Maruja said, "you will draw the direct wrath of Mictlanx and his machine. El Rey will be destroyed."

"We came across the bodies of three Diableros," Brigid commented. "So obviously somebody isn't too worried about drawing the direct wrath of Mictlanx."

"Those killings were done outside of El Rey," Maruja retorted defensively. "Many miles from here."

"How'd they get out there?" Kane asked.

"They were following—"She broke off, glanced worriedly at the men in the shadows and closed her mouth, not answering.

Kane smiled thinly. "You lured them out there, didn't you?"

"In El Rey," Maruja whispered, "even the shadows have ears."

She paused and stated matter-of-factly, "I have my own home in El Rey. I will spend the night there and meet you back here at dawn."

Brigid's eyebrows rose a trifle. "You live right here in the village?"

"You seem surprised."

"From what I understand, most practitioners of *brujeria* live in the wilderness, shunned by townsfolk."

"Perhaps it was that way, many years ago, but we *brujos* are too valuable. Our knowledge of medicinal herbs and healing are highly sought after, as is our practice of midwiving."

She cocked her head at Brigid. "Would you like to see my home?"

"I would, as a matter of fact."

Maruja turned. "Come with me, then."

Kane glanced at the pair of shaved-headed men. "You two go ahead. I think me and Grant will do something about the spies."

Maruja stared at him reproachfully. "Señor Kane—"

"It'll be a nonlethal solution," Kane said. "But they may not be much good for much of anything for a few days."

Maruja looked doubtful but Brigid said, "You can believe him."

She and Maruja walked down the dark street to a small one-story adobe building set far back from the main thoroughfare. It squatted in a barren lot, surrounded by mesquite bushes.

Resting on a wooden ledge above the door was a yellow-brown human skull. Its hollow eye sockets stared down at Brigid. She repressed a shiver, feeling an invisible energy emanating from the structure. Her flesh prickled, and she unconsciously hugged herself as if she was cold. A coyote howled mournfully in the distance.

Maruja glanced at her with a knowing smile tugging at her lips. "Ah, you feel it, too, *señorita*."

"Feel what?"

"The spirits of many generations of *brujos* that find rest here. They are welcoming me back. If you can sense them, you have a touch of the power yourself."

Maruja opened the door, pushing it inward on leather hinges. Surprised, Brigid asked, "You don't lock your door when you are gone?"

The question evoked a chuckle from Maruja. "Who

would dare steal from the *bruja* of El Rey? I have very little to attract thieves, and it is too great of a risk to arouse my anger to violate me in such a fashion."

Maruja took a kerosene lamp from the windowsill and lit the wick with a wooden match. As she adjusted the height of the flame she said, "You may enter."

Ducking under the low doorway, Brigid entered the house. She swiftly studied the single-room dwelling. The adobe walls were covered by stretched animal hides and grinning animal skulls—panthers, wolves and even snakes. Great bundles of dried herbs, dessicated birds and mummified reptiles dangled from the roof beams. Brigid was reminded of pictures she had seen of old apothecary shops.

With a sigh of relief, Maruja unbuttoned the khaki shirt lent to her by Brigid. She shrugged out of it, revealing her high, round breasts, and quickly squirmed out of the pants. She slid into a cotton shirt that she took from a hook on the wall. Brigid was reminded of Domi's unselfconscious attitude about nudity.

She handed Brigid the clothes with a murmur of *"Gracias,"* and then went about the house, lighting candles. As she did so, she asked, "What do you know about the *brujos?*"

"Not much," Brigid said. "Unlike witches in European cultures, the *brujos* are usually respected members of a community, serving as spiritual leaders and doctors. They're sought for their powers of healing, divination and spellwork."

Maruja nodded. "True enough. However, you neglected to mention our powers to cast curses and hexes."

Brigid smiled slightly. "Why haven't you cursed or hexed Ramirez, then?"

Maruja stared at her over the flickering flame of a candle. "I have. Why do you think you and your friends are here?"

"I see." Try as she might, Brigid could not keep a patronizing note from her voice.

"I do not think you do," Maruja replied angrily. "I think you are disrespecting me. Do you believe it is all a sheer coincidence that we met? What are the odds that we would encounter each other in all those hundreds of square miles?"

"I imagine they're astronomical," Brigid said. "But believe me, I'm not mocking you. I'm a woman of science first and foremost."

Maruja put her fists on her hips. "And you think I am just a primitive witch woman, cooking up brews from the flesh of the dead or from live infants?"

"No, of course not. I've encountered folk magic before, Maruja. I'm not dismissing it."

"I am a hex singer," Maruja declared defiantly. "Do you know what that is?"

Regretting her decision to accompany the woman to her house, Brigid edged back toward the door. "I'm afraid I don't."

"It is a tradition among certain members of the

brujeria. We can ward off evil and bring down misfortune by singing hymns."

"Hymns?"

Before Brigid could formulate a response, Maruja took a deep breath, threw her head back and sang in a vibrant contralto voice.

Brigid wasn't quite sure of the meaning of all the words, but she guessed the song had something to do with herbs, the salvation of souls and the saving of the world. The animal hides on the walls seemed to ripple and the candle flames flickered, sending black shadows wavering along the floor and ceiling. The timbre of Maruja's voice touched off sweet vibrations somewhere deep inside of Brigid, making her feel like crying for some reason.

When Maruja fell silent, Brigid said quietly, "Thank you."

Maruja smiled broadly. "You understood?"

"The meaning of the song, if not the lyrics themselves."

"That is all that is important, *señorita.* If you understood the meaning, then all else is mere clutter."

WHEN GRANT AND KANE strolled into an alley between the Toro Bravo and a building they assumed was a blacksmith's shop, they anticipated the two shaved-headed men would follow them.

After taking up position on opposite sides of the narrow passageway and waiting five minutes, they weren't disappointed. But what they didn't realize was that the two men jumped them from above. They leaped from the roof of the smithy's shop and for a handful of painful seconds, all was crazed confusion.

Kane was sent sprawling by a violent blow in the back. He rolled with the fall, drawing up his knees to protect his testicles so that when his attacker jumped for his belly, he tripped and fell heavily beside him. Kane chopped him with the edge of his right hand across the side of the throat, then twisted to his feet as the second man closed with Grant, grappling with him.

Grant misjudged the distance when he swung with a roundhouse right. His adversary grabbed his arm and spun him against the wall, then rained blows on his head and shoulders.

Neither Kane nor Grant expended any time on wondering why the two men weren't using weapons. Grant drove his left elbow into the man's solar plexus at the same time as Kane brought up a knee to parry a kick for his groin from his opponent still lying on the alley floor. He countered with a swift kick of his own, smashing the back of the man's head against the ground. He made no movement afterward.

With a heave of his shoulders, Grant pushed himself away from the wall, heeled around and landed a left hook on the jaw of the man. His attacker staggered backward, then leaped forward, butting Grant in the face with the crown of his skull.

Grant barely avoided having his nose flattened, but the impact against his chin slammed him all the way out of the alley and into a small plaza behind the blacksmith's and the Toro Bravo cantina, where two more shaved-headed men were waiting. Kane pushed the head butter out of the alley ahead of him.

Snarling, he whirled on Kane, a wickedly curving knife appearing in his right hand. With an animalistic bound, the Mexican was on him. Kane twisted aside as the steel blade scraped sparks from the wall.

One of the attackers caught Grant in the belly with a roundhouse kick. He folded over but instead of falling, he threw himself against the other man's legs. Both of them went down in a cursing tangle. Grant wrestled his way on top of the man, then piled a right fist with all of his weight behind it against the man's jaw. Bone broke with a sound like a gunshot. The man's limbs fell away, completely slack.

The man with the knife slashed and thrust at Kane's neck and chest. Kane stood his ground, lightly balanced on the balls of his feet, leaning back from the waist, slapping the Mexican's knife aside. For a long moment, they exchanged a furious flurry of knife strokes and hand slaps. Steel ripped through his shirt but missed the flesh beneath.

Backing up against a recessed doorway, Kane braced his arms against the frame and then, using his hands as levers, launched himself feetfirst. The soles of his boots caught the man full in the chest, knocking him to the ground. Without hesitation, Kane stomped on the man's knife hand and delivered a spinning kick to his head with the metal-reinforced toe of his boot.

As the man fell on his side, Grant rolled to his feet, reaching for the shaved-headed man who clumsily brought his MAC-11 subgun to bear. Lashing out with his right hand, Grant snatched it by the barrel and drove the steel frame hard against the underside of the man's chin. Consciousness went out of his eyes like the snuffing of a match.

Breathing hard, both men probed various injuries and surveyed the bodies. After a moment, Kane said, "I guess we'd better find something to tie them up with."

Grant nodded gloomily. "Not to mention find a place to stow them until we're gone." He cast Kane a challenging glare. "This was easier than just killing them how?"

Kane opened his mouth to answer, closed it, sighed and shook his head. "Maybe you're right. Maybe I *am* getting soft."

Chapter 22

The Cerberus warriors met Maruja and Three-Fingers Lebeaux in the cantina before the sun had fully risen. However, a simple breakfast of coffee and tortillas had been prepared and laid out on the bar by Miguelito's wife, Inez.

"Fill up on these," Lebeaux mumbled around a mouthful of the flat bread. "They don't taste like anything as much as a wet shoe without salt, but they'll get us a long way into the mountains before we need to eat again."

Grant, who had slept poorly in the rear of the Sandcat, glared at the ex-Mag. "You do know you're only along to identify security checkpoints and get us through them, right?"

Lebeaux, chewing noisily, nodded and said, "Ramirez might not know you're here, but he'll want to see you. So I'm helping him as much as you, to keep you from getting lost."

"Thanks so much," Brigid said insincerely. She looked clear-eyed and alert, as did Maruja, who wore a white blouse, buckskin trousers with flared bottoms and embroidered, flat-soled boots.

The sky was just beginning to show scraps of pink and red when the Sandcat rolled out of El Rey. The path swept across empty countryside, the terrain rough and covered with a layer of powdery dust. After driving through a jagged rock defile breaching the first ridge, the path gradually climbed uphill.

The forest receded and was replaced by ragged underbrush. The Sandcat clung to the higher ground at the side of a wide valley. Within three miles, the valley narrowed and the sides became exceptionally steep and rocky. Soon, the Sandcat navigated along a serpentine defile until it became too narrow to drive through.

The Cerberus warriors and their companions disembarked. Three-Fingers Lebeaux gestured forward. "It's the shoe-leather express from here on out."

Adjusting the straps of his backpack, Kane asked, "How far?"

The man shook his head. "That's hard to say. A day's march, less if we're lucky."

"Lucky how?" Brigid inquired, slipping on her own pack.

"Lucky that none of us fall down and break a leg— or our necks."

"Fair enough," Grant grunted.

Long before noon they were deep in the seemingly impenetrable Sierra Madres. When they turned a bend in the canyon wall, it felt as if they were cut off completely from the rest of the world.

They walked beside a rushing streambed, and

entered a deep ravine with cliffs a thousand feet high towering on either side. It was a rugged trail they followed, but Kane felt an exhilaration and sense of freedom in the wildness and isolation of the mountains. He always enjoyed getting away from the vanadium-sheathed confines of the Cerberus redoubt. He took keen pleasure in exploring new lands or trekking through a wilderness, and that made him an exception among the redoubt's residents.

Maruja glanced at Kane and with a knowing smile, murmured, *"El llamade del salvaje."*

"What's that mean?"

Her smile widened. "The call of the wild."

The five people trudged higher into the mountains, into a world of thousand-foot waterfalls and mile-high cliffs. They left the timberline. All around were gigantic masses of granite, occasional crevasses filled with loose shale. They saw very little animal life—a coyote showed its snout momentarily in the brush and a few buzzards wheeled overhead.

The sun at its zenith shone down with merciless heat, but once it slipped behind the looming stone palisades, they felt they walked in perpetual twilight.

They stopped to drink water and rest, but they did not eat. None of them had much of an appetite, which Maruja attributed to the higher altitude and their exertion.

Gazing at Kane, she asked, "What did you do with the spies back in El Rey?"

Kane shrugged. "Like I told you before—we took care of them."

"How?" she pressed.

"Knocked 'em out with some drugs in the Sandcat," Grant replied brusquely. "Tied 'em up and hid 'em in the blacksmith's shop."

"I checked on them before we left," Kane interposed. "They were still sleeping the sleep of the aggressive and stupid."

Lebeaux chuckled mirthlessly. "They're not going to get the jump on us now, but you better hope you don't run into 'em again."

"I think that should be the other way around," Brigid observed sagely.

After twenty minutes, they rose and continued walking, edging their way along a narrow ledge. The only sound was the crunching of their feet as they moved through a thick layer of shale. Kane felt small and insignificant with the mountain peaks looming all around.

Nor did he care to trail after Lebeaux—walking point was a habit he had acquired during his years as a Magistrate because of his uncanny ability to sniff out danger in the offing. He called it a sixth sense, but his point man's sense was really a combined manifestation of the five he had trained to the epitome of keenness. When he walked point, Kane felt electrically alive, sharply tuned to every nuance of his surroundings and what he was doing.

Suddenly the path, instead of ascending, turned and twisted down into a defile. It opened out into a wide, shallow valley. The topography was different—the slopes not as steep, the vegetation much more lush and verdant. Birds flapped in the air and a small herd of deer grazed on the grass.

Pointing to the birds, Maruja said, "Swallows. I know where we are now."

They walked out in the valley, following a trail that snaked through the tall trees. The undergrowth was luxuriant, and long strands of creeper vine dangled from branches above their heads. The air was humid and buzzing with insects. From what Kane could see of the sky through the treetops, he estimated there were still several hours of daylight.

For half an hour, the group marched through the forest. The foliage grew denser and steamier. More than once, they glimpsed the tawny, spotted form of a jaguar slinking through the shrubbery, paralleling their course.

Brigid Baptiste's brisk, almost mannish gait never faltered, despite the heavy pack on her back. Kane couldn't help but reflect that Brigid Baptiste was quite possibly the toughest woman—and one of the toughest people, for that matter—he had ever met.

For a woman who had been trained as an archivist, an academic, and had never strayed more than ten miles from the sheltering walls of Cobaltville, her resiliency and resourcefulness never failed to impress him. Over the past few years, she had left her tracks in the most distant and alien of climes and waded through very deep, very dangerous waters. She, Grant and Kane had come a very long way in distances that could not be measured in mere miles from the day they had escaped from Cobaltville. As veterans of the Magistrate Division, both Kane and Grant were accustomed to danger and hardship, but nothing like they and Brigid had exposed themselves to since their exile.

The five people emerged from an area of dense forest into a small glade floored with flowering plants that sported bright violet petals. The trail vanished among the trees on the far side, but across the middle a huge fissure barred the way.

It was actually more of an enormous pit or cavity than a fissure. Some gigantic upheaval aeons ago had caused the earth to collapse, as though a hole had been punched straight through the crust with a vast pile driver. On all sides trees lined the edges. A flock of birds swarmed above it, darting and diving for insects.

Maruja gestured. "*El Sótano de las Golondrinas*— the Basement of Swallows."

Chapter 23

The five people walked toward the enormous cavity, moving with care through the surrounding brush and clambering over rocks.

"Biggest damn hole I've ever seen," Grant commented unnecessarily.

"It's not really a hole," Brigid said. "It's a shaft leading to a series of caverns."

"My people have many legends about *El Sótano de las Golondrinas*," Maruja said.

"Luis told us the one about the snake-people," Kane replied. "But a hole in the ground is a hole in the ground."

"Except when it's a cenote," Brigid retorted irritably. "It was formed and shaped by the erosion of water in the limestone."

Grant glanced around and then fixed a suspicious gaze on Lebeaux. "I thought Ramirez made his base of operations here."

Lebeaux shrugged. "It's been a long time since I've been here. Maybe they moved on."

"Why would they do that?" Brigid demanded.

Lebeaux smirked. "I couldn't say."

They stepped over fallen logs and a tumble of stones and reached the rim of the pit. The entire earth seemed to have fallen away to unguessable depths. The opening was well over 150 feet in diameter. From their position, they could look down into the vertical round shaft to where it curved to join a horizontal aperture at least a thousand feet below. Sunlight glanced and flashed from the quartz and mica deposits in the rock walls, breaking up into little rainbow patterns.

The abyss was so deep that the blazing sunlight did not penetrate to its bottom, which was little more than a channel filled with house-size boulders. Shadowed, yawning fissures bisected the sheer walls.

Kane experienced a sensation of vertigo, but he closed his eyes against the dizziness. With a studied indifference, he said, "That's some hole."

"Over twelve hundred feet to the bottom," Lebeaux said. "Leastways, that's what I was told."

Brigid carefully eased around the rim, and she stumbled over an object half concealed by a clump of grass. She kicked at it. Metal jingled. "Look at this."

Her companions joined her as she picked up a leather harness. A number of buckles, hooks and fasteners clinked and tinkled.

"A full-body climbing harness," Grant growled. "So that's how Ramirez's crew gets down there."

Kane glared at Lebeaux. "Yeah, but why? What's down there?"

Lebeaux smiled without humor. "The deal was to bring you here, Kane. Do I look like an information booth or some such shit?"

"No," Grant snapped, unslinging his Copperhead. "You look like a slagger who'll be dead in about fifteen seconds if you don't start playing straight with us."

Lebeaux uttered a scoffing laugh. "I played as straight with you as you deserve, you turncoat sons of bitches."

The gunshot sounded like the crack of a breaking stick. Crying out, Lebeaux staggered forward, grabbing for Grant as the slug caught him between the shoulder blades. For a second, he clung to Grant by handfuls of jacket sleeves, his mouth opening and closing like that of a landed fish. Then crimson threads spilled out over his lips and his legs sagged, his grip loosening. Without a sound, he fell away from Grant and plunged over the rim of the pit and silently toppled into it.

The Cerberus warriors lunged for cover. Maruja dived behind a loose heap of shale with thorny weeds sprouting all around it. Kane rolled behind a log, his stomach muscles clenching with adrenaline. Auto-pistol in hand, he looked around, eyeing every boulder, declivity and decent-size bush in the vicinity.

Another shot split the air and gravel gouted in front of Grant's position, a scattering of pebbles stinging his face. "Goddammit!" he barked. "That's a *Sin Eater!*"

KANE DIDN'T REPLY, but he had recognized the sharp, cracking report characteristic of the official Magistrate sidearm, too. Even after all these years, he and Grant often carried them into the field, but recently they had made concerted efforts to wean themselves from the pistols.

A flock of tiny green Mexican parrots came screeching up out of the pit, their rest disturbed by both the gunfire and Lebeaux's falling body. They circled in a flapping, cawing cloud before flying off to the west.

Hearing a rustle of foliage, Kane raised his head just enough to catch fleeting glimpses of movement. "How many?" he asked in a whisper.

"I can't tell," Brigid replied. "But I think we're being surrounded."

"I have counted four men," Maruja said in a voice so calm she might as well have been discussing the weather. "There are probably more."

"I see where one of 'em is," Grant said grimly.

He lifted himself onto one knee, Copperhead jammed against his shoulder, and squeezed the trigger. The stream of 4.85 mm steel-jacketed bullets chopped a line across the ground, knocking up divots of dirt and grass. He kept the snout of the subgun pointed down, since it had a tendency to rise when fired on full-auto.

Starting low on a target and allowing the weapon to naturally track up was the best way to hit the target. The line of rounds intersected with a bush, shearing through leaves and breaches. A black figure reeled into view, crying out in pain and surprise.

The figure resembled a statue sculpted from obsidian, somehow given life and movement. The light struck dim highlights on the molded chest piece and shoulder pads. His face was concealed by a black helmet except for his mouth and chin. A red-tinted visor masked his eyes.

He dropped out of sight, but both Grant and Kane knew he wasn't seriously injured. The molded polycarbonate armor covering the man's chest had rounded surfaces designed to turn heavy-caliber bullets. Still the blunt trauma inflicted by the multiple impacts would cause extreme pain.

Another ebony figure flitted briefly into view among the trees. Kane felt a slight chill. Part of the effect of a Magistrate's black body armor was psychological, instilling fear in not just the criminal but in everyone. Glinting dully on the molded left pectoral was the red duty badge, a stylized scales of justice, superimposed over a nine-spoked wheel. The badge symbolized the Magistrate oath of keeping the wheels of justice turning in the nine baronies. As Kane and Grant knew, more often than not the wheels ground over the innocent and the guilty alike.

The electrochemical polymer of the helmet's visor was connected to a passive night sight that intensified ambient light to permit one-color night vision. The tiny image-enhancer sensor mounted on the forepart did not emit detectable rays, though its range was only twenty-five feet, even on a fairly clear night with strong moonlight.

Kane realized again how the design of the Magistrate armor was more than functional; it was symbolic. When a man concealed his face and body beneath the Magistrate black, he became a fearsome figure, the anonymity adding to the mystique.

There was another reason behind the helmet, the armor, and it was a reason all Magistrates knew but never spoke of openly. When a man put on the armor, he was symbolically surrendering his identity in order to serve a cause of greater import than a mere individual life.

Kane's father had chosen to smother his identity, as had his father before him. For that matter, all Magistrates of their generation had exchanged personal hopes, dreams and desires for a life of service, in order to bring a degree of sanity to the anarchic madness of postnukecaust America.

Another Sin Eater stuttered, and bullets raked a blizzard of splinters from the log sheltering Kane, tearing white patches in the bark. He heard Brigid firing her own pistol, squeezing off two rounds.

"We stay here, we're dead," Grant said. "There's no place to go but down, and it's a long damn way."

Kane nodded, lips compressing in a tight line. "Let me see if I can find us some maneuvering room."

He crawled through the brush, fisting his Bren

Ten, keeping his eyes and ears open. When he reached the tree line, he climbed to his feet. A burst of rounds tore through the branches above his head, showering him with leaves. He ducked behind the tree, feeling it vibrate against his back as bullets pounded into the trunk.

When the gunfire ceased, Kane slid around the tree and opened up, shifting the barrel of his pistol in short left-to-right arcs at a pair of trees a dozen yards away. When the bark exploded into splinters, he heard Grant place a triburst into the left-hand tree.

A small man stumbled out from behind it, carrying an Uzi. He didn't wear armor but was clad in a baggy dark green bodysuit with a rainbow insignia arching across his left breast.

Dropping the gun, his hands clutched a bleeding belly wound. Falling to his knees, he screamed, "I'm hit! Help me!"

A man in Magistrate black sidled around a tree. Angrily, he shouted, "Hawthorne! Shut the fuck up!"

Kane squeezed off one round. The steel-jacketed bullet struck the molded left pectoral of the Mag armor, puncturing the red duty badge and punching a hole through the hub of the nine-spoked-wheel insignia.

The man's arms flailed as the impact pounded him backward. He hit the ground heavily, a little geyser of bright arterial blood squirting up through the perforation in his badge.

Kane took no pleasure in exploiting the major weak

point of the Magistrate armor, but he felt satisfaction at the result, by reducing the opposition even by one.

Return fire ripped into the foliage around him, bullets snapping past his ears like the cracks of bullwhips. Tree bark flew in all directions, and all he could do was hunker down and wait out the fusillade.

While the gunfire was concentrated on Kane's position, Brigid raised herself from behind the pile of stones, leveled her own Bren Ten and ripped off three rapid-fire shots at shadowy figures moving between the trees.

She ducked back down as a swath of bullets chopped fragments out of the rocks.

"You take big risks, *señorita,*" Maruja said breathlessly.

"Part of the job nowadays," Brigid replied dismissively.

Despite her tone, she felt the tingling warmth of excitement as the prospect of danger spread through her.

For a very long time, she was ashamed of that anticipation, blaming her association with Kane for contaminating her. Now she had accepted the realization that his own desire for thrill-seeking hadn't infected her, but only forced her to accept an aspect of her personality she had always been aware of but refused to consciously acknowledge.

Years ago, during her life as a baronial archivist, Brigid Baptiste had prided herself on her intellect and logical turn of mind. She was a scholar first and foremost. Back then, the very suggestion she would have been engaged in such work would have made her laugh. Now she was a veteran warrior, and at some point during her time with Cerberus she realized the moments of danger no longer terrified her but brought a sharper sense of being alive.

The gunfire tapered off, then ceased altogether. After a long moment, a man's voice bellowed, "Hey! We need to talk about this thing before we waste more ammo! It's hard to come by in these parts."

"What's there to talk about?" Grant yelled back. "You shot at us—we shot back!"

"We need to talk about how you should figure out how to stay alive for another couple of hours. Don't know if you've noticed, but you're outnumbered."

"Not as outnumbered as we were," Kane called out calmly. "How about you lay down your guns and leave us the hell alone?"

"Funny guy," the man replied, voice icy with sarcasm. "But no can do, compadre. How'd you talk Lebeaux into coming back here?"

"He volunteered," Grant retorted.

"Bullshit!" The man's tone was full of scorn. "Why the hell would the bastard do that?"

"He thought he'd earn points with Ramirez if he brought us to him," Kane answered.

The response was so long in coming, Kane wondered if the man had heard him. Then his voice demanded, "Why would bringing you here earn points with Ramirez?"

"We'll tell that to Ramirez when we see him," Kane said.

Another man's voice wafted to them, from directly behind Kane's position. "Then start the tellin', Kane."

He froze, recognizing Ramirez's voice.

Chapter 24

"I think this is the part where you drop your gun and put your hands behind your head," Ramirez said mildly. "You know the drill."

Kane didn't move, sensing a gun barrel trained on the back of his skull. "Pretty old trick. Your man keeps me talking and distracted while you sneak up and get the drop on me."

"The old tricks are the best," Ramirez said. "Do what I tell you."

"Even if I do," Kane pointed out reasonably, "you still only have me. There's Baptiste and Grant to be accounted for."

Ramirez chuckled as if he found Kane's words genuinely amusing. "They'll do whatever they need to do to save your life, Kane. They traveled halfway across the country and got into a big-ass battle to rescue you from Area 51. I was part of that, remember?"

Kane sighed. "Oh, yeah."

Area 51 was the predark unclassified code name for a training area on Nellis Air Force base in Nevada. Brigid and Grant had traveled overland from Montana to rescue Kane and Domi, who had been captured by Baron Cobalt and imprisoned in Area 51.

Carefully, Kane laid his autopistol on the ground and linked his fingers at the back of his neck. "Satisfied?"

"For the moment. Stand up. Turn around very slowly."

Kane did so, and he tried very hard to keep from uttering an exclamation of surprise when he saw the man's face. He had not seen Ramirez since they had engaged in hand-to-hand combat in Redoubt Yankee several years before, but he knew the man was nearly a decade younger than himself. Seeing him now shocked Kane into momentary speechlessness.

Although Ramirez wore the Mag body armor, he had dispensed with the helmet, and Kane was afforded a direct view of his face. All of the softness of youth had disappeared, replaced by deep lines of suffering etched into the flesh at the corners of his eyes and curving out from either side of his nose. His shaggy black hair showed a stippling of silver.

A crescent-shaped scar showed lividly on his forehead, bisecting his right eyebrow. Ramirez looked as if he had lived very hard and very painfully in a relatively short period of time. His eyes were dark and as alert and as keen as a hawk's, yet somehow secret, as though the true thoughts behind them would never be revealed.

The bore of a Sin Eater pointed directly at Kane's

chest. Stripped down to a skeletal frame, the Sin Eater was barely fourteen inches long. The extended magazine held twenty rounds of 9-mm ammo. There was no trigger guard, no fripperies, no wasted inch of design. The Sin Eater looked exactly like what it was supposed to be—the most wickedly efficient handgun ever made.

"Mictlanx, I presume," Kane drawled.

Ramirez's lips quirked in a smile. "Tell Baptiste and Grant to surrender."

Kane cleared his throat and called out, "Grant! Baptiste! I've reacquainted myself with Ramirez."

"Yeah?" Grant's voice held a cautious, skeptical note.

"Yeah. He's holding a Sin Eater on me."

Brigid's heavy sigh reached his ears very clearly. "And he wants us to disarm and come out with our hands up, right?"

Kane glanced at Ramirez, who nodded curtly. "That's the general idea," he said loudly.

"Ah, shit," Grant hissed. "Done."

Two men in the black armor closed in on Brigid and Grant's position, forcing them to their feet and taking their weapons. Ramirez marched Kane out of the tree line. As they passed the man wearing the green bodysuit of the Historical Division, he groped for Ramirez's foot with blood-coated fingers.

"Help me," he gasped, writhing in agony.

"Sure thing," Ramirez said, lowering the barrel of his

pistol and squeezing the trigger stud. The Sin Eater cracked. A bullet punched through the side of the man's skull. He convulsed briefly, then lay still.

"We don't have the facilities to treat that kind of wound," Ramirez said by way of an explanation. "I saved him a couple of hours' worth of suffering."

Overhearing his words, Brigid Baptiste said, "I always pegged you for a Samaritan at heart."

Ramirez's eyes passed over her and he grinned appreciatively. "You haven't changed a bit."

"Can't say the same about you," Grant replied. "You look like you've been rode into the ground and then hung out by your heels to cure."

Ramirez ignored the gibe. He eyed Maruja with an enigmatic expression. "What are you doing back here?"

The woman bared her teeth in combination of grin and defiant snarl. "What do you think?"

Ramirez gusted out a sigh. "I set you free but that wasn't enough for you, was it?"

"You didn't set me free," Maruja shot back. "I escaped. You sent three of your Diableros after me, didn't you?"

Ramirez scowled. "What are you talking about?"

Maruja's lips peeled back from her teeth in a sneer. "What do you think? They came into my country and I killed them, hung up their bodies as warnings."

Ramirez stared at her in confusion as if trying to process the information, then said, "So that's what happened to Wilcox, Le Sprague and Ballinger."

He shifted his gaze and gun barrel to one of the men in Magistrate armor standing slightly behind Grant. "That was your doing, wasn't it, Greiner."

The man stiffened. He was taller than Ramirez, lacking only an inch or so of Grant's height. "What do you mean?"

"I ordered you to send those men to track down the workers who escaped, not to go after Maruja."

Greiner snorted out a laugh. "Tuco's scumbags were better suited for that. Your little piece of witchy ass caused us a lot of trouble while you had her here. She's still causing us trouble. Look what she brought back with her."

"Us?" Kane inquired inanely.

The man's glance at Kane was hostile and arrogant. "Keep your mouth shut, Kane. I got no reason to let you live. You cost us two men, one of them a Mag."

Grant grunted. "He shot first."

Kane knew Grant didn't feel quite as callous as he sounded. Although Kane had come to terms with his exile, with his status as an outlander, he knew Grant still grappled with guilt. The peeling away of their Mag identities, the loss of their Mag purpose had been a painful process to endure. Grant rarely spoke of it, but the man was always stoic in the face of pain.

"Why *did* you bring them here, Maruja?" Ramirez asked.

"She didn't," Brigid interposed. "Lebeaux did."

Maruja stepped forward, ignoring the gun pointed at

her. "You don't need to make excuses for me, Señorita Brigid."

"Lebeaux couldn't find his dick even when he had all of his fingers," Greiner declared. "I think you brought him along instead of the other way around."

Ramirez nodded reluctantly. "I think so, too."

In a voice sibilant with spite, Maruja said, "Did you think you could use me and then send me on my way when you had no more use for me?"

Ramirez shifted his feet uncomfortably. "It wasn't that way at all. With Carmenita pregnant, I didn't think you wanted to stay. I couldn't ask you to—"

"Deliver your bastard child?" Maruja broke in, with a contemptuous laugh. "Conceived through rape? Ah, for once you are correct."

Listening to the woman's words and studying the expression on her face, Kane's belly turned a cold flip-flop of nausea. He suddenly understood that Maruja was less a victim seeking redress than a woman scorned, her motivations not much different than those of Clarise in Pandakar.

"All right, enough of this shit!" Greiner's aggressive voice pressed against everyone's eardrums. "Let's just kill this bunch and have done with it. We got business to attend to."

Brigid smiled tauntingly. "Does that business involve tunneling under another barony that has gone democratic?"

Ramirez swung his head toward her, eyes widening.

After a silent couple of seconds, he nodded in grudging agreement. "So that's why you, Grant and Kane are here."

"Did you think Cerberus wouldn't hear about it?" Grant asked. "Mandeville, Palladiumville and then your old stomping grounds, Snakefish?"

"The question is why?" Kane said.

Ramirez chuckled, a harsh, humorless rustle. "So there *are* things you don't know."

"Plenty of them," Brigid stated matter-of-factly, "but we manage to learn just about everything we need to know."

Sweeping his gaze over the four outlanders, Ramirez gestured toward the rim of the pit. "Let's go."

"Go where?" Maruja asked.

"Where else? Down."

Greiner stiffened. "Hey!"

"Hey, shut the fuck up!" Ramirez roared in a sudden fury. "Because of your bullshit, we lost three of our best people and our whole labor force, too—not to mention my baby! You've got no more say about anything!"

Greiner swallowed hard, the pistol in his hand trembling slightly as he tried to control a surge of rage. He did not respond.

Kane, Maruja, Brigid and Grant were marched to the rim of the hole. The other Magistrate picked up the climbing harness and carried it over to a cleft formed by a pair of upward-jutting rocks. From beneath them he withdrew a thick coil of nylon rope. One end was attached to the eyebolt of a metal piton hammered deep into the stone.

Ramirez took the harness from the man, glanced at it with a frown, then tossed it to Kane. He caught it with a jingle of metal. "You first."

"Why?"

"Because I think you're the most dangerous. The longer you stand out around here, the more likely you are to try something stupid and dangerous. If go down into the pit first, there's not a whole hell of a lot of trouble you can cause down there."

"If anybody could manage," Brigid supplied helpfully, "he can."

"No doubt." Ramirez gestured with his Sin Eater. "Do what I say."

Although Kane eyed the piton apprehensively, he slid his arms and legs into the belay loops of the harness. Brigid helped him adjust the straps, and he grimaced when she cinched it tight around his waist.

"You know, Ramirez," he said, striving to sound casual, "you haven't mentioned why we're going down there."

"I thought you wanted answers," Ramirez countered. "You're not afraid of heights, are you?"

"Not so much," Kane replied, threading the nylon rope through the carabiners attached to the harness.

Greiner chuckled disdainfully. "We'll see. Get your ass over the side."

Chapter 25

Slowly, carefully, Kane edged out on the rim of the pit and eased his weight onto the rope. The piton held. He slid farther out, slinging the rope through the loop on the harness until he sat within it. He pushed himself off into empty space, swinging like a pendulum for a long moment.

Although he wasn't afraid of heights, dangling over such a deep pit sent a sudden jolt of apprehension jumping through him. He chocked it down and began lowering himself hand over hand, feeding the rope through carabiners with a prolonged hiss. Swallows poked their heads out of holes on the shaft walls, peering at him curiously.

He glanced up to see everyone gazing down at him, including Maruja, and again he wondered about her motivations. That her and Ramirez's relationship had been more than superficial was obvious, but he had no idea how complex it had been.

Kane continued rappelling down the stone shaft, cold sweat seeping from his pores. A smooth descent was difficult because of the distance. He moved down a few feet at a time, and then stopped to catch his breath and relieve the gnawing ache that settled in his hands, wrists, forearms and crept into his shoulder blades. Every few minutes, he glanced up at the ellipse of light above him, at the comforting sight of Brigid and Grant peering down at him, rather than into the sea of gloom below.

Descending the rope was hard work, and it had been over ten years since he had done any climbing, and then it was part of a Mag training exercise, to upgrade his certification. Three times he had to stop to relax some of the tension in his muscles. The air temperature cooled the deeper he went.

He was pretty certain Ramirez and his crew used another way down into the pit. With what seemed like maddening, infinite slowness, Kane continued to descend into the deepening dark. When his toes finally touched a solid object, it took a few moments to comprehend the fact.

He was conscious of a sense of indescribable depth, as if he had dropped into the very core of the planet, and he felt the ponderous weight of all those millions of tons of stone hanging above him. He stood in a natural amphitheater of stone, surrounded by concave walls.

Glancing around, he saw the body of Lebeaux draped over a boulder, his limbs bent in wrong directions. His torso, from chest to back, looked only a few inches thick. Kane figured every bone in his body had been pulverized.

As he disconnected the harness, he heard a stealthy footfall behind him. He turned quickly and saw a man wearing the green bodysuit of an archivist. He carried an M-11 autocarbine, but he held it negligently, as if he had forgotten it. Kane opened his mouth to speak to him, and then the words clogged in his throat. Nausea roiled in his belly.

Somewhere in the recent past, the man had been hideously burned. A great heat or flame had swept across his features, leaving a raw, puckered mask of peeled flesh. His eye sockets, mouth and nostrils were only dark spots in a livid face. He had no hair and his ears were little more than stumps.

"What the hell are you doing here?" he demanded in a hoarse voice.

"I might ask you the same thing," Kane said, gazing into the cavernous darkness behind the man. "Where did you come from?"

The man jerked a thumb over his shoulder. "That way. You another recruit? Another idiot Ramirez has talked into becoming Diablero?"

Kane didn't answer. He finished removing the harness, gave the rope a jerk and with a clink of metal it was pulled up. He glanced at the man again, realizing the man suffered radiation burns rather than from an open flame.

"What's your name?" he asked.

"Ramirez didn't tell you?"

"Obviously not, or I wouldn't be asking."

The man's face twisted in a macabre travesty of a grin. "Fair to say. I'm Elias."

"An historian from Snakefish?"

He nodded. "I am that."

Kane eyed him closely, his memory flashing back to the burns on Brewster Philboyd's face. "And the local expert on the Subterrene, I'll bet."

"Right again. What gave me away?" He touched his face. "My youthful complexion?"

Kane nodded. "I saw a similar burn on a man in Snakefish. Nowhere near as serious."

Elias peered at him curiously, muttering, "I've seen your face before."

Kane did not respond, waiting for the man to make the connection. He did not wait for very long. Elias uttered a grunt of dismay and took a step backward, aiming the carbine at him.

"Kane," he said. "Kane from Cobaltville, now with that wild bunch from Cerberus. The pix I saw of you was several years old. Otherwise I would have recognized you right off the bat."

"You know what they say—it's not the years, it's the mileage."

Elias sighed. "I knew Ramirez would draw your attention…or the Millennial Consortium's."

"You can't knock down villes for a living and maintain a low profile."

Elias chuckled. "It's not a living, not exactly."

"What is it exactly?" Kane asked.

"I guess we'll just have to wait until Ramirez gets down here. If he wants to explain, he will."

"And if he doesn't?"

"Then he won't. But I imagine he will. Otherwise he

wouldn't have gone to all the trouble of letting you climb down here. He would have just thrown you."

Kane nodded in understanding.

IT REQUIRED OVER AN HOUR for Brigid, Maruja, Ramirez, Greiner and Grant all to rappel their way down to the bottom of the pit. The other man in Mag black, Berger by name, was left topside to attend to the bodies. Kane waited patiently, not making an attempt to disarm Elias. He knew he needed to let the situation play out.

Grant came down last. Working his shoulders up and down and wincing, Grant glanced around, his brow furrowed. "All right, so we're all in the pit. Why?"

Ramirez gestured. "Follow me."

With Greiner bringing up the rear, the Cerberus warriors and Maruja fell into step behind Ramirez and Elias. They entered an opening on the far side of the pit. Exposed wiring and fluorescent light fixtures stretched along the roof as far as the eye could see. Girders of punched steel shored up the ceiling and from these hung cabling. Motorized gurney tracks disappeared down the tunnel where no light could reach.

"When did you make all these improvements?" Brigid asked.

"A lot of it was already here," Ramirez said. "Put here years ago."

Brigid's eyes widened. "Put here by who?"

Elias glanced over his shoulder. "COG planners, probably."

She nodded thoughtfully. "I can see them doing that. Their mission priority was to build underground bases and if there were ones already extant—"

"Exactly," Elias said, turning and extending a hand. "Lee Elias, Snakefish Historical Division. You're Brigid Baptiste, the most famous archivist of all."

Brigid was startled into laughing, but she took the man's hand and shook it. "Famous? Not infamous?"

"A bit of that, too," Elias admitted. "But that only adds to your allure."

Greiner growled, "Cut the chitchat and keep moving."

They continued walking along the tunnel and became aware of a steady drone from far ahead. The tunnel curved, turning almost at right angles. As they walked around the bend the tunnel curved again even more sharply, then turned once more, adding to the Cerberus warriors' growing bewilderment and apprehension.

"How the hell did you find this place?" Grant demanded.

Elias tapped the rainbow insignia on his bodysuit.

Grant grunted in understanding. "Oh, yeah. The archives at Snakefish."

As they made another turn, they were startled to see a patch of light far ahead. Vaguely rectangular in shape and of an unearthly blue hue, it wavered and flickered eerily, at times almost disappearing, at times flaring to a lurid, momentary brilliance shot through with flashes of red and even orange.

The tunnel ended as if on the brink of a precipice.

The three people stared down, through an abyss into a chasm as wide and as deep as the drop-off on the plateau of the Cerberus redoubt. But the walls of the cavern face were sheer, straight and smooth, with no moss or lichens or even cracks marring the surfaces.

Ramirez touched the right-hand wall. "Take a look, touch it. Smooth as glass. Not so much as a scratch from a chisel or a drill bit."

Kane stared and ran his fingers over the soap-slick stone. He could not believe that either natural forces or the work of men could have hollowed out the cavern. Radiance shone down from glass globes tipping metal conduits that sprouted from sockets in the cavern wall. Most of them were dark and others flashed intermittently.

"Impressive," Grant said. "So?"

"So, let's go."

Ramirez inched out onto a narrow parapet, flattening himself against the rock wall. After a moment of hard swallowing, Brigid, Grant and Kane stepped out after him. Maruja, Elias and Greiner followed.

The ledge made a turn to the left after a few steps, and its pitch descended at an increasingly sharp angle. The width of the parapet never varied, and soon they learned the rhythm of walking along it. At first they edged along with exaggerated caution, but with repetition, they became came more confident.

The ledge gradually widened into a true path. The three people breathed easier when they no longer had to inch sideways. The parapet met and joined with an unnaturally smooth floor of a cavern of vast proportions. It had the same glossy surface as the walls.

Ramirez led them forward toward the center of the cavern. Their boots rang on the glassy paving stones, the ghostly echoes chasing one another to the domed roof arched high overhead in the darkness.

They walked toward a black, perfectly hemispherical aperture yawning in the far wall. It was about ten feet high and nearly that wide. Ramirez paused before it and gestured. "After you."

Kane eyed the opening with apprehension. "We'll wait for you, thanks."

Greiner prodded him in the small of the back with his Sin Eater. "He wasn't asking. Get your ass in gear."

Kane stepped through, followed by Brigid and Grant. At the end of a short ramp, light glowed. All of them came to an unsteady halt at a metal railing. High above their heads soared an arched ceiling carved and blasted from gray stone.

The roof was braced in strategic places by towering steel beams of a rust-red finish. The footings of the steel superstructure were sunk deep in the floor that stretched away before them, forming a huge T-shaped platform.

As they edged closer to the railing the Cerberus warriors realized they stood in a position approximately in the center of the crossbar of the T. Ahead, like a stone pier, the stem of the T stretched out into a huge natural channel. In the center of the channel, covered with dozens of thick electrical cables, rested a bronze-colored craft that resembled a giant spearhead.

"I think," Brigid Baptiste said softly, "we've discovered the Subterrene."

Chapter 26

The outline of the low-slung metal-hulled machine resembled a submarine. Its length was close to fifty yards and where a conning tower would be positioned, a streamlined blister rose less than a yard or so above the dorsal surface.

Along the sides of the craft, from bow to stern, ran rows of large oval ob ports just above elongated tracks, like those of the Sandcat. The ports were made of dark blue glass or a similar material, opaque and resembling the shaded lights dangling from the rocky ceiling.

Catwalks and ladderways crisscrossed above them, but they were empty, devoid of movement. The entire cavern looked lifeless. Far down past the Subterrene's bow they saw a high arched opening in the cave wall. The opening was barred by a steel door of thick grillwork.

From behind them, Ramirez inquired, "We'll be happy to give you the guided tour."

Brigid cast a glance over her shoulder. "Do we have a choice?"

Greiner showed the edges of his teeth in a vulpine

grin. "Sure. Take the tour and live—give me trouble and die. I wish you'd choose the second option."

The group of people walked down a metal stairway, their footfalls clattering loudly in the huge, hollow space. As they walked across the body of the T, Kane cast a glance over at Maruja. Her expression was grave but not one of wonder, and he guessed she wasn't seeing anything new.

Nodding toward the machine, Brigid inquired, "I assume that thing was here when you arrived?"

"Why the hell would we come to the asshole of the world?" Ramirez countered. "The data about the tunneler was in the archives, and it said this was where it could be found."

"And not having anything better to do after Baron Snakefish left," Kane suggested, "you decided, 'why not get some of my unemployed Mag pals together, come to Mexico and make myself the warlord of the pit.'"

Elias laughed, and then coughed—a deep, racking cough from the bottom of his lungs. He put a hand to his mouth spit into it, examined the result and flung his hand down. The sputum made a bright pink blob on the floor. With an eerie detachment, he said, "Not long now."

The people reached the channel cradling the Subterrene, and they jumped to the hull. The round hatch gaped open. Ramirez gestured. "Down."

When no one moved, he pointed the bore of the Sin

Eater at Brigid's head. "I don't mind killing one of you to make a point. I really don't."

Ramirez's eyes fixed on Kane's face. "Killing her in front of you would make my point, wouldn't it? I owe you some pain payback."

"I wondered when you were going to get around to mentioning that," Kane said. "You were trying to kill me. I tried to stop you. That's all there was to it. I could've killed you, but I let you live."

Ramirez's face twisted into a combination of sneer and scowl. "Bullshit. You just forgot about me. Hell, I almost wish you *had* killed me. My life turned to shit after I got back to Snakefish."

Maruja murmured something in Spanish and reached for Ramirez, but Greiner hauled her back by a wrist. "Don't move."

Brigid maintained a calm expression, glancing toward the gun barrel as if it was no more interesting than a twig Ramirez pointed in her direction. If she had learned one thing from Kane, and from her association with Grant and Domi, it had been to accept risk as a part of her way of life, taking chances so that others might find the ground beneath their feet a little more secure.

She had never considered her attitude idealism, but simple pragmatism. She had come to understand that death was a part of the challenge of existence, a fact that every man and woman had to face eventually.

She could accept it without humiliating herself, if it came as a result of her efforts to remove the yokes of the overlords from the collective neck of humanity. Although she never spoke of it, certainly not to the cynical Kane, she had privately vowed to make the future a better, cleaner place than either the past or the present. She suspected he knew anyway.

She hoped that somehow she and her friends would be able to negotiate a way out the trap. If not by design, then by luck. Kane and Grant had made something of a minireligion about the matriculation of luck, as if it were a finite resource that had to be periodically replenished.

"What'll it be?" Ramirez demanded.

Kane shrugged and put a leg over the rim of the hatch. "After me."

The gloom of the ladderway closed around him. He climbed down metal rungs to a floor made of interlocking deck plates. It was completely dark except for the illumination filtering down from above, so he stood motionless.

Ramirez came next, followed by Maruja, Brigid, Grant and Greiner. When everyone stood clustered about the ladder, Elias reached over and touched a slick square of black glass inset into the bulkhead. Lights flashed on.

They stood in a circular chamber with electronic control surfaces covering the bulkheads. Tiny lights on the consoles flickered. The state-of-the-art instruments and panels were baffling in their complexity. Underfoot, Kane felt a tingling sensation and the interior filled with a low, resonating hum.

The Cerberus warriors and Maruja were led through a short passageway while a rumble of power vibrated through the hull. They entered the control room. There were no windows or ports, just a forty-inch monitor screen on the fore bulkhead. Six chairs were placed before control boards. Each came with crisscrossing harnesses. Indicator lights blinked in an almost hypnotic rhythm.

"Sit down," Ramirez said, waving toward the chairs. "You, too, Maruja."

As Brigid settled herself, she looked at Elias and asked, "So you found out about the Subterrene by riffling through the archives in Snakefish?"

Elias examined a needle gauge, tapping the glass cover with a forefinger. "More or less. Did you know that there were plans to build a subterranean highway system? It was a very elaborate plan, called the Sub-Global System. Eventually, the COG schemers wanted to go international, with checkpoints at each country entry."

Grant folded his arms over his broad chest. In an exceptionally bored tone, he inquired, "Really?"

Elias nodded. "Really. There were designs and schematics for shuttle tubes that shot trains at incredible speed using a magnetic levitation and vacuum method. They could travel in excess of the speed of sound. Of course there was only one problem."

"Construction?" Kane inquired.

Elias nodded. "That's it. For any of this to have

worked required tunnels over three thousand miles in length. Not an easy undertaking."

"No pun intended," Ramirez said darkly.

"Judging by what I found in the archives," Elias stated, "very few predark scientists took this proposal seriously. There were skeptics that never believed humanity would reach the moon. On the other hand, there was another group who believed that the underground tunnel system was actually being constructed by aliens."

Brigid raised an eyebrow. "Aliens?"

Elias coughed again, but not as violently. "Yeah. There were some predarkers who believed in the idea that aliens inhabited the earth for a long time and liked to live underground, out of sight. Hell, I even saw pix in the archives of ancient alien structures on the damn Moon! If they can do it there, they could come to Earth and build underground habitats, couldn't they?"

Assuming the question to be rhetorical, neither Brigid, Grant nor Kane responded, although they struggled against the urge to exchange knowing glances with one another.

The memory of the mausoleum of the Annunaki that she, Grant and Kane had entered beneath the Moon's surface leaped to the forefront of Brigid's mind. She had no problem remembering how the creatures looked like hideous travesties of humanity. Taller than Grant, leaner by far than Kane, she had passed between double rows of lizard-things propped upright on thrones, their bowed, powerful legs tucked beneath them. The three of them had stared wide-eyed, stunned, shocked, awed and—in her case—terrified.

The Serpent Kings had been buried royally, each one carefully embalmed and positioned upright on a funerary throne, wearing all the trappings of the godhood they had assumed upon Earth. The beautifully polished stone of the ceilings and walls had been carved in reliefs showing events in the lives of the various Annunaki who sat stiffly all down the length of the great hall.

Brigid had easily imagined carpets on the cold floor and a great deal of ornate furnishings. But all of that ancient splendor was long gone. The excavations of the human explorers from the Manitius base had caved in the rock-cut chambers, and the explorers themselves had taken all the funeral finery. Only the thrones and the Serpent Kings remained, shriveled corpses staring into nothingness.

"There were a number of so-called alien abductees who reported being taken to underground bases," Elias continued. "Some of these abductees have described seeing things that really exist in documented underground facilities."

"How was all of this stuff built?" Grant asked skeptically.

Ramirez rapped on a bulkhead with the barrel of his Sin Eater. "With this…and others like it."

"If there were others like it," Elias said doubtfully,

"the Sub-Global System of subterranean highways would have been completed. Instead all we've found are a few tunnels, most of them branching off from here, the Basement of Swallows."

"It was still a great idea," Ramirez said. "The beauty of the Subterrene is that, as it burrows through the rock hundreds of feet below the surface, it heats whatever stone it encounters into molten rock, or magma, which cools after the Subterrene has moved on. The result is a tunnel with a smooth, glazed lining."

"So that's why you were pointing out the walls," Kane said.

Ramirez nodded. "Exactly."

"Let me guess," Brigid said, staring intently at Elias. "For power, to generate all that heat, the Subterrene can use an onboard miniature nuclear engine."

Elias nodded. "There were some cracks in the shielding. We didn't know their severity until we made some runs."

"What kind of heat are we talking?" Grant asked.

"In the neighborhood of 2,000 degrees Fahrenheit," the historian answered stolidly. "The Subterrene works by melting its way through the rock and soil, actually vitrifying it as it goes. The cooled lithium then circulates back to the reactor where the whole cycle starts over. In this way the Subterrene burrows through the rock like a nuclear powered earthworm, but unlike an earthworm, it produces no muck or waste byproducts that must be disposed of. That greatly simplifies tunneling."

Brigid made a "hmm" sound of contemplation. "That also makes Subterrenes very hard to track for the simple reason that there would not be the telltale dirt piles or tailings dumps that are associated with the conventional tunneling activities. If all the debris is used as a lining for the tunnel walls, then it's very efficient."

She paused and added, "Which makes me wonder why you needed a slave labor force."

"Simple," Greiner said. "The way to this installation was buried. Either earthquakes or demolition charges had sealed the passages."

"Oh," Kane said. "But once you reached the Subterrene, you didn't need them anymore, right? So why didn't you let them go?"

"It wasn't that simple," Ramirez bit out, gazing at Maruja and then looking away.

The woman forced a mocking laugh. "No, it was not. Warlords need soldiers to command, and if he cannot have soldiers, then he needs subjects. And if he has subjects, then he needs to rule them. And if he is a ruler, he needs an heir—"

"Shut up!" Ramirez shouted, taking a menacing step toward her.

Maruja stared up at him fearlessly. "Or what?"

Hoping to distract the man from Maruja, Kane interposed, "There has to be more to this undertaking than an underground highway system."

Elias stepped quickly into the opening provided by Kane. "I believe that some of the planners hoped that underground trains would carry nuclear warheads that could strike cities from beneath."

"What about underground rivers and the like?" Grant asked.

"They are constant threats and considerations. Underground rivers breaking through shallow crusts and flooding the tunnels probably happened often. We found a number of tunnels equipped with vanadium-steel, watertight doors. The doors can probably be sealed every few miles in every tunnel, making water-tight compartments."

Kane surreptitiously glanced at Ramirez. The man's temper seemed to have cooled. He no longer glared at Maruja with undiluted rage, so he ventured mildly, "This Subterrene has to have a drill or something on the bow to melt and break the rock, doesn't it?"

Ramirez nodded. "Of course."

"How does it work?"

A slow grin spread over Ramirez's face. He turned toward a row of buttons and pressed five of them in sequence. "Let's give you a demonstration."

The Subterrene shook from stem to stern like a wet dog, metal grinding and squealing at a painfully high volume.

Chapter 27

Ramirez sat down with his back toward the sharp angle formed by the bow plates of the Subterrene. Looking past his head, the Cerberus warriors saw that the viewscreen displayed a perfectly round tunnel, like the interior of a massive pipe. The machine lurched forward, yawing slightly from side to side. Elias adjusted a control stick, and the roar of the engines muted somewhat.

"Where are you taking us in this metal mole?" Brigid demanded.

Ramirez smirked. "This mole was designed to be mobile operations base for a predark construction project."

"What kind of operations?" Kane inquired.

"What kind of construction project?" Grant asked. "Building underground bases?"

"More like cities," Elias replied.

"Cities?" Kane repeated dubiously. "That's a big order, even for machines like these."

Elias touched a toggle switch on the control board nearest his elbow. "Think so? Look."

On the screen, three circular saw blades rose from the prow of the vehicle, attached to multijointed, alloy-coated armatures. Although they didn't spin, it was obvious they were designed to work in perfect sync. Light glittered from sharp points along the edges of the blades.

"Do you know what a kerf is?" Ramirez asked. Judging by the tone of his voice, it was obvious he didn't expect anyone to respond with an affirmative.

"*Kerf* is a term used to mean the width of the saw blade," Brigid stated crisply. "However, the term also includes the width of the cut and the width of the blade plus any wobble created during cutting, plus any material pulled out of the sides of the cut. If you try to use a blade that is too thin you can get excessive wobble and actually get a wider, less precise kerf."

No one gaped at Brigid in astonishment, but Kane repressed a laugh at the disconcerted expression crossing Ramirez's face.

"You can achieve exceptionally precise cuts and kerfs with these blades," Elias said. "They're diamond tipped. Diamond saws are made by combining powder metal with diamond crystals, which are then heated and pressed into a molding to form the diamond segments. They're almost indestructible."

"So," Brigid said musingly, "the Subterrene generates focused heat at the end of a drill, and the saw blades are powered with sufficient force to produce and extend radial cracks in solid rock around the bore by means of hydrostatic pressure developed in the molten rock ahead of the advancing rock drill penetrator."

"Exactly," Elias said, a grudging smile creasing his scarred face. "By thermally melting a boundary kerf into the tunnel face and forming a supporting excavation wall liner by deflecting the molten materials against the excavation walls, it provides a solidified, continuous supportive liner."

Grant scowled. "And you can make underground cities that way?"

"Not just that way," Greiner said impatiently. "A *lot* of different ways."

"This isn't guesswork, Grant," Elias declared. "We're putting to use certain principles of geological discoveries made by predark scientists attached to this project."

"What project is that?" Brigid wanted to know.

"Mictlanx," Ramirez replied promptly. "That's what it was called."

Brigid nodded. "The Aztec god of the underworld. So you took the name of the project and the god for your own?"

Ramirez shrugged. "Seemed an easy way to set up a new identity and get some cooperation from the locals."

Maruja uttered a sibilant sound, like a cat hissing. Ramirez ignored her.

"Are the geological principles about triggering earthquakes?" Kane asked.

Neither Ramirez, Elias nor Greiner answered for a long moment. Then, thoughtfully, Elias replied, "I suppose sharing the totality of our plan will increase your awareness of the long-range result. Since you're now a part of it, you might as well know about it."

Kane snorted, pretending not to notice the menacing half step Greiner took toward him.

"With the Subterrene," Elias continued, "we've perfected a means to quickly and drastically initiate major tectonic events. When shaped explosive charges are placed in the proper depths and positioned in fault lines within the bedrock and detonated simultaneously, the result is the creation of earth tremors and quakes of extreme destructive power. The principle is known as telegeodynamics."

Kane noticed how Brigid's eyes narrowed suspiciously at the word.

"It's basically the same plan as the one the predarkers who drafted the Sub-Global System wanted to implement," Ramirez said.

Ramirez's manner was easy and conversational, but his eyes flicked nervously from the grim-faced Maruja to the Cerberus warriors.

"How will engineering earthquakes benefit you?" Brigid asked. "Why destroy the former baronies?"

"First of all," said Greiner, "we needed test subjects for the Subterrene."

"Second of all," Ramirez interjected, "they were the villes that revolted against unification, against the baronial government. They were populated by traitors."

"They didn't revolt," Grant objected. "The barons are gone. The people left behind tried to build a new society."

Greiner's face flushed and his lips peeled away from his bared teeth. "They were fuckin' traitors to unity, and that's why the villes were destroyed. The people could have maintained unity, the baronial form of rule, but they chose anarchy instead."

"Lies!" Maruja's voice hit a high pitch of angry outrage. "You caused the deaths of hundreds of innocent people, destroyed their homes and ruined their lives, all because you did not like their politics?"

"They made themselves targets," Greiner snapped. "That's all there was to it."

"But there were children—"

"Collateral damage," Ramirez broke in. "Maruja, what the hell did you think we were doing? I explained the plan to you."

"You explained you wanted to build a new world," she shot back, her bosom heaving, "one with order and where people could live without fearing banditos. *Sí*, perhaps I was too amazed by all the wonders you showed me to think clearly. But now—"

"But now that you know you won't be a queen or an empress," Greiner interrupted with a snide chuckle, "now you're thinking clearly, right?"

Turning toward him, Maruja started to push herself up from the chair, but Ramirez said sharply, "Sit down, Maruja. Lay off her, Greiner."

"You're not using the Subterrene to cause random earthquakes. I can guess that much," Brigid said.

Elias crossed the control room to a console, stroked two buttons and a map flashed onto a corner of the big monitor screen. Computer-generated red crosses pulsed in various areas along the Pacific coast, deep into Canada.

"Here, here and here are the most fragile fault lines," Elias said, tapping the screen with a gnarled forefinger. "We'll plant demolition charges necessary to create a single combined earthquake of such immense proportions that it can easily sweep across the northwest. It'll reshape California, Oregon and Washington and destroy large portions of the interior. We estimate the effects will penetrate around three hundred to five hundred miles inland, with lesser tremors and tremblers extending another couple of hundred miles."

Grant frowned. "How do you figure you can plant explosives that powerful and manage to get out range of the effects?"

Ramirez smiled thinly. "We have that covered."

"How so?" Kane demanded.

Greiner chuckled. "We'll achieve our goal, Kane, don't worry about it."

"What is your goal?" Brigid asked impatiently. "So far, you come off more like a group of destructive children, seeing how far you can ramp up the damage every time you leave the house."

"We're going to build a single, unified country

again," Ramirez declared flatly. "Filled only with the best and the brightest, the most fit to survive. That's what the nukecaust was all about, right? Wiping the slate clean and starting over? That's what we're doing again, and that's one of the reasons why we allowed you three to stay alive."

Striving to sound nonchalant, Kane said, "This may be a wild guess, but I get the distinct impression you're looking to fill your new society with a bunch of ex-Mags."

"Not ex-Mags," said Greiner defensively. "We never stopped being Magistrates…or at least, not all of us."

"Excuse me." Elias tapped one of the pulsating crosses on the map, like a school teacher demanding the attention of unruly students. "Do you know what this is?"

"No," Grant growled. "But I'll bet you're going to tell us."

"This is the Hayward Fault Zone. There are several fault lines connected to it that run from the Pacific tectonic plate to the North American plate. Explosive charges planted throughout this zone will trigger quakes throughout the Continental Divide, causing landslides, avalanches and even volcanic activity."

Brigid stiffened in her chair, inhaling a quick, startled breath.

"What?" Kane asked.

"The Triple Divide Peak in Montana is the point at which two of the principal continental divides in North America converge."

She did not need to add that the peak was located very close to the Bitterroot Range and the Cerberus redoubt.

Greiner chuckled. "So, congratulations are in order, Kane. You've been chosen for a singular honor—to plant that specific charge."

Kane stared at the man in disbelief for a long moment and then grinned crookedly. "I don't recall raising my hand."

Ramirez matched his grin. "Yeah, I know. Next you're going ask me how I can persuade you to do such a thing."

Before Kane could answer, Ramirez nodded toward Greiner, who stepped beside Brigid, pressing the bore of the Sin Eater against the side of her head.

Kane and Grant swiftly rose, but Greiner didn't move.

"You two used to be Magistrates. You know there are ways to overcome reluctance in cooperation," Ramirez said calmly.

Greiner jerked the barrel of his Sin Eater toward the door to indicate that Brigid should follow him. "Move it."

Brigid cast a swift glance toward Kane and shook her head ever so slightly, her lips moving almost imperceptibly. "Wait," she mouthed.

Kane caught the signal and struggled to contain his rising anger. Brigid had indicated that they should ride out the situation a bit longer.

Getting to her feet, Brigid accompanied Greiner out of the control room. Ramirez gestured toward the chairs. "Please be so good as to sit back down. I want you in a place I can keep my eyes on you for the next couple of minutes."

"All of a sudden," Kane said darkly, "I'm not feeling inclined to do anything you say."

Ramirez's face reddened with a sudden anger. Moving with a surprising speed, he lunged from his chair and slammed an armored forearm across Grant's broad chest. The big man stumbled backward, his knees hitting the edge of the seat. He dropped heavily into the chair, snarling, "You son of a bitch—"

Metal bands snapped out from the back of the chair and crossed over his chest, immobilizing his upper body. He strained against the harness.

"That's an emergency feature in case the ride started getting rough," Ramirez said. "It won't hurt you…much."

He turned toward Kane. "Sit your own ass down, Kane."

Jaw muscles knotted, Kane eased himself into the chair. With the faint whine of an electric motor, identical metal bands encircled his torso. "Where the hell are you taking us?" he asked.

"Mictlanx," Maruja said softly. "The underworld."

"Actually," Elias said smoothly, "we've just arrived."

The thrumming of the engines ceased, followed by a sensation of coming to rest. Ramirez gestured to the viewscreen. "See for yourselves."

In stunned amazement, Kane and Grant saw that the Subterrene had emerged into a huge underground metropolis. The sprawling city's main arteries were not paved streets, but instead were composed of gleaming monorail tracks, laced out in every direction.

Trains thundered along the rails, coming and going through a labyrinth of tunnels fifty feet in diameter. They saw no real buildings as such in the city, only windows in the cavern walls. Milk-white fluorescent tubes extended the length of every tunnel. Small caves were recessed into the walls, and each one was illuminated by the neon tubes in uninterrupted links.

"This entire region is honeycombed with interconnected levels, tunnels and chambers," Elias declared. "We're talking hundred of miles worth of tunnels, all of them branching off from this central nexus point."

"What do you think of the capital city of Mictlanx?" Ramirez asked.

Kane gazed at the vast vista of machines and tunnels and replied sarcastically, "Very nice—if you like capital cities with no citizens."

"Why do you think he wanted children?" Maruja said bitterly.

Chapter 28

Kane suddenly realized that like every would-be ruler, both Elias and Ramirez were egomaniacs. Whether this was due to cause or effect, he had never been able to determine. But he was sure it had been true since time began, from Alexander through Attila, Hitler and all of the overlords lusting to control and enslave others.

The air within the huge enclosed space smelled and tasted stale. Grant, Kane, Elias, Ramirez and Maruja strode along a catwalk stretching from the Subterrene. The vault-walled chamber surrounding them was of such huge proportions that its nether end was lost in the shadows. Although he looked for them, Kane could see no sign of Brigid Baptiste or Greiner.

"How deep are we?" Grant wanted to know.

"Approximately three thousand feet," Elias replied. "It's difficult to be precise."

"How did you find this place?" Kane asked.

"Actually," Ramirez answered, "the Subterrene found it. Once we had the thing up and running again, there were several preprogrammed destinations encoded into the autodrive. This was the first stop."

"What about the other places?" Grant inquired.

Elias made a dismissive gesture. "They don't really concern us. This one apparently served as the main hub, sort of like a roundhouse in a predark railyard. It's surrounded by observation posts and monitor stations, sort of like suburbs around predark cities."

"And now this hole in ground is the capital city of your new Great Society, eh?" Maruja asked, a sneer in her voice.

"More like a Great*er* Society," Elias retorted with a note of pride. "Even if I don't live to see it come to fruition."

Kane and Grant made an exaggerated display of looking around with frowns of disapproval on their faces. "Still doesn't seem like very much," Grant commented. "It's just another leftover COG facility, one of about a dozen we've visited over the past few years."

They continued along the narrow walkways that paralleled all of the gleaming rails stretching through the labyrinth of tunnels. Trains raced past, the flatcars holding long metal cases emblazoned with Danger! High Explosive! labels in bright red.

"High explosive?" Grant inquired. "Not nuclear?"

Ramirez shook his head. "No. We found a huge cache of Semtex, TCAP and Astrolite-A here."

Kane's shoulders stiffened as a cold hand seemed to stroke the base of his spine. "What was it used for?"

"To build the subterranean freeway system," Elias replied. "To every part of the Western Hemisphere to blow a wall down here, expand a tunnel there, open a cavern there. The links apparently always existed. To the predark scientists, anything was possible."

Grant smiled tauntingly. "Do you think you're the first scavengers to come along and try to kick-start some predark tech so you can build an empire?"

"The difference is," Ramirez said, nodding toward Elias, "we have somebody who knows what to do with the tech."

Elias waved his arms at the ceiling, toward the tunnel openings. "Look at the lights, glowing in the center of the Earth! Smell the air! All of it atomic generated. Eternal day in an eternal, impregnable city. Who wouldn't want to live here?"

Maruja stared at him in disbelief. "Do you really think people will lead better lives in an underground world?"

Ramirez chuckled smugly. "Hell, no. We'll return to the surface when everything is ready."

Kane's lips quirked in a challenging half smile. "Your idea of everything being ready is after you've destroyed most of it through earthquakes?"

Elias coughed and said, "More or less. And when the surface is cleansed, we'll rise up there and repopulate it with the magnificent kind of society the Earth should have."

"Cleanse it of who and what exactly?" Grant demanded.

Ramirez shrugged. "Muties, for one."

Kane rolled his eyes ceilingward. "Oh, come on."

"Enough of this guided-tour shit," Grant snapped. "Why don't you just come clean with us? We've already guessed most of it."

Elias started to laugh, then put a hand over his mouth as he coughed violently.

"How about sharing your guesswork, then," Ramirez suggested.

Grant came to a complete stop on the catwalk, turning to face Ramirez and Elias, oblivious to the threat posed by the Sin Eater pointed at his midriff. "The people your Diableros abducted were used first to get the Subterrene operational, and because the radiation shielding was inadequate, a lot of them died, didn't they?"

When no one answer was forthcoming, Maruja said, "*Sí,* that is what happened." She pointed to Elias. "And it is what happened to him, too."

"You also needed mules to plant the explosive charges," Grant continued. "What was the method—dig the tunnel, then strap the bombs to the poor bastards, drop them off with the promise to fetch them back before the explosives went off?"

Defensively, Ramirez said, "Something like that, but the ones we used for that purpose were already dying of rad poisoning."

Kane shook his head in exasperated frustration. "And this is all because you want to rebuild the old baronial system?"

"Why the hell not?" Ramirez snapped. "Do you really think it's better now—anarchy, outlanders running around free, Roamers and Farers everywhere? Kane, Grant—you two were a couple of the best Magistrates in the history of the Mag Divisions. Even you have to admit that things are out of control and need to be put right. We need another Judgment Day."

Neither Grant nor Kane responded for a long, thoughtful moment. True enough, life in Cobaltville had been predictable, and they sometimes missed the monotony of routine. They knew Brigid often longed for it, as well. Their whole lives, from conception to death, were ordered for them, both at work and at home.

With a degree of wistfulness, Kane said, "I'm not going to deny life was simpler or even better in some ways with the barons in control—but it was only better for a very small fraction of people."

"The barons chose their elite carefully," Elias said. "We can do the same. Men and women like you, Grant and Brigid Baptiste will mean a great deal in the new order."

Grant snorted disdainfully. "The new order is exactly the same as the old one—inferiors supporting the masters on their backs."

"That's the way of the world," Ramirez said coldly. "The way it was in the baronies."

"Only the division was made scientifically," Elias interposed. "Not based on anything as common as race or ethnicity, but on purity control."

"We know all about purity control," Grant said. "It's not going to work here."

Smirking, Ramirez jabbed the barrel of his pistol into the small of Kane's back. "Let's go."

The walkway entered a white-tiled corridor. The air smelled fresher, and it was much quieter. Ramirez herded Maruja, Kane and Grant toward a bright green door.

"You're right," Ramirez said. "Purity control won't work here. That's why we're going to rebuild the elite the old-fashioned way—and Brigid Baptiste will be one of the architects."

Before Kane could turn and demand an explanation, the door slid aside, revealing a room so dimly lit it was like a grotto. His eyes quickly adjusted to the murk and the first thing he saw a cushioned daybed. Strapped to it was the naked figure of Brigid.

Chapter 29

Brigid's long slender arms were drawn up over her head, with metal cuffs encircling her wrists, the short chain between them stretched over a crossbar above the bed. Her willowy figure was taut and stiff, her long sunset mane of hair screening her face. Her back was arched, thrusting her full breasts forward. When she shifted her legs, Kane saw that she wasn't completely naked—she still wore her thick-soled jump boots.

Greiner lay on the floor at the foot of the bed, more naked than Brigid, since he wore nothing at all. He lay on his side, clutching at his groin with both hands, rocking back and forth. Blood glistened on his lower face, flowing copiously from a mashed nose and split lips.

Kane took a step forward, but Ramirez placed the cold bore of the Sin Eater at the back of his skull. "As you were, Kane."

At the sound of the man's voice, Brigid twisted around, lifting her head and shaking her hair away from her eyes. They glittered like polished emeralds, bright with fury.

"This is how you make citizens of your new empire?" she snapped. "Rape?"

Murmuring in Spanish, Maruja rushed to her. Ramirez didn't object, not even when Maruja looked around, found a silver key on a bedside table and unlocked the cuffs. Brigid sat up, rubbing her wrists. Glaring at Greiner, she said, "The overstimulated asshole should've immobilized my legs first."

Maruja picked up Brigid's clothes from a heap on the floor, handed them to her and knelt beside Greiner. As Brigid dressed, Maruja gently pulled Greiner's hands away from his testicles.

"Let me see, *novio*," she whispered soothingly. "I can help. I am a healer—I can help."

Whimpering, Greiner allowed the woman to examine, crying out once when she probed his scrotum with a forefinger. She eyed the livid, swollen flesh at the juncture of his thighs, then threw back her head and laughed in spiteful triumph.

"Greiner, it is my medical opinion that you will never impregnate any woman ever again," she said.

As Maruja rose, she pursed her lips and spit full into the man's blood-coated face. He wailed in dismay and agony.

Brigid buttoned her shirt with sharp, angry motions, not bothering to turn her back. She had learned the hard way that modesty was a variable, an artifice. Staring unblinkingly at Ramirez, she demanded, "Did you do the same thing to Carmenita?"

Ramirez didn't answer. Kane couldn't help but grin. Elias saw and declared, "Smirk, smile and mock all you wish! If your intellects fail to grasp the potential of underground cities and freeways opening up the world, that is your deficiency. It will be the death of you."

"Maybe so," Grant said with a forced geniality. "But it doesn't take a brilliant mind to see that your plan is shot full of holes."

"Yeah," Kane agreed. "The kind you can drive trains through."

"Shut up," Ramirez snarled. "Everybody get over against the far wall. Elias, cover them."

Kane, Brigid, Grant and Maruja moved farther into the cell as Ramirez handed his pistol to Elias. He helped Greiner to his feet and hauled the moaning man out of the room. Over his shoulder, he called, "Maruja, come with me."

"No," she said defiantly. "I'll stay with them."

"No, you won't," Ramirez shot back. "Elias—if she doesn't come out, shoot Baptiste in the knee."

The man's radiation-ravaged face twisted in a smile. "Which one?"

"Your choice."

Blowing out a sigh, Maruja stalked across the room and out into the corridor. Elias backed out, too, and the door slid shut after him. It closed with a click of locking solenoids. Grant pressed his hands against the metal surface, then his shoulder.

"Locked solid," he announced.

"Big surprise," Kane said, turning to face Brigid. "Are you all right?"

She nodded, hugging herself as a shudder shook her frame. "He threatened to knock me unconscious and rape me anyway if I didn't cooperate, so I figured it was in my best interest to do so…up to a point."

"To the point of your boot?" Grant inquired.

"That's the one," Brigid said, smiling wryly. "I suppose I could've told Greiner I was barren, but I don't think it would have mattered to him."

Kane nodded. "Probably not."

Even though her expression and tone didn't reflect it, Kane knew the topic was still a sensitive one for Brigid. Over five years earlier, on a mission beneath the Black Gobi desert in Mongolia, she had been exposed to an unknown type of radiation and suffered chromosomal damage. She had been rendered barren.

Grant paced the cell, running his hands over the walls. "You cut down on the opposition at least, but I'm not sure where Maruja stands. She still has feelings for Ramirez, I'm guessing."

"Could be," Kane agreed. "I was hoping we could trust her."

"I think we can," Brigid said confidently.

"Why so?"

Brigid's wry smile expanded to one of amusement. "You're still not up on the whole woman-scorned dynamic, are you?"

A bit nettled, Kane countered, "I haven't had to face it too much, Baptiste."

"Except when Beth-Li Rouch shot you," Brigid reminded him with an acid edge to her words. "You remember that, don't you?"

Reflexively, Kane's hand touched his right hip where Beth-Li's bullet had torn a gouge, but he did not respond. He retained vivid memories of the incident, and it was one reason he was reluctant to become involved with any of the women who were permanent residents of the Cerberus redoubt.

"It's not going to matter too much about Maruja," Kane commented. "Ramirez still plans to use you and Grant as hostages to force me to be his mule, riding on his warhead delivery trains."

Brigid nodded thoughtfully. "That might be his plan, but whether it works is a different story."

Grant paused in his inspection of the cell. "Why do you say that?"

"Do you remember when Elias referenced something called Telegeodynamics?"

"Yeah."

"Do you remember the briefing about Nikola Tesla?"

Grant and Kane's memories flew back several years to the mission involving the HAARP array in Alaska and the twentieth century's scientist involvement with it.

"To a point," Kane said cautiously. "What about him?"

"Tesla was always experimenting with so-called perpetual-motion machines," Brigid explained. "At one time, he constructed a simple device consisting of a piston suspended in a cylinder, which bypassed the necessity of a camshaft driven by a rotating power source, such as a gasoline or steam engine. In this way, he hoped to overcome loss of power through friction produced by the old system."

"Fascinating," Kane said dryly. "So?"

"So, that device also enabled Tesla to try out his experiments in vibrational resonance."

"What's that?" Grant asked.

"Every substance has a resonant frequency that is demonstrated by the principle of sympathetic vibration. The most obvious examples are the infrasound wands—you remember those, right?"

"Why would we, Baptiste?" Kane demanded, his voice heavy with sarcasm.

"Yeah," Grant growled. "It's not like we were almost killed by the damn things more than once."

Kane thought back to when they had first encountered the slim silver wands used with such deadly accuracy by the hybrids. He remembered the harplike instrument played by Aifa in Ireland and a similar device Sindri claimed had been found on Mars, a relic of the Tuatha de Danaan.

All of the devices were related in that they operated on the same principle of sound manipulation. The infrasound wands wielded by the hybrids converted electricity to ultrahigh sound frequencies powered by a miniature maser.

He recalled how Sindri had described the Danaan harp as producing energy forms with balanced gaps between the upper and lower energy frequencies. He explained if the radiation within particular frequencies fell on an energized atom—like living matter—it stimulated it in the same way a gong vibrated when its note was struck on a piano. Harmony and disharmony, healing and death.

"Well, then," Brigid declared, "you know that when a vibrational frequency is matched and amplified, any material may be literally shaken to pieces. Tesla perfected a vibrating assembly with an adjustable frequency and his experiments with it caused trouble in around his laboratory in New York City."

Interested in spite of himself, Kane asked, "How big was this resonator?"

"Small enough to carry in a satchel according to the reports of the time," Brigid answered. "At one point, he put his little vibrator in his coat pocket and went out to hunt a half-erected steel building. He found one—ten stories of steel framework without a brick or a stone laid around it. He clamped the vibrator to one of the beams, and adjusted until the structure began to creak and weave and the steelworkers fled the site, panic-stricken, believing that there had been an earthquake. Police were called. Tesla put the vibrator in his pocket and went away. Ten minutes more and he could have laid the building in the street."

Knuckling his chin, Grant sank down on the edge of the daybed. "So you think there's more to this earthquake machine of Ramirez's than tunneling and explosives?"

"Could be," Brigid stated. "But there's only way to find out."

She sighed heavily, running her fingers through her hair. "Unfortunately, we're locked up for the duration. What's that old proverb?"

"There's no place like home?" Kane asked sourly.

Brigid smiled. "No, the other one, about where there's life there's hope."

Kane frowned. "I'm not familiar with that one—"

The door suddenly slid open.

Chapter 30

Brigid, Kane and Grant kept close to the tiled walls, not running but not skulking, either.

"Somebody opened that door," Kane whispered, eyes flitting back and forth. "So where the hell are they?"

"They must have done it remotely," Brigid replied.

Grant grunted. "I'm betting on Maruja."

The Cerberus warriors slowed, walking more cautiously as they neared the end of the corridor. Beyond, where the passageway opened into the huge cavern with catwalks and tracks, they heard the rumble of the trains sliding along the silver rails.

They stood and watched, seeing no one. "This is all running on automatic, isn't it?" Kane whispered.

Brigid nodded. "That would be my guess."

"But where are all the trains going?" Grant asked.

Brigid shrugged. "There's no way to tell. It's quite possible that when the power was restored here, the trains just picked up from their old programming. Elias and Ramirez don't really know how to shut it down or alter it."

Kane eyed the tunnels. "Do you think that this was

all part of the Telegeodynamic plan you were telling us about?"

"It very well could be… If so, it makes more sense than a long-range plan to build underground highways and blow up cities. Tesla claimed his device, properly modified, could be used to map subterranean deposits of oil."

"And that was important to predarkers?" Grant inquired.

Brigid smiled slightly. "You have no idea. A vibration sent through the earth returns an echo signature using the same principle as sonar. This idea was actually adapted for use by the petroleum industry, and was used in a modified form with devices used to locate objects at archaeological digs.

"Anyway, even before Tesla had mentioned the invention to anyone he was already scaring the local populace around his loft laboratory. At one point in his research, Tesla happened to attach the device to an exposed steel girder in his brownstone, thinking the foundations were built on sturdy granite. As he discovered later, the substrata in the area consisted of sand and ash—excellent conductors and propagators of ground vibrations.

"After setting up the little machine, he proceeded to putter about the lab on other projects that needed attention. Meanwhile, for blocks around, chaos reigned as objects fell off shelves, furniture moved across floors, windows shattered and pipes broke. The pandemonium didn't go unnoticed in the local police precinct house, where prisoners panicked and police officers fought to keep coffee and doughnuts from flying off desks. They raced to Tesla's lab and found him smashing the vibrator to bits with a sledgehammer."

Interested in spite of himself Kane asked, "And then what happened?"

"He apologized for the inconvenience. He later told reporters that the very Earth could be split in two by his oscillator, given the right conditions. The detonation of a ton of dynamite at intervals of one hour and forty-nine minutes would step up the natural standing wave that would be produced until the Earth's crust could no longer contain the interior. He called his new science Telegeodynamics."

Grant nodded as if she had explained everything. "That figures."

"In a way it does," Brigid replied. "Tesla posited a series of oscillators attached to the Earth at strategic points that would be used to transmit vibrations to be picked up at any point on the globe and turned back into usable power. Since no practical application of this idea could be found at the time that would make money for big investors or other philanthropic souls, since you can't effectively meter and charge for power derived in this way, the Telegeodynamic science was largely forgotten, written off as crackpotism."

"But somebody revived the idea?" Kane wanted to know. "Somebody who thought it would be a good idea to trigger earthquakes using the oscillators."

"Not exactly. Tesla and a few geologists proposed that the creation of small, relatively harmless temblers could relieve tectonic stress, rather than having to wait in fear for nature to take its course."

Grant's lips compressed. "The idea didn't remain just idle speculation, did it? The whitecoats of the Totality Concept probably used it to trigger earthquakes to control or wipe out unruly populations."

"Let's talk about it later," Kane said impatiently, edging closer to the end of the corridor. "Speaking of safe bets, I think we can bet our lives on the fact there are vid monitors fixed on all these tunnel openings."

"More of the new order that's just like the old one," Brigid remarked dourly. "But if Maruja unlocked the door to the cell, maybe she deactivated the vid spy eyes, too."

Grant nodded. "My thought, exactly. So we're going to have to chance it."

Kane inched closer to the mouth of the corridor. With a sigh, he whispered over his shoulder, "Shall I be the decoy this time around?"

Brigid and Grant exchanged glances, then Brigid said, "Why not? You've got the classic profile of one."

"Thanks," Kane murmured snidely. He drew in a breath, held it, set himself, then bounded out of the passageway and into the cavern, down in the area where the monorails crisscrossed and ran parallel to one another. He wended his way around cargo carriers and support stanchions.

Reaching a central junction, he stopped running. He stood, looking around. Nothing happened, no alarms howled and neither Ramirez nor Elias appeared. He waved to Grant and Brigid.

They hesitated and then left the corridor. "I feel like I'm carrying a target on my ass," Grant said quietly.

"Just keep moving," Brigid whispered.

"They must have seen us on the spy eyes by now—they can't all be deactivated."

"I have a feeling we'll find out about that at any moment. Ramirez likely has his own way of handling situations like this."

Grant scowled. "You don't believe in filling a man's day with sunshine, do you?"

Brigid declined to reply. She and Grant strode across the cavern to the head of a long train. The engine, like all the others they had seen, was little more than a bullet made of burnished bronze. A transparent Plexiglas canopy enclosed the pilot's compartment of the engine. A flatcar holding a four-foot-long metal-walled container was coupled to it.

Kane examined the interior, noting only a hands-on joystick type of control attached to the floor. "It seems simple to operate."

Grant glanced around uneasily. "Yeah, but we don't know where it will take us."

"I submit our destination is the least of our concerns," Brigid said.

Carefully, Grant and Brigid climbed aboard, sitting

behind Kane. He slid the canopy over their heads, rubber seals squeaking faintly. Cautiously, he gripped the hand control and eased it forward. The engine suddenly emitted a high-pitched whine. Oxygen hissed into the compartment from small tanks attached to the inner walls.

The train slowly eased into motion. The whine rose in pitch and with a slight lurch, the train slid almost silently along the rail. It swiftly built up speed and plunged toward one of the tunnels.

A subgun stuttered from a catwalk overhead. Bullets ricocheted off the nose of the engine, sparks flaring from the point of impact. They heard the muffled voices of both Elias and Ramirez raised in angry shouts.

Kane pushed the control stick forward, and the train moved faster along the rail and entered a tunnel. The train shuddered, seeming to tip over on its side as it slid around a sharp bend. There were swerving curves in the rail, but the train did not slow as it slid along them.

"I don't know where we're going, but we're on our way," he said loudly.

Overhead light fixtures flicked by so rapidly that they combined with the intervals of darkness between them to acquire a strobing pattern. Grant turned, watching the central junction recede in the distance. He glimpsed three figures at the foot of a spiral staircase, and then they were lost from view as the train rounded a curve.

Leaning forward, he asked, "How fast do you figure this thing can go?"

"At least a hundred miles an hour," Kane answered, adjusting the throttle.

"Probably a good deal faster," Brigid interjected.

Kane grinned at her over his shoulder. "Let's find out."

He pushed the handgrip control forward past the halfway point. Grant and Brigid braced themselves in the swaying engine as the train picked up speed, shooting like a projectile through the tunnel. The whole length of the train shivered and shuddered as it took curves in the rail, but Kane did not slow.

The voice of Elias suddenly filled the interior of the engine, making them all jump and swear in surprise. "Do any of you really think it matters? No matter how far you run, how fast you force the train, you can't outrun us!"

They looked around for a speaker and finally Kane located a tiny grilled disk on the floor of the cab. "Can you hear us, Elias—Ramirez?"

"Yes," came the crisp response from Ramirez. "There's no point in you taking off. You're carrying a load of TCAP you know."

Kane felt sweat form at his hairline. After a moment, he said, "If you could detonate it, you would've done so already."

"Don't be so sure."

Hitching around, Grant stared out of the rear of the canopy, down the long tube of the tunnel. He glimpsed a flicker of faraway movement. "I think they're coming after us."

Kane thrust the throttle all the way forward until it locked into place. The train shuddered, seeming to lie on its side as it slid around a hairpin curve. "Let 'em try to catch up."

Brigid leaned against the bulkhead of the cab, staring through the canopy as the fantastic underworld whipped past the screaming train. Bizarre rock formations sped by, like fragments from a dimly remembered nightmare. A rushing river swirled to their left, alive with mud-colored fish. She realized that Elias hadn't lied about the fantastic subterranean world, filled with valleys and riverbeds.

The train plummeted into a tunnel so narrow that the walls seemed to press against the streamlined exterior of the engine. It slid down the center of a canyon. Up ahead, red lights flashed in a hypnotic rhythm.

Elias voice shouted over the transceiver, "Do you see those lights? They're warning signals. You've got to obey them!"

"We'd rather not," Kane retorted. "Once we get started, we like to keep moving."

Peering forward, he saw a barrier of metal painted in red-and-yellow stripes bisecting the track. Over his shoulder, he announced, "I can either slow down or ram. We might be derailed."

"Ram," Brigid said calmly. She glanced over at Grant with an arched eyebrow.

Grant shrugged. "Ram it."

The engine's blunt nose drove into the striped barrier

Warlord of the Pit 299

with a clanging crash, uprooting it from moorings in the tunnel floor and knocking it askew. As the train roared past, a hot barrage of machine-gun fire spewed from emplacements in the wall, striking notches and sparks on the rail on which they traveled.

Two bullet holes starred the canopy and a suction began, snatching at Kane's hair and drawing it toward the punctures. A whistling like a teakettle on full boil filled the interior as the engine zoomed over the notches and nicks in the rail, shuddering and rocking.

Brigid handed Kane a wadded-up bandanna and he crammed it into the holes. Their ears registered the change of pressure as the high-pitched keening abated.

Elias's voice filled the cab. "Mr. Kane? Miss Baptiste? Mr. Grant. Do you hear me?"

"We're here," Kane said, "despite your security precautions."

"You're traveling far faster along the rails than the designers intended. Otherwise the guns would've chopped you to pieces in a cross fire. Listen to me carefully—I shall warn you but once. Stop the train immediately. Put it in reverse and return. You won't be harmed."

"Sorry," Brigid said, leaning over the seat and speaking loudly. "You must know we're not going to do that."

Elias voice wheezed out of the transceiver. "Arrogant to the last."

"You're wasting time," Ramirez blurted angrily.

"Time is running out for you, Ramirez, not us," Grant said.

"That's where you're wrong again, Grant. It's running out for Maruja."

Chapter 31

Maruja's unsteady voice said, "I am in the train with Ramirez. I had no choice."

"Where's Elias, then?" Kane demanded.

"In the control room, back in the cavern. While he was busy, I opened your cell door so you could escape."

"A stupid plan," Ramirez snapped, "hatched from a stupid bitch."

"For her sake and your own," Elias declared, "I urge you to listen to me and stop throwing away your last chance to surrender. Stop that train before I am forced to destroy it."

Kane frowned at the transceiver grid. "Afraid you're missing an urgent point, Elias. You may well destroy this train in order to keep us from escaping, but it doesn't really matter whether we die in your train or at the hands of Ramirez, does it?"

Elias barked out a laugh. "I know you idealistic types too well, Mr. Kane. You'll face death cheerfully, but you won't force innocents to die with you. Will you sacrifice Maruja in your foolish attempt to escape, an attempt that I assure you is doomed to failure? Must she die, too? That is your decision."

"No," Grant growled. "It's *your* decision, yours and Ramirez's."

"You'll be the ones to have doomed her," Ramirez chimed in. "Are you able to live with that?"

"She was your lover," Brigid pointed out. "Are you able to live with being her executioner."

Ramirez chuckled coldly. "*Was* is the operative term here, Baptiste."

The Cerberus warriors fell silent. The train whipped through a tunnel so small that the white light tubing was only inches from the sides of the canopy, an endless glow worm stretched out eternally through the subterranean maze.

The speaker crackled. Elias's voice increased the tension inside the cab. "I must ask you to make your decision quickly. Your time has nearly run out."

Kane drew a deep breath. "Sorry, Elias. I think you and Ramirez are bluffing."

Elias snarled wordlessly, then half shouted, "Do you remember passing a river?"

"Yeah."

"Then it should have been a warning to you."

"Why?"

"I mentioned to you that we live in constant threat of underground rivers breaking through shallow crusts and that a system of safety locks were installed. In less than one minute, I will activate the controls that will close and magnetically seal all the vanadium-alloy doors ahead of you. It will be like driving your train into a solid wall. You will die instantly."

Kane bit his lower lip, then said, "And what about our cargo of TCAP? That's a shock-sensitive explosive. There will be a hell of lot more damage than a destroyed train, especially if you're worried about flooding."

"I'm getting sick of this shit, Kane. Make up your mind," Ramirez rasped.

Kane inhaled deeply and turned to glance at Grant and Brigid. They did not speak, their faces showed nothing. Exhaling, Kane drew back on the control stick.

"You win, Ramirez. We're stopping. Come and get us."

He waited, but there was no utterance of triumph over the transceiver from either man. The train slowed by degrees. Gazing through the canopy, Kane saw gleaming metal plates in the distance, completely blocking the tunnel. The train rolled to a steady stop, the blunt nose only a couple of feet from the watertight wall of vanadium.

Kane swiftly unlatched the canopy and climbed out, moving to the flatcar. Gripping the metal-walled crate by one end, he said to Grant, "Give me a hand."

Grant stared at him baffled, and then his expression twisted into one of incredulity. "Oh, no…don't tell me—"

Kane grinned, tugging on the crate. "Yep."

Clambering out of the engine, Brigid's face showed alarm. "You're going to try to blow that door down?"

As Kane and Grant wrestled the crate off the flatcar, Kane said between clenched teeth, "Why not?"

Brigid opened to her mouth to speak, closed it, shook her head, then said, "At the moment, I guess I can't think of any reason."

The two men carried the crate to the front of the engine, pushing it down between the nose and the vanadium portal. They quickly inspected the position, and then Kane climbed back into the cockpit. Brigid and Grant sat on the flatcar as he adjusted the control stick and put the train into slow Reverse.

When it approached a bend in the tunnel wall a hundred yards down the line, Kane braked the vehicle to a halt and he climbed out, but kept his hand on the stick. Turning to face Brigid and Grant, he said, "Start running. I'll catch up."

They hesitated and then did as he said. Kane shoved the control stick forward, released it and waited to make sure the train rolled smoothly along the rail. Then he turned and began running. He did not run far before the tunnel seemed to lift in a soaring gravitational shove that lifted him from his feet.

Kane realized, as the detonation of the explosives was directed mainly at the vanadium door, he would be caught in the back blast and he could not escape the rock slide that roared down toward him. He glimpsed Brigid turning to gaze at him a split second before a shower of shattered dark rock poured down from above.

Kane flung himself aside and the shock wave of the

detonation lifted him clear of the tunnel. It was like being bludgeoned by an invisible massive club. He fell heavily against the monorail, but he reflexively turned his fall into a roll.

Springing to his feet and shielding his head with his arms, he ran toward a fissure in the wall. He felt rocks pelting him from all sides. The avalanche cascaded down and bowled him off his feet. He felt the masses of shattered stone crashing behind him, but by his last-second lunge into the cavity he avoided being crushed by larger chunks of rock.

He lay, pinned by the weight of the fallen stone, hearing the roar of the collapse vibrated deafeningly against his eardrums. Finally, after what seemed like an interlocking chain of eternities, the reverberating thunder and crash of falling rock ceased.

Kane strained against the stone, trying to lever himself free but it was a useless effort. His legs were pinned and though he felt no distinct pressure at any one point, an ache seemed to penetrate his entire body. He couldn't see or hear anything except the rasp of his respiration. He could only hope that Brigid and Grant weren't caught in the cave-in and buried like him.

Carefully, he pushed against the wall and loose rocks shifted away from his body, clattering loudly. Perspiration trickled into his eyes, burning them until he blinked out the sweat.

"Kane!"

Grant's voice penetrated through the rock, far more clear than he thought. "Here!" Kane called.

"Are you all right?" Brigid asked anxiously.

"Don't know yet. I think so. How about you?"

"Think so," Grant said, his voice drawing closer. He coughed. "I think I see where you are. Hold on."

Kane heard the feet of his two friends skidding on pebbles and crunching on gravel. He caught a glimpse of a shadow, and then Grant and Brigid began digging him out. It didn't take long. Kicking his feet free of loose rocks, Kane stumbled, squinting through the thick planes of dust and smoke. Most of the light tubes had been shattered, but a few of them still provided a weak illumination.

He squinted down the tunnel. "Did it work?"

"We don't know yet," Brigid said. "Let's go see."

Kane slapped at the layer of dust covering his clothes. "I don't think Ramirez was close enough to have been damaged, but the rail is definitely screwed. He can't make it down here."

Brigid nodded uncertainly. "Remember what Elias said, that there were side tunnels and galleries honeycombing this whole area. Ramirez could have diverted into one of them."

They reached the point where the vanadium-steel barrier blocked the tunnel. It hung loosely, bent almost double by the explosion of the TCAP. Of the train, there was no sign except for a litter of metal. Brigid pointed to the gap between the edge of the door and the tunnel wall. "We can squeeze through there easily enough."

Kane eyed Grant's burly body and said, "Some of us, anyway."

Grant scowled but did not respond. His weight gain over the past couple of years had become something of a sore point. Still, he had no trouble following Kane and Brigid through the opening. Most of the tunnel was clogged with tons of stone that had collapsed from overhead.

The Cerberus warriors crab-walked along a narrow passage between the rockfall and the tunnel wall, their feet stirring up dust. Jagged edges of rock caught at them. The passageway curved slightly to the left, then suddenly opened into a vast space.

They received the impression of standing in a dome-roofed cavern, but it was in almost absolute darkness. Only a faint ray of light from above seeped into the place, but it was sufficient for a slow, silent survey of their surroundings.

They stood on an elevated table of rock, not more than ten feet wide. They saw gloomy chasms and labyrinthine connecting caverns all around. There were endless vestibules and antechambers to explore, but none of them looked particularly inviting.

In a whisper, Brigid quoted, "'From the land of the light to the land of darkness, to the Netherworld she descended.'"

Kane glanced at her with a combination of irritation and curiosity. "What's that from?"

"*The Song of Inanna,* a Sumerian epic, about the goddess who went weeping down into the netherworld, the 'Great Below,' to implore the King of Shadows to return her beloved to the upper world again."

Grant shook his head. "I thought you would have had enough of Sumerian epics about gods and goddesses by now."

Brigid smiled, moving closer to the edge of the table of rock. "Know thy enemy."

Faintly they heard the sound of rushing water, but they couldn't place its location in the gloom.

"That must be the river Elias told us about," Brigid murmured. "Close by and running fast."

Grant made a growling sound deep in his throat. "I can't see that this situation is any better than the one we left."

"Theoretically," Brigid replied, "we could follow the river to the surface."

"Yeah," Kane grimly said. "If we could see the thing and had a boat—"

White light, intolerable in its brilliance, suddenly blazed all around them. For a panicky half second, Kane thought they had been caught in a secondary explosion. They clapped their hands over their faces, but not fast enough to prevent their optic nerves from being overwhelmed by the incandescent blaze all around them.

They felt no heat and heard nothing like a detonation, but the light pressed against them from all sides.

Elias, his voice rich and smug, announced from somewhere beyond the blaze, "It's like I told you. There's no escape."

Chapter 32

The door slid open and Elias heeled around from a control panel when Brigid, Kane and Grant walked in under the gun of Ramirez. Maruja sat in a chair on the far side of the room, her wrists handcuffed behind her back. Her dark eyes seethed with fury and sorrow.

Elias gestured. "I told you there were many secondary outposts and monitor stations. This is one of them. You ended up exactly where I wanted you to be."

"I'm glad we could help you out," Kane said deadpan.

Elias wheezed with laughter. "The three of you have helped more than you've hindered."

"It's not too late to change that," Maruja said angrily.

Elias laughed again, in breathless exultance. "I fear it is, my child. Everybody has done well."

He swung his arm toward a bank of vid screens. "Take a look. There they go, racing on our own underground railroads. Three trains on automatic pilot, three trains set to explode simultaneously when they reach their destinations."

"I thought I was supposed to go on one of those," Kane said, as if disappointed.

"It's not too late, Kane," Ramirez said flatly. "You destroyed the fourth train, but we can find another for you."

Grant, Brigid and Kane gazed at the screen, watching the little trains rush toward their targets. Elias peered at them, as if taking happiness by their demeanors of defeat.

"You've seen enough," he announced. "Ramirez, take them out and kill them. Shoot them in the head. Put their bodies in the river."

Ramirez raised his Sin Eater and gestured toward the door. "You heard him."

"Maruja, too," Elias said.

Ramirez hesitated for an instant, then grabbed Maruja by the upper arm and hauled her to her feet. He stared at her for a long moment, and then turned toward Elias. "No."

"Do it! I gave you an order!" the scarred man bellowed.

Ramirez glared at him contemptuously. "An archivist doesn't give a Magistrate orders."

"I'm telling you to kill her!" Elias raged.

"And I'm telling you to go to hell."

Elias snarled and lunged for her, hands reaching for her neck. Maruja struggled to get away, her knees buckling. Ramirez fired once.

Kane bounded forward, slapping the gun barrel upward. The pistol shot reverberated in the control room like the striking of a huge gong.

Maruja sagged forward, a splotch of blood spreading across the bodice of her blouse. Brigid stared at her, unable to believe that Ramirez had shot her, even accidentally. The woman sank slowly to the floor.

Ramirez leaned down trying to hold her up, to keep her head from slamming against the floor. She stared into his face and whispered, *"Buenas noches, mi amor."*

She stopped speaking, but her eyes remained fixed on Ramirez's. She died very quickly and quietly.

Grant spun on Elias, driving his right fist into the man's jaw. The man staggered, falling against a control console. He clutched at it as he slid to the floor. Brigid ran along the banks of panel controls until she found the one she sought.

Elias stared at her, his eyes glassy. Gasping for breath, the man could barely speak, but he husked out, "Ramirez! Stop her!"

He said it again, hopelessly, but Ramirez ignored him, cradling Maruja in his arms.

Brigid ran her hands over the controls for the flood doors. She pressed every button, slapped at every toggle switch, closing all the vanadium bulkheads in every tunnel branching off from the city of Mictlanx.

"This ought to bottle things up," she stated flatly.

"What are you doing?" Elias cried out.

Kane turned toward him. "Rearranging your city."

He grabbed up the chair Maruja had sat in and smashed it down on the main console. Lights flared through the glass-covered indicators, and then they went dark.

Elias slumped against the base of the console, staring at Brigid and shaking his head. "The doors…they can never be opened again."

Ramirez raised his head, his eyes dull. "That was the idea, you crazy bastard."

Barely able to speak, Elias said, "When the trains smash into those vanadium-steel doors, this whole city will be destroyed…perhaps this whole region…everything!"

Kane stared first at Elias, then at his two friends. "In that case, it's best we get out of here."

He turned toward Ramirez. "You, too."

The man looked up at Kane, his eyes dry but full of grief. "I'll stay with her." He inclined his head toward Elias. "And him, too."

Sobbing for breath, Elias tried to get to his feet, and then slumped back down against the console. "You fools, where do you think you'll run to?"

"There's an emergency lift down the catwalk about thirty yards, then take a right," Ramirez said bleakly. "It'll take you to the surface."

Elias's mouth hung open and he breathed through it wetly. He reached out for Ramirez, then covered his head with his arms. He stayed that way, rocking back and forth, sobbing and gasping.

Grant, Kane and Brigid Baptiste ran across the control room, past the computer stations and out onto a catwalk. None of them looked back as they raced along it, following Ramirez's directions. They saw a huge lift recessed into the cavern wall and they leaped into it, Kane striking the up button on his way in.

The thick doors rumbled shut and the elevator shot upward. Brigid and Kane stared at each other, bracing themselves for the time when the first explosions erupted from below, when the first of the trains plowed into the vanadium barriers.

The elevator raced upward. The Cerberus warriors became conscious of barely breathing despite their exertion, of the sweat of tension flowing from their pores.

A gigantic *boom* cannonaded upward and the elevator shuddered brutally. It struck the upper latches and held. The doors slid into grooves, opening to reveal a long incline toward a lighted exit. Another explosion hammered the ground beneath their feet. They staggered but kicked themselves into a sprint.

A series of thundering blasts knocked Brigid to her hands and knees. Kane grabbed her arms, lifting her and half carrying her toward the opening at the end of the passageway.

Grant glanced back and saw the elevator car disappear, swallowed up by the earth as the shaft crumbled inward. A billowing ball of flame-laced smoke flung itself from the throat of the lift shaft like a boulder launched from a catapult.

A brutal column of concussive force rushed down the passageway, slamming into them like an invisible tsunami, buffeting them up and bowling them off their feet. They flew up and out into clean air, rolling painfully over the rocky ground.

Kane looked fearfully up at the mountain looming above them and saw how the face of it shook and trembled. Stones and dirt, shaken loose, sifted down. The ground heaved and shuddered. A fissure opened up around the mouth of the passageway with a clash of rending rock.

The mountain did not fall, and within moments the sounds of the subterranean blasts were only muffled echoes. Kane rose, brushing himself off, looking around. The sky darkened with approaching nightfall, the sun a blazing orb of yellow orange dipping toward the horizon.

Heaving himself to his feet, Grant glanced around at the terrain. "Does anybody have any idea where we are?"

Brigid massaged her shoulder and winced. "Still in Mexico, I imagine."

Kane sighed. "It's going to be a long-ass walk home."

Brigid smiled wryly. "Hopefully, Lakesh will be able to pinpoint our positions through the biolink transponders and send somebody."

"Hopefully," Kane agreed. "Wouldn't count on it, though."

"We've made long walks before," Grant declared. Turning toward Brigid, he asked, "What was that Maruja said to Ramirez right before she died?"

Brigid Baptiste's mouth jerked as if she felt a sudden stab of pain. Softly, she quoted, "'Good night, my love.'"

Kane glanced again up the sky. "All things considered, appropriate last words."

The Executioner®
Don Pendleton's
CODE OF HONOR

The Black Cross are a ruthless and unforgiving group of assassins who, until recently, were the best operatives working for the U.S. government. When someone begins targeting retired American servicemen, Stony Man decides to send Black Cross a new recruit: Mack Bolan. Charged with taking the entire organization apart, he'll do it the only way he knows how—Executioner-style.

Available December wherever books are sold.